T0166065

QUEST I

QUEST I

(THE DIRTY ONE)

Stroke T. Renigade

Copyright © 2011 by Stroke T. Renigade.

ISBN:	Softcover	978-1-4653-8855-1
	Ebook	978-1-4653-8856-8

All rights reserved. No part of this book may be reproduced or transmitted in any form or by any means, electronic or mechanical, including photocopying, recording, or by any information storage and retrieval system, without permission in writing from the copyright owner.

This is a work of fiction. Names, characters, places and incidents either are the product of the author's imagination or are used fictitiously, and any resemblance to any actual persons, living or dead, events, or locales is entirely coincidental.

This book was printed in the United States of America.

To order additional copies of this book, contact:
Xlibris Corporation
1-888-795-4274
www.Xlibris.com
Orders@Xlibris.com

ONE

ZANDORIA; LIVING IN A FANTASY

OVER SIX FRILLION LIGHT YEARS from the edge of our solar system there is another known as Libysha. Now in case you've thought to perhaps pay these folks a little visit, well, here are the directions: First you need the fastest ship…Wait! Better make that spaceship like a Millennium Falcon model ZX14 which you can usually rent a pretty good one with an 8 track stereo and forty-seven thousand eight track tapes. But I have also heard that if your dealers name is Sammie, he can get you a nice new silver Silver Edition, which comes in Dog, Hawk, and Eagle, and all are equipped with every song ever written in the universe. The collection updates at a rate of about 10,000,000 new songs from about the universe every day. It also has quadrofuci sound throughout the ship. But no matter which you choose it is still going to be a very long journey without a little magic. You see in order to travel one frillion light years you set the ship on haul arse and you travel at that speed until you get tired, that will be about one frillion, now you continue at that same rate of speed until you become tired five times more than you were before. Got that? Then you veer hard to the right for a quarter of a ways more, also you should take the ship off of haul arse and put it into neutral, you should be able to cruise in from here. Now you got to drop down a little and you should be right on top of the Twin Suns.

The system of Libysha is similar to ours, yet different. Libysha has two suns with six of its twenty planets being suitable for life, as we know it on earth. Those planets are filled with fantastic mystery, magic, and beauty. The names of these planets are: Anemeg, Vindol, Trimelva, Benthelia, Aireoliga and Zandoria, a splendid and peaceful planet. There has not been a major full-scale war between neighboring planets since the Council of Oligarchy was gathered together by the great King Xortep. It began in the eighth millennium, the peace they had—and from the beginning, the prophets, told of the end. They told of an unstable balance in the universe, the evil that would interrupt the peace and where it all would come from, and the good that would be the beginning of its end.

Even though, some of the more traditional residence tend not to always agree with the contemporary studies and advancements allowed by the Council, all approved of the simplicity that has been maintained, such as the medieval setting, Monarchy rule and the sorcery.

The Council of Oligarchy consists of descendents of the original council. Today they are; King Estiob of Anemeg, King Yoral of Vindol, King Lardu of Trimelva, King Lanhem of Benthelia, King Ecneraelc of Aireolia and King Revilo of Zandoria.

Each king rules his planet with other kings controlling designated sections, somewhat like generals. The one that they must answer to is King Revilo, who is the descendant of King Xortep.

King Revilo has had his Palace in Talmory, where annually the Council gathers to celebrate peace and pay their respects to King Revilo. This year the people of Talmory have more than the annual visit to prepare for. They must finish arrangements for a very special birthday and wedding ceremony, all to take place in Talmory, in seven days, after the full day of darkness caused by a total eclipse of the two suns.

In Talmory, everybody is excited and go about their tasks painstakingly, for all understand the importance of having everything ready before the eclipse of the two suns. To the people of Zandoria this is a Holy Day, which of course there will be no work done on that day.

It has been said that many strange creatures lurk about the land on the day of darkness, only to return to their lair when the light shows once more.

THE FIRST DAY

Two wagons travel along Prince Street, a main road in Talmory. The wagons continue on their way, while a group of small children run behind trying to catch a ride on the back of the tailing wagon. The children soon cease their advance near the Palace gates.

The gates to the Palace are closed only at night. During the day it is the responsibility of Erdna, Captain of the Guards, to make sure all is secure. The driver of the first wagon will have to report to him in order to receive permission to enter.

"HALT!" shouts Erdna, moving from his post just inside the gate. "What business do you have here? What do you have on those wagons?"

The driver of the first wagon lifts his old beaten straw hat from his head calmly, and then wipes the sweat from his brow. "How are you doing today, Erdna?"

"I am doing just fine. Even though my health is not in question, and the question still stands."

"I have brought a delivery," announces Otep, lifting the cover for Erdna to see. "These two wagons are loaded with Bonda Berry Juice brewed especially for the King of Anemeg."

Erdna develops a fiendish thought, 'I was just about to take a break. Now, I can have my break and a little of the King's personal Bonda Berry Juice as well.'

"Okay, Otep," says Erdna, climbing aboard the lead wagon. "Pull your wagon behind the Butchers' cot." Erdna points out the direction he wants the wagon driven, and then remembers to leave someone in charge.

"Egott, you are in charge until I return." Erdna sits up straight as he thinks of the enjoyment that he is about to experience.

Through the front door of the palace walks a handsome young man with long dark hair. His name is Cush and he is the son of King Revilo. Cush was about to go into town to get away from all the confusion, but he sees Erdna riding aboard the wagon and decides that this matter is more pressing than his immediate departure. Cush walks down the stairs towards where Erdna has ordered the wagons driven.

Erdna dismounts and notices a few soldiers lounging near the stables. "You there! I want the five of you to unload the barrels on the wagons and take them to the wine cellar."

As the driver of the wagons busy themselves with the lines securing the loads, Cush casually walks up behind Erdna. "What were you doing on that wagon, Erdna?" asked Cush.

"I was showing Otep where to unload these wagons."

"And what, is on these wagons which is so important that it requires a personal escort by the Captain of the Guard on the inner grounds of the Palace?"

"Bonda Berry Juice," says Erdna with a grin. "Bonda berry Juice made especially for the King of Anemeg."

"So you thought you should guard it with your life to make sure the King would not be shorted. Is that correct?"

Because of their friendship and their relaxed conversation, Erdna has forgotten Cush's authority as the King's son and starts to explain. "Well, not exactly. I have not had a break all day, so I thought…"

"Silence, Erdna, and get at attention."

Erdna makes a quick change from relaxed to locked spurs. Cush walks around behind him to allow himself a chance to cover his amusement.

"You have not had a break all day, you say, well neither have I! They have been running me around just like a little errand boy, 'Cush do this, Cush do that'."

Erdna remained at attention and listened as Cush paced back and forth.

"Well, I want you to know I am fed up with this feces. I want you to go over there and grab a barrel from the wagon and follow me, Captain."

"Yes, Sir," said Erdna before turning to walk to the led wagon. Cush stands watching while still doing his best to keep from laughing. Erdna returned with a barrel as ordered and stands once more at attention with the barrel across his shoulder. Cush moved to lead the way to the cellar doors with Erdna close behind. As they enter the cellar, Cush points out a far place in the corner of the room where there is a table and chairs.

"Hurry, Erdna, and get the barrel open, while I find something for us to drink out of."

"Yes, Sir."

"Now I know I left those cups back here," said Cush, as he tried to push a shelf from the wall. "Erdna, come over here and give me a hand."

"Yes, Sir."

"Stop calling me sir."

"Yes, Sir. I mean Cush."

Erdna is more than happy to give Cush a hand. They find the cups Cush had stored in a cache' on one of his other visits to the wine cellar, Erdna smiles broadly for he knows his break is going to be even more enjoyable than he had imagined, for no one likes to drink alone.

Inside the palace, two men are also having themselves a drink. The two men are King Revilo and his closest friend and confidant Balaam.

The King has a strong majestic face; he is a fine looking man of about fifty-five, who looks more youthful than his years. Richly, even magnificently dressed in a long and full white shirt, which is casually embroidered in gold, with a large belt around it hanging low over his fawn colored tights. He sits watching Balaam, who looks even younger than the king and his jet-black hair does not show any signs of gray. His face was florid with good living, but his waistline was as athletically trim as a man of twenty-five. He was about to finish up his turn and give the king a chance to win a game, which looks like backgammon; only the fifteenth stone has been replaced with a king from a chess set.

The king takes his roll, and he gets double five and then he looks across at Balaam with the grin of a child on the seventh day. For the first time since he and Balaam were much, much younger men he has beaten him at this game.

"Come, my friend, no need to look so sad. I deserved to win this game."

"Yes, my lord, you have played exceptionally well. I am glad you have broken the longest losing streak in the history of the game."

"If you are happy for me, then why do you look as if someone has just stolen your favorite spell stone? Tell me what is on your mind, my friend."

"I have been having a little trouble with a new spell I found in a book given to me by King Lardu's sorcerer, Haadel. I cannot seem to work it out. The only reason why he gave me the book was because he could not work it either."

"Come now, Balaam, are you trying to tell me what you have found a spell which you cannot work? It cannot be true! Everyone knows that you are the best in three galaxies."

Balaam knows he should have used another excuse; still anything would be better than telling the truth of what was really on his mind. It was not time and it was not his job to disturb what was being written in the book. He must continue his story. "This is by far the most unusual spell I have ever encountered, my lord. So if you please, I would like to return to my work shop to practice on it for I believe I almost have it worked out."

"I was thinking to play another game, but if you really feel a need to leave you may go. "

"Thank you, you will be pleased with the outcome of this."

"Wait! There is one condition to which you must agree."

"What is the condition?"

"You must return when King Lardu arrives."

"As you wish, my lord," said Balaam as he fades slowly from the high backed chair he was sitting in.

King Revilo watched as Balaam used his power and shook his head, "Sorcerers are so hard to understand." The king poured himself another glass of Bonda Berry Juice and sipped slowly.

Suddenly, a young lady entered gracefully through the door of the King's study. She was wearing a yellow chiffon gown. It is hard to tell how she looks for her face is covered by a scarf, but her movements indicated she had been well established. She becomes very excited as she sees the king.

"Father, you must come to your window," she insisted with a voice as smooth as satin, while grabbing the king by his arm.

The king has a choice; he can join her at the window or he can have his arm pulled off.

"It is so wonderful, father, the carnival has arrived outside the city."

"Yes, it is wonderful," said the king as he saw what had made her so excited.

"Oh, father you must have their performers appear this evening at the palace."

"Ricki, you know Prince Derrag is coming tonight with King Lardu and Queen Neeves. So that may not be such a good idea."

But the princess knows how to make him comply, just one kiss on the cheek and as always before he will change his mind.

"Okay, okay you win. I will have Cush run out and tell them to be here at eight bells."

"Thank you, daddy."

"By the way I sent Cush to check the guard post and he has not returned yet."

"Father, you know how he gets whenever you ask him to do something, as soon as he can, he sneaks off into town and drinks Bonda Berry Juice all night."

The king looks down from his balcony toward the guard post." Now I see Erdna has also disappeared."

"If you ask me, Father, the two of them are off together somewhere getting drunk. Daddy, you know he hates Derrag. Cush will probably be gone the rest of the day," she said leading him away from the balcony.

"You are probably right, my dear," he sits down at the table and begins to write. "I want you to take this note to one of the guards and have him to present it to the owner of the carnival."

The princess grabs the note, gives her father another tangling kiss on the cheek, then she is off to find a guard.

Princess Reikciv walks hurriedly down the hall in her excitement. Suddenly she feels weak, very weak and her weakness causes her to experience tunnel vision.

" I have got myself too excited, " says the princess as she stops to rest in a chair. "I better lay my head on this table and rest a while."

She falls asleep and dreams of standing in her sleeping chambers looking out of the window, when suddenly she sees a series of flash candles fly high into the sky. As the light begins to fade, she hears loud noises of confusion coming from a lower level of the palace. She stands trying to make out the sounds; someone enters her room undetected by the princess and begins to walk slowly and quietly up behind her. He is close enough to reach out and turn her about.

She is so surprised by the presence of the intruder that she cannot speak. He said not one word he only looked deeply into her eyes. Then the intruder's hand begins to move up toward her face, until he is almost touching the scarf.

The images fade away.

"Ricki, dear are you alright?" Asks the Queen as she brings her around by shaking her gently.

"I must have dozed off, "she says.

" Maybe you should get some rest. "

" Yes, Mother, I am a little tired, " she says as she stands. " I must get something to eat. "

"You will, just as soon as you go up to your room. I will have one of your attendants bring you up something to eat."

"I must give this note to one of the guards," says the Queen holding out her hand to receive the note.

"I want you to go to your room and do not leave until I send for you, "says the Queen holding out her hand to receive the note.

"Yes, mother, as you wish," she said handling her note as she passed her on her way to the lift, which would take her to an upper level. "I will be glad when I get my own place."

Queen Sesma walks through a lower level of the palace where she finds a guard on his way out of the palace." Guard, come here!" she commanded.

"Yes, your highness, "he said and hurried over.

"I have a note which needs to be delivered at once to the owner of the carnival."

"Wait!"

"Yes, your highness?"

"If you see Cush, tell him to return to the palace at once."

"Yes, your highness," and he turned once again and picked up a double time out of the palace and made his way quickly over to deliver the invitation.

Riding hard through the town the guard, His name is Bodel. Bodel slows as he reaches the out skirts of town where the carnival workers are busy setting up. Bodel dismounts and walks his mount over to where a few men busy themselves setting up tents.

"You there! Where can I find the owner of the carnival?"

The men say nothing upon seeing a palace guard in uniform addressing them, they only point towards an area where three men stand talking.

Bodel walks where those men are, but they still continue their conversation. He tries to casually draw their attention by clearing his throat, but he is still ignored. So he speaks. "I have a note from King Revilo which one of you is in charge?"

A man with thick black hair to his shoulder, who looks to be about forty-seven, average height and dressed in all black leather with a lot of shiny chains and things, turned to find Bodel waving the note about.

"I am," he said taking the note.

The King had written:
You are invited to perform at the palace tonight.
Bring your tumblers to entertain the Princess Reikciv.
Come to the palace at eight bells.
You will be handsomely rewarded.

The man nods his head. "We will be there at eight bells."

"Very well," said Bodel pulling his mount about. He is soon riding hard once again, this time back from where he came.

The man begins to smile as he looks over the note once more, then he turns to his companions. "Well, my brothers, it seems our work is almost done."

"Zenon, your plan is working just as expected," said the youngest looking of the group.

"Yes…Beezubul will be pleased," Zenon proceeded toward a wagon only a few feet behind them and the others followed. Upon entering the conversation resumed.

"Should I send a messenger to tell Beezubul when we are going to the palace?"

"No, Elnun, what I want is for you to ride out to the base camp and tell Beezubul in person…. Tell him we will light the way for him."

"I will ride to him now."

Beezubul has his men hidden in the hills far outside the city. His men are ready to move with stealth on his command. Beezubul if not for his evil nature would be considered a handsome man. He has the appearance of early forties, but his looks are deceiving. A glance from his strange eyes could strike fear in the heart of the bravest man. Beezubul was banished to a remote area in the Land of Excilo when he tried upon his curious arrival to overthrow the Council of Oligarchy. But he has had time to plan another offense.

Beezubul has pure thoughts of evil and he knows how to use intimidation to get what he wishes. Beezubul has a new plan and this time he has the help of Nud, the Lord of Slime and his Deacons, the Slime Dwellers. These deacons pray not to your GOD or mine; they pray to the chaos; they pray for anarchy. With their help, their support and their prayers Beezubul is confident that he will succeed.

It is dark now.

Balaam knows all that is about to take place in the next few hours, but it is not for him to interfere. Yet as the book unfolds itself he can help things along to try and eliminate some of the confusion that will develop when time comes for him to bring Quest back. But before I tell what he is planning to do next I will explain a bit about the book.

Many many, yes it was a long time ago, when what I am about to explain took place. There was a great writer of stories, whose stories were known throughout the land. He was a teacher and a prophet, and when he told his tales all listened. He was a teacher and a prophet and when he told his tales all listened. He had forty men who copied his works for sales and those sales made him a very wealthy man. But then he woke one morning with an ideal for a book, which he could not write and his copiers could not copy. He ordered his copiers to bind the finest pages in the finest leather and lay the title in the finest gold. Twenty-five thousand copies he demanded, of course, this meant that more copiers would be needed insisted his chief copier until he was handed the Master's copy. It was more than two hundred sheets of blank pages – there were no words, no marks, no corrections, nothing but blank pages – still he insisted that this was the most important book that had ever been written. He titled it Thee book and it sold out as one of the biggest conversational pieces ever. There were even a few attempts to duplicate the original twenty-five thousand but all could tell the originals from the fakes.

Then a group of thinkers presented an argument to the judges that what he had written, or supposedly had written, or not written, or whatever was a mockery. And the argument they presented, and the defense presented by the author, cost him his life, and the book was banned and anyone found with one in their possession…would be instantly put to death. Many of the books were destroyed, buried, placed in personal vaults or lost. But Balaam was given one, which he had kept under glass and used for a conversational piece, whenever he had guests over. Well, until three nights ago when he was working, yes on the spell from the book Haadel had given him, then suddenly the glass about Thee Book exploded and the book was lit up with an eerie glow, it opens and begins to Write it self- the words were appearing slowly displaying the events that are now occurring.

The seventh bell tolled as Balaam began to force him into a very deep trance. He knows what he is about to do will require complete concentration, his magic must travel a great distance to a far, far, far, far away planet.

He must locate a special renegade, and then Balaam's power shall borrow his will to survive and have it pay a visit to Zandoria. The visit will be short because Balaam's power will weaken once the princess is gone and the forces of evil become stronger, and the Quest will begin.

The eighth bell has been tolled.

King Revilo and Queen Sesma have welcomed King Lardu, Queen Neeves, and Prince Derrag to the palace. Princess Reikciv has not yet been summoned from her chambers; she dares not leave and disobey her mothers' wishes.

The guard at the main gate of the palace has been told to expect the performers from the carnival. So they are allowed to enter without a hassle from Erdna, who has not yet recovered from his afternoon break with Cush, who had gone into town to enjoy the company of one of his lady companions for what he thinks will be another PEACEFUL NIGHT IN TALMORY.

Erdna escorts the owner of the carnival and his troopers perform feats of magnificence all through the palace on their way to the grand hall where the Royal Party await drinking goblets of Bonda Berry Juice, as the sounds the yells, timbres, cymbals, strings, harps, bongos, and drums echo all throughout the palace.

"Wait here!" Erdna enters the grand hall. "Good evening, your majesty's," he said with a bow.

Zenon raised his hand and his troops broke it down a little.

"Good evening, Erdna," said King Revilo. "Tell me why are you doing the job I assigned to Cush?"

"It is my duty, sire."

"Your duty reassigned by Cush I assume."

"Yes, sire."

"I want Cush back within the hour, I want the guards doubled."

While this went on Zenon had men to move the flash candles into position against the windows facing toward the setting suns.

"Zenon you better be good, his majesty is in a difficult mood." said Erdna, as he tossed him a small bag.

Zenon moves forward as his troops follow him in further ahead.

"THANK YOU, SIRE, FOR YOUR INVITATION. THERE REALLY WAS NO NEED FOR PAYMENT FOR WE ARE ALWAYS HONORED TO PERFORM AT YOUR REQUEST, YET THANK YOU FOR THE GENEROUS PURSE. WE WOULD LIKE TO LIGHT UP THE SKY WITH JOY."

Then he nods to Vodon for him to do his little number and he sends off a flash candle, which indeed lights up the sky over Talmory with a glow, which can be sighted from far outside the city.

Beezubul has waited for Zenon's signal, they will fly fast and quiet on the backs of their Rodagons, and when the light of the flash candles glows high in the night sky, the Slime Dwellers moved quickly. Beezubul moves swiftly towards his Rodagon.

"COME DEACONS, THE TIME IS NOW!" He shouts as he and his Rodagons take to the air. The assault has begun.

In the palace the royal families watch the lights as they begin to fade. Then all turn their attention back to the performers.

"It is not I, whom you should thank, but Princess Reikciv," said King Revilo and for the first time he realizes she is not present. "WHERE IS THE PRINCESS?" shouts the King.

"I sent her to her chambers, "replies Queen Sesma, "She was not well."

"Ricki wanted to see this and I know she would not want to miss it for the worlds. ERDNA, HAVE THE ESCORTED HERE NOW!"

ERDNA moves to follow the king's command. But as he is about to exit, there is a huge cloud of purple smoke caused by Zenon throwing three small bombs on the floor. In the thick of the gas Edna feels a blade sliding across his throat.

The kings are not able to make out what is taking place as the gas immobilizes them. But the Slime Dwellers move well wearing their protective masks and continue to dispose of a few of the guards before they even know what is going on. King Revilo and King Lardu, knowing that this is not a part of the show they were expecting; draw their swords, but they do not rush into the choking gas. They remain close to protect the queens.

Prince Derrag tries to fight alongside the guards as they attempt to counter attack the impostors who have perpetrated the fraud. Derrag and the guards are not able to move sufficiently through the thickness of the purple gas. Prince Derrag and his guards are dead before they can kill. Both kings are soon disarmed, but spared for Beezubul to do with as he wishes once he finishes his carnage, which has already begun in the palace courtyard.

Beezubul and the Deacons have completed their assault. Their swords are dripping wet with blood as they march across the courtyard of the palace. Other deacons are in the progress of scaling the outer wall of the palace, under a balcony, which belongs to the chamber of the princess. They reach the ledge of the balcony the same time the deacons inside conclude their mad pillage through the palace and force their way into her chambers through the huge doors.

They find the princess is not there and the person they find does not wish them to know where she is and he begins to fight to maintain. He is out numbered, but it does not matter to him, he fends off the attackers only to feel the hilt of a sword against the back of his neck. They swarm down on him like mad hornets. But instead of the sound of his cry as their blades cut deep into him, there is the dull clinking of the metal as it made contact with the hard floor where the stranger had fallen.

While a few of the deacons stand puzzled and unsure of what they have just experienced. The Coadjutor discovers Ricki in her hiding place and drags her out of the room. Reikciv struggles trying to see what had happened to the man who tried to save her. The coadjutor leads the way out as they escort Reikciv to where Beezubul now awaits.

The grand hall of the palace, Beezubul finds bliss at the success of his plan for he has the princess as a reward and what a sweet reward indeed." Take her out to my steed and prepare to travel to Mount Seficul."

"BEEZUBUL, YOU KNOW THERE IS NO WAY THIS IS GOING TO WORK. I AM GOING TO..."

"YOU ARE GOING TO WHAT?" He asks cutting the king off and speaking loudly with his back to him, and then he turned to face him. "I WARN YOU NOT TO TRY ANY RESCUE ATTEMPTS FOR ALL WILL FAIL AND THERE WILL BE A HIGH PRICE TO PAY FOR THOSE ATTEMPTS."

He continues to speak addressing all his words to King Revilo as he moves slowly toward Prince Derrag lying on the floor. He kicks him for assurance and smiles.

"It is really terrible I did not run into my young friend Cush. He would look good lying alongside the prince here," Beezubul strokes his fingers through his long blonde hair, then walks to where king Revilo has been restrained to his throne.

"BY THE WAY, ALL ARE WELCOME TO MY WEDDING TO THE PRINCESS. YOU KNOW THE TIME AND THE PLACE IS MOUNT SEFICUL," Beezubul walks closer to King Revilo, and then he slashes him across the face with his sword. "To remind you of the time your ancestors sentenced me to in Exilo. YES TO THE PAIN!"

With his left hand Beezubul points the way for the deacons to exit as he takes lead way out the grand hall in front of the palace.

In the courtyard, the deacons mount their Rodagons. The princess struggles against the ropes which have her secured to the back of the Rodagon Beezubul is preparing to mount. She attempts to kick him as he tries to mount; he avoids the offense and manages to slap her unconscious.

"SHE MUST BE RED!" explains Beezubul as he mounts to the sounding laughter of the deacons. Then he and the Slime Dwellers are on their way to the fortress of Mount Seficul.

"TO THE PAIN!" He shouts.

Balaam fades in to find things a bit worse than he had expected. The dead are being cotted out, King Lardu and Queen Neeves had long made their cry for vengeance and now mourn the loss of their son as they prepare to take his body back to Trimelva for burial rituals. Queen Sesma has retired to her chambers for she was so overcome by grief her mental stability is greatly threatened. King Revilo has paced about the palace most of the evening worried about what to do to get his daughter back where she belongs. As a reminder he has not allowed anyone to dress the facial wound he received from Beezubul, but what he has done is think and prepare his plans while walking the throne room floor as he used his sword as a means of support, he slowly begins to realize if he is to think properly, he must allow himself to calm down for his anger has overridden his sense of reasoning. So he sits where he has as always when faced with a difficult situation; on his throne, which was his fathers' before him, and his father's father and so on and on.

There he sat when he awaited her birth. King Revilo holds his head down in his hands over her lap; his crown falls off his head and rolls across the hall in to Balaam's left foot.

Balaam picks up the overly jeweled crown and walks toward the king with the crown held in his up turned palm.

"I can help," he said, trying to hold back his emotions from seeing all the dead.

The King looks up to see Balaam standing in front of him. "YOU CAN HELP. I CALLED FOR YOU AND YOU DID NOT COME. WHERE WERE YOU WHEN ALL OF THIS TOOK PLACE, MY FRIEND?" Asked the King, looking around the room. "I WILL TELL YOU WHERE YOU WERE; OFF PRACTICING YOUR CRAFTS. LEAVE ME! I HAVE NO NEED FOR YOUR SKILLS NOW."

"But I know what we must do."

"HOW DO YOU KNOW?"

"It is all written in Thee Book."

"IF IT WERE ALL WRITTEN IN YOUR BOOK, WHY DID YOU NOT TELL ME EARLIER, SO ALL OF THIS COULD HAVE BEEN." King Revilo pauses for he remembers Balaam's behavior from earlier today and his excuse about a spell…he could not perform. Then he remembered Balaam had never had a problem with spells before, even new ones always came to him so easily, "YOU KNEW! YOU KNEW ALL THE TIME. DO

YOU KNOW WHAT YOU HAVE DONE? LOOK AT ALL DEATH HAS TAKEN WITH HER. YOU KNEW ALL OF THIS WAS GOING TO HAPPEN, BUT YOU DID NOTHING AND YOU EVEN LEFT TO SAVE YOUR OWN SKIN…YOU ARE NOTHING!"

"REVILO, YOU DO NOT UNDERSTAND. I COULD NOT INTERFERE. PLEASE, TRY TO UNDERSTAND. HERE TAKE YOUR CROWN," pleaded Balaam holding out the crown to his friend.

The king stands with his blade and slaps the crown from Balaam's hand. Then he prepares to bring down yet another blow, this time aimed for Balaam's head.

"MY FRIEND, YOU ARE HISTORY."

But as the king attempts to use his sword against Balaam. He uses his magic to stop the advance of the sword in full force. King Revilo realizes his anger has caused him to swing on a friend. He drops his sword and drops down into his throne.

"Why have you done this to me?"

Balaam knows he will not understand because of all the loss he has suffered; yet he must tell him. "I had to let it happen. There was nothing I could do to stop it. Will you let me help? Thee Book…"

"I don't care what was written--I don't care about the story of Thee Book."

"Thee Book is writing."

"What?"

"I have a copy of Thee Book and it is writing. It is writing as we speak and continues the story as the times continues."

"You have a copy of Thee Book? Do you know that anyone with a copy of Thee Book is to be put to death?"

"Anyone with a real copy of Thee book right now is watching to see what will be written next. What you will do and what you will say."

If this book of yours knows all, which is to happen, then I want you to tell me what is going to happen to Beezubul, now that he has my daughter."

"He will die."

"HOW WILL HE DIE? AM I TO GO TO SEFICUL MYSELF TO RID THE UNIVERSE OF THIS FOUL?"

"No! He will die at the hands of Stroke Renegade."

"Stroke Renegade? Renegades are causing the problems. Why would

I wish to employ one? I am sure that will be next; calling in a high priced savage warrior."

"This renegade and his friends have unknowingly been preparing for this day and those to follow all of their lives. Preparation, which has took place on a little blue green planet too far away to describe. And Quest.

"What are you talking about now?"

"It is not a what, sire. The prophecy of Thee Book describes them as: '…a band of five men with the will to survive no matter what the cost.'"

The king has had a slight change of heart. If Balaam's books has indeed began to speed out the story, which he knows, then it is time for him to go forward with the will of what is to be.

"If all is as it is said to be, then we must move forward. We must keep things on course. Bring Quest back here as soon as you can."

"I am way ahead of you, sire. There is a ship waiting for me with all the proper men for this mission. If we leave at this moment we should be in their solar system by morning. But I must take them at the correct moment or the mission will fail."

"There is no room for failure. You must succeed."

"Tell the people, that five men of Quest shall be the ones to save the Princess for it is all known and it is being written in the Thee Book," then Balaam holds out his left hand with the palm turned up, places his right hand on top palm side down and flips his hands over. Balaam slowly begins to fade out, he rematerializes at the city's dock for the intergalactic ships.

"We are ready to leave on your order, Balaam," said Keiop, Balaam's apprentice.

Balaam turns to take one more look at the palace. "I will not fail and Quest will not fail, either. They will be victorious, "Balaam then turned to board the ship

The ship Deliverance soon slowly begins to lift off and then accelerates as it cuts through the clouds.

TWO

THE LOW COUNTRY

SEPTEMBER 28th

THE FLUFFY WHITE CLOUDS DRIFTED lazily across the pale blue sky over the Atlantic as she allowed her waves to touch gently on the beach. The weather was typical for this time of the year, even though it had been unusually hot all summer. It was a day when some would say the coming of winter was going to be extremely harsh. But this was for those who cared to take note of the forecast. Others simply enjoyed the weather and continued with their own business as usual on this small island known as Hilton Head, in an area the locals referred to as the Low Country.

The people of this island community enjoyed living here. And most would live nowhere else. A man working in one of the last few Full-serving service station had just given a trucker from out of state the weather predictions, and he was taking time out while making deliveries to the local Pizza Inn to watch a boat on waters ideal for sailing. As the playful couple beached their craft on one of the many privately owned beaches. This particular beach has the scenery of a large hotel in the background; where inside preparations are being made for a birthday celebration. A party for someone the employees of the hotel consider very special.

At the registrations desk, two men stand talking. One is Black, very handsome and stands about six feet six. His name is Solomon. The other is a few years younger, he is white with blond hair and unusual looking blue-green eyes, very handsome, but he is dressed as if he has a serious case of poverty chicness. He stands about six foot or so and he is called The Rebel.

"Okay, Solomon, you know what to do. So don't be all day about it."

"You have the easy part, young man. All you have to do is wait for me to come down."

"You're his big brother, and besides, you know how suspicious he is whenever I'm too nice to him. He'll just think I'm trying to set him up. So The Rebel is going to walk himself over to the bar and have himself a cup of coffee, " said Rebel, before leaving Sol still standing there.

These two men have a very special party planned for their brother Stroke. But first thing first . Sol must lure Stroke down to the Auditorium. This should not be a major factor, for not only is Sol the manager of the hotel, He has known Stroke for many, many years. He knows he can handle it. But before he leaves, Sol remembers another part of their plan and turns to one of the Bellhops.

"Follow me to Stroke's penthouse, then take his bags to the roof."

"Yes, sir!" He knew what to do when he got there.

Upstairs Stroke has just finished packing his bags; He zips one shut and picks up his favorite yellow sweater. Before putting it on, He turns his attention to the beautiful view outside his hotel's window then walks over to the mirror.

Stroke really didn't consider himself all that handsome, but many females had told him differently - it was probably the money that they liked. His money! He had worked three and even one period four jobs at a time. Nothing but a stressed out young man, who had learned to endure the pain. So anyway, as this young man stood looking at his shell in curiosity, he paused a little more and took special note of his hair which had been cut short enough on the sides for waves, then allowed to grow as long as he dared over the rest of his head until it fell back to form a braid down pass his shoulders. He has a bronze skin color and piercing eyes, which were yellow tint mixed in with black. All seemed to give him the added look of mystery he had wanted for years. What Stroke saw in the mirror made him smile in admiration of his well-toned six-foot frame. While he stood facing himself in the mirror.

Sol walked into the room unnoticed. "I can't understand it, either."

" And what can't you understand?" Stroke asked, while pulling on his sweater.

"How such a funny looking kid could grow up to be so popular with the ladies."

"I guess that's because I know how to please."

"Well at least you haven't forgot what I taught you."

Stroke smiles and develops an oriental accent. "Ah, practice, make ah, perfect," said Stroke as he splashed on a year's supply of Halston Z-14.

" Are you ready? " Asked Sol trying not to laugh at Stroke's lost humor.

"Always, Big Brother."

"Well then, get moving," Sol turned toward the Bellhop, "Get Stroke's bags."

"Good morning to you, too," said Stroke, as he fingered his hair in the front. "Nice uniform. You look like Mike Starborne."

The bellhop takes this as one of Stroke's humorous compliments. "Thank you, sir," he said standing with the bags next to the door. Then waited there as Stroke and Sol exit the room in order to close the door behind them.

Stroke walked down the hall trying to keep stride with Sol's long legs." I hate it when they call me 'sir', " he complained.

"Well you have to expect that when you own a fifth of the hotel."

"Basically, I think you have a point...By the way, have you seen Rebel? I had the craziest dream last night and I wanted to tell him about it. Maybe we can write a song about this. It was wild. Anyway, it will keep until the trip."

"The way the two of you were all zooted up. I wouldn't be surprised if you had dreamt about being on another planet," said Sol as he pressed the button for the elevator.

"Man, you ain't ever lied. We were gone. Did you see that girl Rebel left with?"

"Yeah, Man! A-real-land-walking-air-breathing' underwater-seamonkey."

Solomon has got off a good one on Rebel, and he knows it, they hardly stop laughing to enter the elevator, and the laughter is allowed to die slowly.

"Have you seen him this morning?"

"Yes. And you would have as well if you had made it down for the breakfast conference. But, I guess your Underwater-seamonkey was showing you her under-cover breathing equipment," said Sol, as he and the bellhop once again laugh loudly.

Stroke did not like Sol using the same joke on him and he gave the bellhop a very evil sequence, which caused him to cease his laughter. Then he turned back to face Sol, "That shit ain't funny. Don't you know any good looking women, because I know there are plenty here."

"There were a few there last night. But like I said, you and Rebel were both too wired to see them," Sol polished his nails on his beige camel hair sports coat, "I know I left with two myself," he added as the elevator doors opened revealing they were now on the ballroom level, where the Auditorium was located not far down the hall.

"Come on. Rebel is waiting for us in the Entertainment hall."

"You mean the auditorium?" he replied following Sol down the hall.

"Yes, smart ass."

"Why is he waiting for us there?"

"Why not?" responded Sol and before Stroke could argue his point, Sol pushed the doors open and disappeared inside.

"Hey now! Why is it so dark in here? I know we paid the electric company this month because I saw the bill. "

"WE TURNED THEM OFF SO NO ONE WOULD SEE HOW UGLY YOU ARE."

Now he needed no light to know whose voice that was. "WELL, REBEL THAT WORKS BOTH WAYS, YOU KNOW. BECAUSE NOW NO ONE WILL KNOW THAT IT'S REALLY YOU WITH THE BAD BREATH." He begins to laugh at his own humor, as the house lights come on. He sees that the room is filled with the employees of the hotel, whom are all standing on the stage to give him one very big...

"SURPRISE!"

Stroke is overcome by the sight of his entire staff applauding his entrance, not to mention the two men responsible for all of this standing there in the middle. He begins to walk slowly down the aisle toward them. "I'M GLAD TO HAVE A HOTEL WHICH CAN RUN ITSELF. BECAUSE I SEE ALL THE EMPLOYEES ARE HERE READY TO PARTY." He looks over the faces of all his friends, with a big smile on his face. He looks toward Solomon and Rebel; both are pleased by his reaction.

Rebel is a member of Quest and part owner of the hotel. Without him none of this would have been possible, and Stroke knows it. Rebel approached as he climbed the stairs to the stage. "Happy birthday, dude," said Rebel, giving Stroke a strong handshake, then a big hug. And on n that note the Chef and members of his kitchen staff roll in a huge cake with HAPPY BIRTHDAY RENEGADE spelled on it. The walls tremble as everyone in the Auditorium joins in to do their rendition of 'The Birthday Song'. At the end of the song Rebel gives Stroke a small box. While Stroke rips savagely at the wrappings, Rebel takes the floor.

"THROUGH HARD WORK AND DEDICATION, WE AS A GROUP KNOWN AS QUEST HAVE MADE OUR DREAMS COME TRUE. NOW WE ARE DOING WHAT MAKES US MOST HAPPY, WHICH IS SHARING OUR MUSIC AND WORDS OF SURVIVAL WITH OTHERS, WHO KNOW JUST WHAT WE ARE TRYING TO RELATE TO THEM."

Stroke has managed to remove the wrapper from the box and he instantly recognizes the object in the box as the 18kt gold cross which belongs to Rebel's mother. Stroke looks at Rebel as he turned to face him. "You know I can't take this. It belongs to your mother," he said attempting to give the box back.

"No, Stroke, Mom wants you to have it to protect you, and remind you that it was GOD, who made all of this possible for Quest." Stroke remembers how he had once told her how beautiful he thought the cross was when she had shown it to him. But the cross was in the box - the same box. Of course, this was long before Rebel could afford a chain of quality for such a fine work of art. And now that he could afford just about anything he wanted for his mother, She wanted him to have the cross. But since he didn't believe in GOD he decided to pass it on to Stroke for his birthday.

"ALL RIGHT, ENOUGH IS ENOUGH," interrupts Sol trying to lighten the air. "Here. Stroke, you haven't opened my gift," he said, trying to pass another box similar in size. Stroke dropped the chain around his neck, and then wasted no time opening the second box. This time he finds four keys carved of gold, which Stroke holds for all to see. "Thanks, Sol, just what I always wanted…Spare keys to the homes of four of your finest women," Stroke turns the box upside down and begins to shake it. "Where are the addresses? "

Solomon starts to comment on Stroke's last foolish statement. But, today is his birthday. So he goes about things as they were planned. "TEE, WHAT YOU HAVE THERE ARE THE KEYS TO ADVENTURE. "

" I KNEW IT, " adds Stroke, still deciding there was something more behind those words. But he also knows whatever it really is; he will just have to wait to find out. The chef motions for Stroke to come over and cut the cake. Stroke moves over toward the Chef standing by the cake and he can feel all of the eyes on him. He starts to say something as the Chef hands him the knife, but he finds himself at a loss for words, he looks around the large room at them as a lump forms in his throat and his stomach begins to hatch butterflies. He starts to speak, but his mouth has gone dry, he clears his throat. "I don't know what to say."

"How much do you have to say to cut a cake?" asked Rebel, allowing him enough time to regain his composure.

Stroke laughs as he was about to become very emotional, He cuts the cake, then hands the knife back to the Chef, who will finish the job started by the small indent made by Stroke.

"Thank you. THANK YOU ALL VERY MUCH, FOR YOU HAVE MADE THIS A DAY TO REMEMBER AND TOMORROW NIGHT GOING TO GIVE YOU A CONCERT YOU WILL NEVER FORGET," Stroke is interrupted by applause. "COME ON NOW, HOLD IT DOWN. IF WE'RE GOING TO DO THAT REBEL AND I HAD BETTER GET HOME AND TAKE CARE OF SOME BUSINESS."

As Stroke exits the auditorium he was still very excited about all that had happened. Rebel takes up his part of the plan; he will distract Stroke while Sol sets him up for the big one. "Yo! Stroke, I drove up you should drive back."

"NO WAY, you know I don't need the cops running a check on my driver's license in South Carolina."

"Man, I told you I had all of that mess cleared up a long time ago."

Solomon knows Rebel's argument Stroke about who is driving back is more than enough to get his curious mind off the keys to adventure. Still he to take over with something else Stroke should know, "Stroke, before you go, ah, I think we should discuss the plans for the new club we' re planning to build in Slovannah."

Stroke has been very enthusiastic about the construction plans for the new dub ever since he came up with the idea for the multi-million dollar project. The elevator arrives and Solomon decides to casually change the subject. While Sol works Stroke, Rebel pressed the button for the elevator to take them to the roof.

"But before we can talk about that, I have a little bad news for you."

"Wait, Sol! I thought we weren't going to tell him until tomorrow?"

"No. I think it would be better if we told him today."

"Tell me what?"

"It's like this, Stroke, the promoters have decided to decline our proposal for them to buy the new bird," said Sol.

"OH SO THEY GONNA FLIP ON ME!" He shouted, then he decided to get smooth, but he was pissed. "Look, I told those suckers that this band they pay so much money to promote - could save all sorts of time on travel, if we just had our own bird. But that's cool. How much longer do we have on this contract?" The elevator doors opened. "What the hell are we doing up here? This is the roof. "

"No shit, Cherokee, " Sol replies.

Rebel exits the elevator and starts up the stairs to the roof; he knows what is there.

"Well, Stroke, don't you want to see it?"

"See what?"

"ADVENTURE, HOME TEAM."

Stroke remembers their conversation; he pulled the keys from his pocket, while at the same time taking to the stairs. He almost cleared them all in one leap. Rebel stood holding the doors open as he slowed his pace in awe of what he saw. Because there on top of the roof of the hotel was Adventure, a beautiful mid-night blue Black hawk with 'ADVENTURE 1' on the sides in bold yellow letters.

"DAWG GONE! IT'S THE SAME DAMN BIRD I'VE HAD MY EYE ON."

"I wanted to give you something you could use."

"How did it get up here?"

"I flew it up last night before the party," said Sol.

"Can I take her up?"

"Take her up? You can take her home. This one is all yours. Well, after a few more payments. But yours just the same."

"But I need to get my gear."

"Don't worry. I had it taken care of already. There is also music and a chest of cold ones aboard."

Rebel drifts around to the far side of the chopper and pulls the door open. "COME ON, DUDE, LET ME SEE YOU FLY YOUR NEW BIRD BACK TO SLOVANNAH. LATER, SLIM."

"How many times have I told him not to call me 'slim'?" asks Sol, as he tries to pretend he doesn't know what is going to happen next. "WHAT ARE YOU WAITING FOR? AN INVITATION?"

Stroke smiles, and then gives Solomon a big brotherly hug. "Thanks, slim," he said then moved out smartly to avoid any painful physical reaction Solomon may have wished to share with him for being called 'slim' twice in such a short span of time. Solomon watched as he made his escape toward the chopper. "HAVE A GOOD TRIP AND BECAREFUL."

He stopped outside the chopper, then turned to wave and smiled in appreciation for the bird. He then came to attention to give Captain Solomon a proper military salute, He executed an about face and climbed aboard the chopper.

Inside the cockpit Stroke strapped in quickly, then pulled on his headphones. Next he slowly fingered the controls touching each and every switch skillfully, taking care as if it were a woman. The motor sounded sweet as it begins to kick up.

Rebel reached inside the cooler and pulled out two-goose neck Budweiser's.

"Captain Renegade, over?" said Rebel using the proper style of in flight communication, as Stroke begins to maneuver the chopper from the landing pad. " No, ah, not while I'm flying. Break. But I would like to hear some music. Over."

"Ah, Roger that," said Rebel as he made use of this shirt to help twist the top off.

Stroke looked over to see Rebel taking one straight from the muscle instead of turning on the radio, Stroke was flying in a south bound direction heading straight for Slovannah, he managed to maintain control while reaching over to turn on the radio, then he searched out a decent station. And he found a freq. one that he was familiar with 91FM the run is mostly classical but from time to time there was a chance of some excellent jazz. This brings a look of displeasure from Rebel as the same sound, which Stroke was digging, passed through his headphones as well.

"WHAT THE HELL IS THAT? OVER."

But before Stroke could answer the programmer announced. "Dave Brubeck Take Five. And we're going to take a few as well. I'll be right back after these messages."

Rebel reached over and eased the volume down very low. "There is no way. Break. I'm going to listen to that all the way to Slovannah. Over."

"Okay, chief, why don't you see what Sol packed in the tape box? How's copy?"

Rebel picks up the tape box. "Ah, that's a good copy." Rebel began to mumble out the names of the artist within the case. "Let's see, now Franks? No. Grover? No. Chic? No. Cannonball Adderly? O no." Rebel didn't mind a little jazz when he was in the mood, but he wasn't in the mood. "Stroke, there ain't nothing in here but jazz. Over."

"That's what I'm going to listen to all the way to Georgia. Over," said Rebel, tearing the wrapping from around a cassette of their latest releases.

"I wonder what the Boys are doing now? Over." He asked while Rebel popped in the tape.

"The Boys are down on the Street handling a little promos with the local stations. Break. WHAT THE HELL IS WRONG WITH THIS THING? Over." Asked Rebel in his fury with the cassette player for not producing any sound.

"Why don't you try turning it back up, professor Groover. Over?"

"Roger that," said Rebel as he leans forward to correct the volume control and

'There She Goes Again' starts to jam through the headphones.

THREE

L.O.C. OPEN FEAST ON RIVER STREET
SLOVANNAH, GEORGIA.

IN SLOVANNAH THERE HAVE BEEN many changes since General James Oglethorpe founded her in 1733, but the way the river flows has not. And there is no one to my knowledge, who could tell you exactly how many ships had sailed these waters right off the top of their head, or even the number of times the Waving Girl had put out. There was a new face, which had been placed on this river, which borders Georgia from South Carolina. The work, which had been done on the Street, bared the last name of a man who had been Mayor of Slovannah almost as long as Stroke had been a Slovannahnian.

Here on this very famous river, along the cobble stoned street a large crowd had gathered. Not a crowd on the scale of Saint Patrick's Day in Slovannah, where over two hundred and fifty thousand people walked the street, but about the size of a first Saturday Celebration in July. And all these folks have come down to see three Home Boys, who were members of one of the fastest rising bands in the world.

Patiently, Sledge stands admiring the view as a few young girls try to get his autograph. This is all too new and wildly different for this handsome young man to really get use to. He tries to see what Blaze and Diddily are up to, but it is rather hard for him to see over all the heads for he is only five feet seven inches tall. But he tries and manages to spot the two of them, as he gives away his last tee shirt.

Blaze and Diddily were doing the promo thing like they were supposed to. Well, actually Diddily was doing his own thing as usual. They had taken advantage of this opportunity to invite a few girls over to the beach house on Tybee Island (Slovannah Beach). But now Blaze was trying to make the younger Diddily understand what he had already warned him about once before.

"But look at all this dough, and they are still happy."

"Wrong! You were to give them the tee shirts not sell them."

"Ah, but mine were all autographed by the members in the band."

"Ah. How much did you make?"

"Twenty-five hundred." He said showing him a phat knot.

Blaze whistled and shook his head. "Give it up."

"Give it up?"

"Give it up or I'm telling Sledge."

"Here take it! Take it all," he said passing him the roll.

"Thank you. And what about the girls? Did you remember the girls?"

"What?"

"Look, kid you've got to pay attention."

"I thought I was."

"Don't go there."

"All right, now what about the girls?"

"Okay, here it is; you don't have to worry about how old the girls are to ask them to party, because you're in college and that makes most of them safe for you. But in order to keep Sledge and myself from looking like 'Chester the molester' you've got to let us know if any of your guests are San Quinton Quail. Understand?"

Diddily has a look on his face that could only mean. "No, I don't understand."

"And what don't you understand, now?"

"How am I supposed to know if she has a bird?"

Blaze is raged and unraveled by Diddily's question and he runs his fingers through his long sun bleached hair. "San Quinton Quail is not a bird."

"It's not?"

"No, it's not."

"Then what is it?"

" It's jail bait. You know girls under age. "

"Oooooooo."

Blaze thinks he understands, so he turns Diddily around to point him in the direction of the girls. "Go get'um, tiger, and tell her the party starts at four."

"Why four?"

"Because, Stroke and Rebel are coming in around five. Just be cool, kid, they are still grinning and looking this way."

Diddily smiles, "Yeah, I should have sold three more tee shirts."

"No, kid that's not what a smile like that means."

"Well what does a smile like that mean?"

"It means she is still on your jock. So close your mouth and stop wasting time, kid move out!"

"Okay, I'm gone."

As Blaze watched him make his approach, he was not sure if Diddily would ever receive his hawk wings, which is the ranking ability to score with any female you want.

Blaze turns to see how he can make his way over toward Sledge, who he observes to be in obvious hawk composure, as he watches him finishing up a conversation with a very well built red head. Sledge turns and sees him coming and shows a smile of an experienced hawk.

"So what's happening, dude?"

"Diddily that's what's happening," said Blaze pointing a hitchhiker's thumb toward Sledge's young brother. "Man, the kid is slow. I was trying to explain to him that we could have all the females to ourselves at the party. And the kid didn't get on the bus until I was about to close the door," Blaze finds his remarks about Diddily very amusing. But Sledge has just sighted a very important city official coming toward them.

"Cool out, Blaze. The Mayor is heading this way." Blaze moves to stand on his left. He is impressed that the mayor has taken time out from his busy schedule to pay them a visit.

"Well, if it ain't J.P." smiles Blaze, like he and the mayor were drinking buddies.

The Mayor was not close enough to hear Blaze's last statement. But just like any good politician his hand is already being offered to them as he listened to his aide to make sure he calls their names correctly.

"Blazes and Sledge, I'm so glad to meet such talented young men. Steve's tell me you have one of the best selling albums so far this year."

"Yes, sir, and we have another which will be released while we are on tour," explains Blaze.

"You young men must be very creative to produce such great sounds."

"I guess you could say we are. But there are three more members of Quest; there is Diddily, the youngest members standing with those young ladies", Sledge pointed Diddily out for the Mayor. "The other two will be returning from Hilton Head later today."

"I hope you won't mind that I have taken liberty to throw a reception in your honor. It will be a grand affair. Can I expect the five of you there?"

"Yes sir. We will be more than happy to attend," said Sledge accepting the invite, even though Blaze had nudged him in the ribs to remind him of their plans.

"Fine shall we say about seven?"

"Ah, why don't we make it about eightish?"

"Eight will be good. Steve will make the arrangements for the limos.

Well, I've got to get back to City Hall. I'll see you later." He said before turning to leave, waving at a few of the citizens as he made his way back up the cobble stone street.

"How many cars will you require?" asked Steve, pulling out a red memo pad to make a note of their request.

"Two Rolls would be nice," Sledge assured him with his arms folded across his chest.

"Is the band still staying at the beach house?"

"Yeap."

"Fine. There will be two Rolls Royce arriving around seven forty-five," Steve turns to travel the path the mayor walked back up to City Hall.

Sledge rubs his hands together and smiles. "This is going to be great."

"What do you mean?" asks Blaze, "Why didn't you tell Mr. Mayor there that we already made plans for this evening?"

"First of all," Sledge was using his right index finger to make the indication. "It's good publicity for the band. Second, when the mayor offers to give a party in your honor, you don't refuse. Well, unless you have a better offer."

"The mayor of Slovannah is giving us a party?" asked Diddily catching only the tail end of the conversation.

"No. The Mayor of India," said Blaze.

"Don't talk to the kid like that."

"The kid is a friend of mine and I can talk to him anyway I please," Blaze places his arm about Diddily's shoulder.

"Thanks, Blaze."

"You're welcome, kid," smiles Blaze looking at Sledge. "So, I guess you want to cancel the party on the beach."

"No. But we're gonna have to cut it short."

"Cut it short! Cut it short? Over thirty young ladies and you say cut it short?" Blaze shakes his head. "Look we've finished our business here for today. So why don't we head for the beach."

"Sounds like a good idea to me," adds Diddily.

"Shut up, kid. Blaze and I have some business to discuss."

Diddily is hurt by his brother, who still won't treat him as an adult member of the group. He walks slowly behind them as they start through the crowd. As they discuss what Diddily believes to be very important business, a man wearing black raincoat, sunglasses, and a wide brim hat walks up behind Diddily and taps him on the shoulder, then hands him a folded piece of paper.

"You are our only hope."

Diddily reads the note, and then runs to catch up with Sledge and Blaze. "Hey Blaze! Check this out."

"What does this mean? Quest you are needed," Sledge reads the note over Blaze's shoulder.

"I don't know," says Diddily. "It was handed to me by that man over there." Diddily turns to show them the stranger, but he is no longer there.

"What man," asks Sledge? "Come on, kid, you've been running with Stoke and Rebel too much."

"You're right, Sledge. They've got him trying to play one of those stupid paranoid trips on us."

"It's not a trip!"

"Yeah, yeah, yeah. Get in the truck, or we're gonna play a trip on you called - walk to the beach. Ha ha ha. Hey, Sledge, did you hear what I told him? Walk to the beach."

Diddily climbs into the back seat of the gold blazer with its outlawed black tinted windows and sits there quietly without sharing in their laughter, he crumples the note, then tosses it pass Sledge out the window at a wastebasket. It goes in.

Sledge and Blaze enjoy the sound of Van Halen "Unchanged" during their trip to Tybee Island. Diddily stares out the window quietly trying to cool off.

Sledge turned away from the view outside the window to face Blaze.

"I sure hope the boys didn't have any trouble making a settlement before they left."

"You know Stroke."

"You're right."

"I hope they don't smoke it all before they get back. I could sure use a little something right now, as a matter of fact." Sledge turns around to call Diddily into the conversation. "Hey, dude, where is that doobie I gave you to hold for me?"

"It's in the ashtray."

Sledge hurries to remove the joint from the ashtray.

"Yes, this is definitely the way to take a road trip," Blaze was watching Sledge as he put a little fire to one end of the doobie.

With Blaze driving it's a surprise they arrive at the beach house without incident. Pulling into the driveway, no one noticed the dark blue 1975 two door Cutlass Supreme Oldsmobile with a white Landau half top, which has been following them since their journey to the beach began. Sledge does notice that one of his favorite tunes is about to start on the radio. But they have reached their destination; so Blaze turns off the trucks motor.

"Man, how can you turn that off? That was "Ramble On.""

"Come on, you guys, let me out! Sledge, if you want to hear it so bad, you can run inside and listen to it."

"Ain't no biggie. I've got the tape I can hear it later. "

"Good, now let me out." insisted Diddily.

While Sledge and Diddily begin to remove their gear from the truck.

Blaze sees two people standing in front of the house and he knows they are waiting for him and he can tell from their faces that they are still having trouble with the stage designs. "Damn! Looks like more work."

"But now they work for you, " said Sledge, as he tugged at the weight of the bag thrown across his shoulder.

Blaze finds himself surrounded by questions as he approaches the Stoop. Both men are wanting to be answered at the same time. And he answers them both with, "Can't I at least put my bags inside before you start? "

Diddily wrestles with the front door and it seems to give him a troublesome time as he tries to hurry to catch the phone ringing inside. "I'll get it, " he says as he finally forces the door open.

"Well I guess I'll just pop up stairs and have a little drink," thought Sledge trying to avoid the activities.

"SLEDGE!" shouts Diddily, catching him as he reached the first step. "IT'S FOR YOU."

"Tell them I'm busy."

"NO CAN DO. IT'S THE PRESS."

Sledge walks over and takes the phone from Diddily, then he muffles the receiver. "Hey, kid, how about fixing me a drink? "

" Sure, " said Diddily picking up Rebel's sky blue acoustic guitar to diddle a little Muddy Waters ' Hoochie Coochie Man' on his way up the stairs. Sitting quietly at the bar Diddily can hear bits of both conversations.

"No, no, no! I told you yesterday, this set was not designed for birds. And we want all the costumes in the dressing rooms because no one has decided what colors they want to wear... " Explained Blaze.

" Of course we still want the banner to fall before the questioning begins. It would not have the same effect if it didn't..." insisted Sledge.

Diddily takes time to mix himself up a little drink and he sucks it down quickly.

"HEY KID, I'M STILL WAITING ON THAT DRINK!" Shouts Sledge, using his left hand to muffle the phone.

Caught by surprise Diddily sends the drink down the wrong chute and he almost drowns as he answers Sledge. "I'M COMING, SLEDGE!" Then he quickly pours Blaze a drink so he won't have to make the trip again. He throws his guitar across his back and starts down the stairs with the drinks. As he steps from the bottom step Blaze passes in front of him, as he had just let the set managers out.

"Here you are, Blaze," said Diddily with a slight slur from the drink he slammed.

"Thanks, kid, You must have read my mind.' said Blaze taking hold the glass, then he walks over to find himself a quiet spot to relax for awhile.

Sledge finishes his conversation with the pres s crew and turns to find Diddily holding a glass out to him. Diddily tries to stand without swaying, so Sledge wouldn't know he has been drinking. But Sledge had something else on his mind. "Hey, kid, how about a smoke?"

"Okay, " he agrees, sitting down to play Rebel's guitar.

" Have you any papers? " asked Sledge looking over the top of the glass at Diddily stretched out on the couch.

" No. Did you ask Blaze? "

" No. I didn't ask Blaze, He never has papers on him, but he always has a light. And there aren't any in the house because I checked for some earlier. "

"Well?"

"Well, I guess you'll have to go and buy some. ""Why don't you wait? One of the girls may have some when they get here," said Diddily not willing to admit he is in no condition to go to the store.

"Come on, kid, how many girls do you know that carry papers in their purse? And besides you know we don't smoke in front of the guest Now, stop making excuses, You could have been back by now."

"How am I supposed to get to the store? "

"Take a taxi or ask Blaze to let you drive the truck."

"Yeah right, you know Blaze won't let me drive that truck."

"He will if you tell him I told you to."

Diddily laughs, " Sure he will."

" All you have to do is tell him you' re going to the store to get some… papers, so we can have a little smoke. You dig? Now hurry up, kid, you're wasting time."

Diddily starts toward Blaze, who is sitting playing a game of Backgammon alone; because everyone knows he cheats. Blaze ignores Diddily as he stands waiting for him to acknowledge his presence. Diddily decides to be forceful. "Blaze, give me the keys to your truck. "

"For what? " asks Blaze not bothering to look up from his game?

"Sledge told me to go to the store."

"Oh, is that all? Why didn't you say so? You better start walking," Blaze snaps his fingers as he rolls the dice. "Yeah!"

"I'm going to the store to buy some one-point-five's."

"Now that's what you should have said the first time, " Blaze reached in his pocket for his keys. On finding them he throws them toward Diddily. "Okay doesn't turn on the radio. Don't drive too fast. Fill the tank and hurry back."

Outside the house, two men sit waiting for them to make their next move.

"Sieron, why didn't we just garb them and go?" asks brother Sajem.

"Those are not our orders. Our orders are to give them the note from

Balaam and wait until they are all together in one spot, and then let Balaam know and he will do the rest. Look, one of them is coming out."

"Yes. He is the one I gave the message to."

"Then we shall follow him."

Diddily walks over to the truck mumbling the orders Blaze gave. As he drives away from the house he is too preoccupied to notice the additional weight. Diddily is determined to defy at least one." Well, I want to hear some music, "Diddily turns on the radio and he hears Lynard Skynard's Free Birds. He cruises with the radio turned up so loud he can hardly hear himself think. Diddily continues the short distance to the store waving at anyone who waves at the familiar truck. He sounds the horn at all the girls he sees along the way. His drive is fast, fun and quick. He parks the truck in front of the store located on the first and only curve on First Street. He was about to dismount when he remembered Blaze's request for him to put some gas in the tank. So he drives the blazer over to the pumps and fills it up. He still hasn't noticed the two men in the car, but they pay dose attention to every move he makes. When he finishes, he drives the blazer over to the front of the store then goes inside.

Sajem gets out of the car and follows him over, but he remains outside on the walkway. Diddily stands in line behind a customer until it is his turn to be served.

A young, very attractive clerk smiles at Diddily." And what can I do you for today, Diddily? " She asks.

"Hi, Angie, first you can give me some One-point-Five's and a carton of Marlboro's in the box. Then you can deduct it from this, " he said passing her a fifty dollar bill." Oh yeah, I also got gas."

"Diddily, what about that date you promised me? "

"Don't worry, baby it's gonna happen just as soon as your husband stops wearing that police uniform."

"Here's your change, " she says with a smile.

"See you, Angie."

Diddily turn s to leave and sees the man he remembers from earlier standing outside smiling at him through the glasses window of the store.

"Damn!" he says pushing the door open so that he may confront the stranger. "Look, dude! I think you had better stop following me."

Sajem has other orders from a higher source." We need you. You must tell your friends, because they must also come. Can we talk?"

"No, dude, you must be on shit, because dope don't make you that crazy. I believe that whatever type of party you have planned you had better leave me and da Boys out of it. So, if you don't mind I want be telling them anything. And I suggest you stop following me before I call the cops!" Diddily turns to walk toward the blazer.

Sajem runs back to the car, where Sieron is waiting. "What happened?"

"Nothing."

"Did you tell him again? "

"Yes. But he said he was not going to tell the others anything. He also said that if we continue to follow him he is going to call the cops. Sieron, what are cops?"

"I don't know, but if he calls them we will find out." Sieron pulls the gearshift into drive.

Diddily knows he is being followed and that's what he wants, because as soon as he gets back he's going to show them to the Boys, then he's going to call the law.

Diddily enters the house and finds Blaze and Sledge patiently waiting.

"What took you so long? " asks Sledge, "And where are those papers?"

Diddily throws Sledge the small pack of rolling papers. "Do you remember the guy I told you about?"

"What guy?"

"You know, the guy on the river, who gave me the note."

"Come on, kid, don't tell me you're going to start that shit again.
I told you it's not going to work," insists Blaze.

While Diddily tries to convince Blaze that he is telling the truth.
Sledge rolls one.

"But I'm telling, you these guys are real nuts."

"What? So now there's more than one? " Asked Blaze.

"Well if you don't believe me just look outside and you'll see two men wearing dark sunglasses in a dark blue Olds."

Blaze starts toward a window in the front room. "Okay, kid, I'll check it out."

Sledge starts behind him with the joint hanging from his lips. "Does anyone have a light?"

Blaze turns to face him with butane lighter, turned up so high it looks like a torch, he gives Sledge a light, then they both walk towards the window in order to investigate Diddily's story.

"Dark blue Olds, two men wearing sunglasses. The kid was right, " says Blaze taking the joint form Sledge.

" Now what do you plan to do about it? " asked Sledge.

" What do you think? I'm going to call the Police; that's their job."

" Well, you go right ahead, " said Sledge, taking the number from Blaze." While I stand here and finish this, before they get here. Better still, ask for someone we know. "

"Okay, while I call the cops, you roll another one

"And why not?"

"Because there is no more to roll."

"You mean I went all the way to the store for papers, and all you had was one lousy joint!"

"Not jus t one lousy joint, one joint of Ses, " said Sledge passing the joint to Blaze.

"And that's what makes the whole thing worthwhile, " said Blaze, taking in a big toke." Kid, go ahead and call the cops. Sledge and I are gonna stand here and, ah, keep an eye on those friends of yours. O yeah, you better ask for Deputy Jenkins."

Rebel and Stroke were now in Georgia, and had just flown over the mouth of the Slovannah River. The beach house was only a few minutes away.

"I know the guys will be happy to see this new chopper. They will probably throw a party to celebrate the arrival of a bird to Quest's collection of fun shit,"grins Rebel.

"If I know the Boys, like I know the Boys; they are already planning a big party anyway. But luckily for them I won't be staying."

"That's fine by me, leaves more women."

"Yes without me being there one of you might get laid, " He looks at Rebel with a big toothy grin.

"There you go again with that Superman shit."

"You know it's true. Hey, dude, why don't you take the tape out so we can hear what's been happening in Savoo while we were gone."

Rebel reaches over to eject the tape, and then tunes the radio to the freq of I-95, which is a very popular local rock station. What Rebel finds on the radio is another song about to start, a song that was wrote by Stroke and himself. Rebels turns to look at Stroke, who is already looking at him. They are thinking the same thing as usual.

"That must be a very popular band around these neck of the woods," says Rebel.

Adventure begins to shake from their laughter. Just as they start to really groove with the music, Stroke brings the bird into position for landing and begins to hover the helicopter over the private beach in the back of their house on Black River.

Blaze is the first to notice the chopper landing on the beach.

"HEY, DUDES! THERE THEY ARE NOW," He says rushing out to The Sun deck to greet them.

Stroke lands the chopper, then helps Rebel unload his gear; carrying his bags up a few yards toward the house. Rebel carefully removes the case that contains his favorite Washburn guitar, which he rarely allows anyone to touch. Blaze stands on the beach as Stroke and Rebel run toward the back of the house.

"WHERE DID YOU STEAL THAT CHOPPER?"

"We got it from Joe."

"Joe. Joe who?"

"Joe Momma." Blaze does not find this funny. But he asked for it.

"I'll see you guys later, " said Stroke as he hands the bags to Sledge.

"I know you will. " Adds Sledge giving the bags to Diddily.

"We have to attend a party given in our honor at the Hyatt."

"O yeah! Who says?"

"The Mayor of Slovannah, that's who. "

"Cool, I'll be in Liberty City, so just give me a call later."

"Well, it won't be too late, He's expecting us at eight o'clock," Sledge hears the doorbell ringing. "Are you sure you don't want to stay? There are a few girls coming over. That's probably the first load now. "

"No. I've got a couple of stops to make before I go in."

"Well, since you don't want to party with the Boys, I think I better get inside and check on things, " Sledge added with a wink, and then stepped off.

With everyone else headed in the house Diddily had a chance to talk with Stroke.

" Stroke, I need to tell you something, "

" I know what you are thinking, kid, you' re worried about the excitement and fear over our first big concert. It's gonna be just like diddling at home. So don't worry."

" Stroke, you don't understand."

" Yes I do, kid, I' m a little edgy myself right now. But once I hit the first Crash tomorrow night, hey! They had better be ready. So relax, kid," Stroke pats Diddily on the back, then runs off toward the chopper and he wastes no time getting airborne.

Diddily stands waving at Stroke. Happy to know he is back, yet unhappy Stroke talked all over him when he was trying to give him a warning about the two weirdoes.

Blaze watched from the back door to the sundeck as Diddily climb the stairs.

"Don't worry, kid, Stroke can take care of himself. Besides, you should know why he was in such a big hurry."

"But I don't."

"Wake up, kid, it's his birthday and he wants to go out and hurt someone's daughter. You know, get some birthday poonthang."

"Poonthang?"

"Come on, kid. You've still got a lot to learn."

Blaze tries to explain to Diddily the facts of life, as he leads him back inside the house.

Sajem runs back to the car after watching everything that happened from a different observation point, because the Cops made them move after giving them a warning citation for trespassing.

"Sieron! Call Balaam. I have seen him. But he is leaving."

"Balaam is not going to like this. We were to let him know as soon as they were all together."

"We could not help it. The cops were in charge of the situation at that time."

Sieron pressed a button on the radio, which resembled any other radio in any other Cutlass Supreme Olds. But this is not a regular stock Olds and what is revealed is a monitor screen with a two-way speaker. Slowly an image appears; it is Balaam answering the radio signal from the Deliverance.

" Balaam! Stroke has been here at the house, but he has left, "Sieron informs him.

"We are following him now," adds Sajem.

"Good and where are the others?"

"They are all inside the house. And from what I could see they were about to have a feast," said Sajem, still keeping his eyes on the chopper.

" Good. They will be busy for a while. I want you to keep your eyes on

Stroke. We will come in closer to observe the others. Do not worry the time was not right when they were together. "

"I think we are going to have some trouble keeping up with Stroke."

"What type of trouble are you talking about?"

"Just the fact that he is in…" Sieron pauses then looks at Sajem.

"Sajem what is that, again?"

"A helicopter."

"Okay, just keep an eye on him until we come in closer. Then we shall continue observation from the ship."

"Yes, your mystic."

There is no way their car can continue to tail the chopper long without them losing sight of it and to add to their difficulty Stroke begins to veer to a more southbound heading. Still Sajem does his best to maintain visual contact.

"Sajem," calls Balaam," we have just made the tracking. I want you to return and watch the others. We will follow Stroke from here."

"Yes, your mystic."

Sieron nudges him. "Why did you not ask him?" Sajem says nothing. "I thought you were going to ask if we could go get something to eat? You know how hungry I am."

"Yes you may go get something to eat," answers Balaam over hearing Sieron's sniveling. "But I want you back as soon as soon as possible to watch the others."

"Thank you, all great and powerful one," said Sieron. But Balaam did not hear this for he had turned his radio off after he gave them their orders.

FOUR

BROWN SUGAR, OR SMILING EYES?

THE BOYS WERE GLAD TO be busy entertaining so many guests all of which were very pleased to have been invited to party with the Boys. There were a few more people than the Boys had expected, but due to the fact that they were all females, well, none of the Boys really seemed to mind at all. If they did mind, well they didn't have time to complain.

Diddily is still concerned about those two men, he cannot think of a reason they would have for bringing so much attention to themselves. He wonders if his older brother Sledge has any idea what they may have been talking about." Sledge, what do you suppose those two guys wanted? "

"Probably your body, dude, " said Sledge in a very serious tone. Turning away from Diddily Sledge resumed his conversation with the five young ladies he was talking to before he was interrupted.

"So you think they were only a couple of Homo's after my body?"

Sledge turns back to look Diddily over. "Nah, kid, I doubt it. So don't get your hopes up too high. The kids' first brush with fans," explained Sledge addressing the small group of women he has about him. At this time another woman draws his attention as she enters the front door and walks in as if she owns the place. "Here comes trouble. The Devil's baby girl."

Blaze is not slow moving to cut her off on her way through the house.

Because she has an evil look in her eyes and the smile on her lips is only an appetizer.

"Hi, Kathy."

"I heard through the grape vine that you guys were having an orgy, "

" Not an orgy, Kathy, just a small get together with some friends."

"Well isn't that's how L.O.C. starts all its sets."

"How can such ugly statements fall from such a beautiful mouth?"

"Save the bull shit for someone who wants to hear it."

"Okay, Kathy, what can I do for you?"

"Well, for starters you can tell me which room Stroke is in, and save me the trouble of looking."

"He's not here."

"Come now. All these girls, and you say Stroke is not here. Don't try to cover for him."

"Kathy, you know I wouldn't lie to you."

If the look Kathy was giving him had been translated into words, it would probably say, 'don't even try it.' Blaze decides what he really need is a good lie.

"Look. Stroke got a new chopper for his birthday..."

"What? I forgot. Today is the twenty-eighth. It is Stroke's birthday," said Kathy, cutting Blaze off at the beginning of what was to be a tacky lie. Blaze is going to use her forgetfulness to his advantage.

"Well, he said he was going to stop at Sol's house to change and then he was gonna pick you up, and the two of you were going out to celebrate his birthday. And that's the truth; Blaze had his fingers crossed behind his back.

The Rebel had been watching Kathy from the time she entered, until the doorknob almost hit her butt as she exits the house. He has been waiting to find out what happened at the upstairs bar. There was no need for him to go to Blaze, because as soon as she started for the door Blaze started for the stairs. Blaze walked up to where Rebel was leaning against the bar.

"Well?" said Rebel.

"Well, what?"

"I know you didn't tell her where he is."

"Yeah I did," said Blaze, pouring himself a drink.

"That makes you an accessory. Because you don't put fire out with gasoline."

"Well if I hadn't told her where he was this party would have ended like the last one when I tried to cover for Stroke."

"You're right. I don't know why he had to fall for a black belt in Judo, anyway."

"Adventure?"

Stroke has decided to see if an old friend he works out with is at home. Even though his friend lives in a very quiet neighborhood, Stroke takes advantage of Alfred's spacious front yard to land his chopper; which almost vibrates the windows form the frames of the nearby homes. The sight of the chopper landing on his property shocks Alfred.

"Who in the hell is landing a helicopter on my lawn?" He steps out on to his front porch and sees Stroke running around the front of the chopper. "WHY DIDN'T YOU CALL?"

"I was flying over the neighborhood. So I thought I would drop in to see if you wanted a good work out."

"Are you going to wear what you have on or does that bag contain what I think it does?"

"Very observant. And they always said you were slow."

"Come on in. I think I need to kick you in your head a little so Alfred leading Stroke into the house. "I want you to know my gardener is going to be pissed when I tell her how those tracks got in her lawn."

Stroke and Al both change and soon were seated Adventure I.

"The usual spot?" asks Stroke

"Where else?" said Al taking time out from looking at all the devices inside the chopper." This is a nice little toy you've got here."

Stroke smiles and turns on a little Cannon Ball Adderly for him to enjoy.

"Yeah. It's okay. Just a little something for puttering above town in."

On the other side of town, there sits one very angry young lady. Kathy has driven to Sol's house in Liberty City; she is upset because she has not been able to catch up with Stroke. She begins to talk to herself.

"Thanks, Blaze, for lying to me. But all you did was delay what's going to occur when I see you and that no good friend of yours."

She speaks aloud as if there were someone there beside herself. She leaves with plans of returning.

At Lake Mayor's Stroke and Al enjoy their workout, which they began with a series of stretching exercises, then a quick lap around the lake's mile and a quarter track. After their warm up, Stroke is able to release a little tension as he finds his inner strength via their practice of Korean Karate. Both are very alert, and from the accuracy of their kicks, it appears they both hold at least a Black belt in their forms. The way they move seem more like ballet, even though every other blow or kick could have the forces to cause some very serious damage if not blocked properly.

They have done this together hundreds of times before. And they continue for about forty-five minutes, then AI uses a move he had used many times before: A spinning back-kick with perfect execution, and out of it to a front leg take down. The exercise is over.

Alfred helps Stroke to his feet. "Why do you fall for the same move every time?"

"Because it's the only move you have perfected, and when you use it I know you're tired."

"That was a good excuse, and you know what I've said about excuses."

"Yeah, yeah, yeah! Excuses are a sign of weakness," Stroke uses his hands to brush away the dirt and grass from his yellow and black sweats.

AL only shook his head as he followed Stroke over to the chopper. Stroke flew AL back to his house, and then started the trip for his final destination in the chopper for the evening. But his travels were not unseen; Balaam had been watching him since the time he told Sieron and Sajem he had a track on him.

Of course he does not know he is being watch as he drops the bird at Sol's house, His only concern is taking care of his new baby. So he tops off the tanks with fuel from the reserve tanks they had stored there for the old bird, before it was considered unsafe by the Federal Aviation Commission. After securing Adventure I for the night, Stroke grabbed his bags and started into the house through the garden room door and walked into the kitchen.

He knows his chances of finding something to eat in the house are slim and none. Sol only had canned goods there, because usually no one stayed there for long periods of time, but Sol always had plenty cold beer on hand, just in case of a 'National Emergency'.

He takes a cold one from the refrigerator, then stepped through the kitchen into the den and walked on toward the entertainment center to activate the master switch in order to hear a little music; jazz or in this case Michael Frank's Passion Fruit. Hanging out here was really getting to be a habit with Stroke; it was a place where he could come to get away from it

all; the parties, the crowds and the attention. Well sometimes, it becomes a
bit too much for him and he had just about moved in. Just about.

He sat down to enjoy a cold one with hopes of relaxing his sore muscles
and having a quiet evening. He thought: maybe next time I won't take the
chopper, then maybe Al won't kick me so hard.

Five albums and four beers later. Stroke's thoughts are disturbed by
the sound of his fifth beer bottle hitting the table with a hollow and empty
sound. "Man can't live on beer alone, either." He said revealing his line of
thoughts. He pulled himself up from where he had been sitting on the floor
since the time he arrived; he had moved occasionally to change the music.
He started towards the garden room. The front door bell rings. It continues
to ring as if there were an urgent matter.

"HOLD YOUR DRAWERS! I'M COMING!" He shouts taking long
strides through the house toward the front door. As he opened the door,
Kathy grabs him around his neck and gives him a long wet kiss. The phone
begins to ring on the other side of the house.

Breaking from the kiss, Kathy looks Stroke in his eyes. "Are you going
to invite me in?"

"I would. But I'm actually on my way out for something to eat."

"Is the girl you went to see earlier in-the house?" asks Kathy, knowing
well Stroke hates accusations. So she answers her own question.

"She is isn't she? That's why you're telling me you're on your way out."

"Don't be childish and immature. If someone were here, don't you think
they would have answered the phone by now? "He said and the phone stops
ringing. He smiled.

Sledge was on the on the other end of Stroke's ringing phone. "Well,
Stroke's doing it again. He's not in yet."

"He may be in deeper than you think," adds Diddily with a big smile.

"What are you talking about?"

"When the Kat-woman came by today, Blaze told her where he was
staying, so she could give him a little birthday poonthang. I guess that's
why the phone wasn't answerer."

"Yes, you may be right. Well I guess we'll just have to cover for him as
usual. I'm gonna have to have a talk with him about responsibilities."

Stroke understood his responsibilities and he really had no intentions
of missing the party. He was doing his best to get rid of his favorite girl
without hurting her feelings. But she wanted to make up for forgetting his
birthday and the accusations about the other women by fixing him up a

home cooked meal. She had begun to scramble about the kitchen, and since she had been here before on many occasions in the same type of situation, she knew where to find what she needed. Stroke decided to let her stay long enough to cook.

"STROKE, WILL YOU PLAY SOME MUSIC FOR ME?" She asked, calling him from the kitchen. Stroke puts on another one of his favorite albums, Earth, Wind, and Fire's 'That's The Way of the World'.

At the beach house. The guys entered the limousines sent by the Mayor's aide. Sajem reports their activities to Balaam. "The four here are leaving. What should we do?"

"I want you to follow them where ever they go."

"Understood."

At the Hyatt Regency Hotel, Rebel, Diddily, Blaze and Sledge arrive at the hotel, decked out in tuxedos. And the boys look extraordinarily sharp. They feel the magic as they exit the vehicles and start towards the automatic doors. Making their way casually through the crowd of people, still trying to use clout to enter the exclusive affair.

Entering, they see most of the people there are the rich and or influential members of Georgia, South Carolina, and Florida. The Boys move slowly taking notice of Slovannah's key officials and distinguished citizens, who are lurking about the balcony of the Ballroom floor. All the elevators are in use. And they watch as another capacity crowd is lifted to the floor of the main party, while the others wait in the long lines for their chance to board.

"Man! Look at all those people waiting for the elevator. I think we better take the escalator," said Diddily leading the way over.

"J.P. must have invited every Big-to-do in Georgia," Sledge tells them.

"Look! Isn't that the Governor of South Carolina standing there?" asked Rebel.

"Just as long as he hasn't forgot to invite plenty of rich and beautiful females," said Blaze.

The others agree as they board the escalator, which carries them up to the Ballroom floor. The Mayor sights them on their way and moves over to hail them.

"WELCOME, QUEST! I thought there were five members."

"There are," said Rebel accepting the Mayor's hand.

"I didn't meet you today. Did I?"

"No sir, you didn't. I'm the Rebel."

"Well, Rebel. Where is the other member?"

"Stroke was suddenly overcome by something unexpected."

The Boys were amazed at how well Rebel had worded that.

"That's okay, as long as he feels better tomorrow night."

Blaze pulls Sledge over so he can whisper something in his ear.

"If I know Stroke, he is already feeling something better," The Mayor escorted them into the Ballroom. There was no need for formal introductions, well not until they had a little refreshments.

"Drinks, gentlemen?" asks J.P., as a waiter with a tray of Champagne approached him. They all declined. "You mean, you don't drink?"

"We drink, we just don't drink Champagne." Sledge told him.

"Well, there is a wet bar over to your left and the waiter can bring you whatever you wish from the bar."

The waiter looked at them one at a time and the answer was the same four times. "Draft."

The Mayor even decided he would have a beer. As the waiter goes to get the beers, Rebel must satisfy his curiosity. "Was that's the Governor of South Carolina I saw when I walked in?"

"It certainly was," The Mayor told him. "I see she is over talking to our Governor. Hey! Why don't I introduce you? Since they are all here to meet you anyway."

After the Mayor introduced Rebel to the two Governors, he decided to make a formal introduction of Quest to all the guests. J.P. steps onto the stage.

Diddily is still concerned about Stroke not showing up. "I wish Stroke had come."

Sledge smiles as he looks at Diddily. "He probably already has, kid."

At Sol's house, Stroke is just finishing the dinner Kathy prepared for him, and must now try to get rid of her, so he can attend the Mayor's party.

"Would you like some more?" Kathy asked watching him slide his plate forward. "I made enough for five people; in case the Boys popped in."

Stroke stands, and then walks around the table to where Kathy is sitting. He bends over and kisses her lightly on the lips. "Thanks, Kat, but I've got to bathe and get ready for the Mayor's big party. Would you like me to draw your bath for you?"

Stroke sees through this sudden charm and he knows he is about to be played, but he does not know what her next angle will be. "No. But thanks anyway, Kat," He said hoping she would decide to leave. "I'll take care of that. Besides I've got to check to see if Sol has an extra Dinner jacket or Tux; that will fit. So I guess you'll be leaving now?"

"How do you expect me to leave? I haven't even cleaned up this kitchen."

"Really, Kat. You don't have to do all of that. Dinner was enough."

Stroke gets no answer as Kathy disappears into the kitchen. This was an argument he would only lose. So, he throws up his hand walks down the hall towards the bedroom, while she makes her way about the kitchen to 'All About Love' as it plays on the system. Stroke stops in the bathroom before going to the bedroom to begin his search for something sporty to wear to the party.

She cleans up the kitchen, and then starts to fold away the dishtowels. She hangs them away carefully on the racks under the sink, and she reaches inside the cabinet as far as her arm could stretch to pull out a bottle of wine she had hidden there on her last visit. Kathy walks out the kitchen and removed two wine glasses from the ceiling rack over the bar in the den. Then she stopped momentarily in front of the bar, and smiled fiendishly at herself in the mirror.

Stroke has laid out his attire on the bed. He grabs his grooming kit and goes into the bathroom to turn off the water, then checks the temperature with his bare foot. "Perfect," he says, then begins to undress. He has one leg out of his sweats when he remembers to close the door, which he does just before pulling his pants to the floor. He removes his tank top tee shirt, and then climbs down into his bath. Feeling the warmth and comfort of the water on his aching body, he begins to forget about Kathy.

Suddenly the sound of Earth Wind and Fire was shut off and Stroke thought, 'What in the hell is she up to now?' Then he could hear the beginning of 'Still Loving You' by the Scorpions, which begins Kathy's favorite mood tape, a tape that happened to be a very long reel-to-reel.

Kathy walks into the bedroom and sees that Stroke has laid out what he plans to wear.

"The Renegade won't be needing these things tonight," she says, as she hangs the clothes back in the closet. Then she removes her own clothes to reveal something she knew Stroke could not resist.

Stroke knows what ever Kathy has planned, she is starting now. But he thinks himself safe, because she would not come in the bathroom...Or would she? Stroke begins to ponder the thought. Then he realizes the door is unlocked.

"Oh no!" He grabs a towel and jumps from his bath. But before he could reach the door, the doorknob turned. Stroke backs away slowly as the door open, Kathy comes in with a bottle of wine in one hand and two wine glasses in the other.

"Guess this mean I won't be going to the party?"

Kat smiles, and holds the glasses out for him to spill the wine, while she holds the glasses. "I thought you might want me to come in and scrub your back."

He reached for one of the glasses; he took a sip, and then nodded his head in approval. "My back, please," insisted Stroke as he climbed back down in the tub.

Stroke smiled up at Kathy in admiration of her finely constructed body wrapped in a yellow Teddy. Kathy knelt down beside the tub and removed the scrub brush from a hook on the wall.

"Where is the soap?"

"It's in the water," he said pointing to the area he thought it might be.

The look on Kathy's face tells him she does not mind feeling for it there. She leans over to the edge to kiss Stroke while she feels for the soap. Stroke decides she might as well join him in the bath, so he pulls her into the tub and they continue to kiss.

Meanwhile back at the Hyatt, Blaze was standing alone as he turned up his ninth beer. He spotted a very attractive young lady over the bottle while it was still turned up. The other guys were preoccupied with various young ladies they had met, so he knew they would not be any problem as far as competition. Suddenly Blaze realized his stares were being returned, and when he motioned for her to come over, she only did the same back at him. So he tries to make her understand. He will meet her half the way. She agrees and they meet out on the dance floor in the middle of the crowd. Just as the band starts in with a slow selection written by Jimmy Lord Brown and Brick.

"Perfect timing. I would say. My name is Crystal. And you are Blaze?"

"Sometimes," said Blaze trying to add a little mystery. As he takes her into his arms. While the band plays their rendition of 'Hello' by Brick.

Blaze and Crystal hold on another close, even after the song stopped playing. Blaze knew what the next lines of an experienced 'hawk' should be.

"I've got an idea. Why don't the two of us get away from this crowd and go somewhere a bit more exciting?"

"In Slovannah?" she asked with a curious smile. "Where did you have in mind?"

"The beach house."

"Yours or mine?"

Blaze looked over toward the others. "Yours will do just fine."

"Excellent. I'll get my wrap," she kissed him, and then rubbed the red lipstick from his cheek, stroked his face one more, and then walked away.

"Wait, Crystal. Do you have a car? I rode here with my boys in a rented limo."

"Now, don't you worry, Sugar. Crystal rode here in a limo as well, but hers belongs to Daddy," she said, ending her statement with a sexy little wink before she turned once more to retrieve her wrap.

Blaze tries not to smile as he turned to walk over to where the Boys were standing talking over the plans for what remained of the evening and they were receiving a few suggestions from their lady friends. The Rebel had been watching Blaze and Crystal long enough to make a typical assumption. "Shot down Hawk?" asked Rebel with his arm around the waist of a very attractive female with long auburn hair. Blaze holds his arms up to show Rebel the secret Hawk club sign. And no more needed to be said. Rebel removed his arm from about the young lady, and then walked with Blaze so they could talk away from the group. "Okay, dude. Here is the plan…"

"Forget it. I've already made arrangements to join Crystal. SO I will be retiring to her beach house," Blaze paused to wave to Crystal." As you can see. She is ready."

Rebel turned about to see Crystal standing in her electric blue evening gown, with her white full-length mink thrown across her shoulders.

"Look if it doesn't work out. Just remember who looked out for you."

"Right, I'll ask her if she has any rich friend girls."

Blaze starts to walk off, then he turns momentarily. "By the way, don't wait up!"

Meanwhile back at Sol's place. Stroke and Kathy had made their way to the bedroom, and as they stood at the foot of the bed touching one another. Stroke allows his gentle kisses to flow across her wet body. First her ears, then her neck while he used his hand to gently caress her breasts. As Stroke's hand left her breast, well, it continued down a little further and it was careful, but strong as it moved downward across her belly, only coming to rest on the soft curling hair of her genital mounds. He could feel her attempts to adjust her waist as she moved her legs apart to give him more room to work. He felt a slight thrust of her hips; a gentle, uncontrolled grinding motion, while at the same time he was giving her even more pleasure by using his mouth on of her breast.

How much longer would he continue to torture her like this? She thought as she clenched to his sides and held it so tightly that her nails seemed to break skin. Once she released her grip. He moved his head even further down, until it was on the same level as they rested on her hips. The damp warmth of the quivering erect mystery of her driving him on. Her hip ground in small circles thrusting up into his face with urgent demands. Then she suddenly stopped him and pulled him up to an upright position. She lowered her hands from his face and touched him on his manhood. She scratched her fingernails lightly over the length of it, as she traced a line of kisses from his chest down, then she lowered herself to better please him. Stroke could feel the hot moistness of her breath flowing over the smoothness of his skin. He swallowed deeply, then trembled with emotions as the please she gave him sent chills through every nerve in his body. And he thought how glad he was he had missed the Mayor's party.

At Crystal's place. Blaze finds himself taken by the lovely blonde goddess to a beach house not far from his own. But the size showed she had possibly been born in money, for it was one of the newer homes along Black River, and it appeared to have all those accessories the Realtor had offered the Boys when they remolded the Rheem joint.

Rheem Joint is the name for Quest's beach house. But none of it really mattered to Blaze, at the moment.

Crystal through her mink to the side as they walked into the living room.

"Blaze, ah, sugar, if you don't mind," Crystal pressed a button on a console she lifted from the couch, and pointed toward the well stocked bar which revealed itself as Blaze moved closer.

"Would you mind pouring me a scotch and soda?"

Blaze moved on toward the well stocked bar and poured Crystal a scotch and soda, then he poured himself a smooooth glass of Jim Beam, neat. He poured it slowly down his neck as Crystal disrobed in front of him. Blaze walked over seriously admiring the way she filled her camisole, then he handed her the drink she request. In appreciation she removed his tie and helped him to remove his jacket.

"Sugar, would you please light the fire?"

"That's exactly what I had in mind," Blaze moved forward and kissed her. But she breaks the kiss off with a smile.

"This fire's already lit, sugar. I mean the fire in the fire place."

Blaze stirred up a decent fire and pressed another button on the console, which caused the lights to dim. Then she entered seven numbers accessing her to a very hi-tech system.

"Bob Seager…I love Seager."

"Me too."

At the Rheem Joint Sledge, Diddily and Rebel have made their trip back to the beach house with their lovely party guest. All of them had been Debs. Sledge makes his way drunkenly to the overhead light switches, while Rebel shouts out orders to Diddily.

"Hey, Kid, make the girls a few drinks."

One of the ladies acts as spokesperson for the rest of her friends.

"What we really want is something to smoke. If you know what I mean?"

Rebel reaches for his stash box and pulls out a doobie. "Now tell me! What would you girls do for some red?"

Another young lady stood up and pulled her dress over her head.

Sledge looked over at Rebel. "Man, we would have a gold mine if you had said gold."

Rebel lights up as the girls do as their friend has done. "True, yes that is true. But I can survive mining silver." Rebel unrolls two long strips of condoms.

"Ladies! Let the party begin."

FIVE

PSYCHOTIC COMPOSURE

B ALAAM AND KEIOP ARE CHATTING about the mission and the time being wasted waiting for the moment.

"We should grab them and go ahead with the first stage of our mission," said Keiop. "We need waste no more time."

"I have told you. We must wait for the right moment. When they are all together and have the most energy. Even you will know the time, because our energy will be coming from a mass of sources, but they will all seem as one, then their will shall be so strong…It will make what we came here after easy to get."

"So, what shall we do in the mean time?"

"We shall do nothing, but wait and let things happen as it is written. Try to relax; Sieron and Sajem are going to send us beer and oysters from a place called W.G. Shuckers. So I think you should get some rest. Tomorrow it will all happen and we must be ready," explained Balaam.

Stroke soundly sleeps after, well, you know, he and Kathy had finished. But while he sleeps Balaam begins an incantation, there will be no need for Stroke's will to travel back through space.

Stroke finds himself walking in darkness, he sees a dim light just ahead, it is not an electric light but the glow is given off by what he recognizes to be a torch. He also recognizes his surroundings as some sort of corridor, which would be found within a palace. He continues to walk down the corridor. He feels as if he knows this place and where he is going, or maybe it is déjà vu. But something wants him to stop, so he does. He reaches for two large doors to his left and opens them. The room is dimly lit; he senses the presence of another. He steps further into the room where he sees someone standing in front of a window, he can tell it is a woman by the shapely figure, he approaches slowly walking carefully so as not to be detected.

He is close enough now to touch her and he turns her around. He sees a smile in her eyes like he has seen in no other before. But the eyes are all he can see of her face because she is wearing a scarf. He wants to see her face. He must remove her scarf.

As he starts to remove the scarf, He hears a disturbance at the door and looking over the railing of the balcony he sees men attempting to scale the outer walls. He must protect her, He must protect himself. Quickly he hides her away, and then readies himself, just as the doors swing open. He knows there are too many, but he tries as anyone in this situation would. Besides he still believes this to be only a dream.

He uses Korean Karate with the help of a six-foot candleholder and catches the first few who try to rush him by throwing the candleholder and knocking their legs from under them. He then grabbed the twin to the first candleholder and used it to fend off the attackers. He proves himself to be a worthy adversary against so many. He even appears to have an advantage as he uses the moves he has practiced so many, oh so many times before, and with the aid of the second candleholder he continues well. They close in on him and he is rendered unconscious by a blow to the back of the head.

Stroke awakes with his body covered by his own sweat. Quietly he tries to slip his arm from under Kathy in order to ease off the bed. She stirs slightly in her sleep and turns over as he creeps away. He goes into the bathroom, turns on the light, and then turns on the cold water. Using both hands; he splashes the icy water on his face, then stands up straight with a little support from the sink. He turns the water off and looks at his eyes while rubbing the back of his sore neck.

"Either Kat hit me during the night, or that was one serious dream." He opened the medicine cabinet, then grabbed the Tylenol bottle, pops the top and dropped a couple of pills into his hand, then he turned to leave.

Walking down the hall he finds where the wine bottle was left when it died last night. "Shit…Got damned!" He said as he banged his little toe against it.

He limped the remaining distance into the kitchen to open the refrigerator in search of a 'Private Stock'. He starts to reach for a mug from the tray, and then decides to drink it straight from the muscle. Stroke tossed in the pills behind a mouth full of brew as he made his way into the den. He stirred up a fire, then pulled a couple of throw pillows from behind the sofa and piled them on the floor in his favorite spot in front of the fire he had built, but before he can relax.

"Stroke, where are you?" CAN YOU HEAR ME?" She asked calling all through the house across the intercom system.

Kathy scrambles out of bed and pulls on the sweater that Stroke was wearing earlier, as she made her way through the room, then she starts down the hall blindly. "OOOOOOOWWWWWWEEEEEE!" She screams bumping her toe on the same bottle.

He laughs, but tries not to show that he knows what has happened to her toe, as he sees her limping down the stairs. "Are you okay, Kat?"

"I'm fine. What's wrong with you?"

"I couldn't sleep, so why don't you join me down here?"

Kathy walked over and he adjusted himself so she could find a comfortable spot. She lowered herself sleepily on him, and he remembered the pain in the back of his neck. "Tell me, Kat, did you hit me while I was sleeping?"

"No, but if you'd like, I could hit you now," she told him with a very broad smile.

"Go to sleep."

Stroke stares into the flame as she dozed off. He knows it will be difficult for him to sleep before the sun comes up. He sips on his beer and holds onto her as she snuggles tightly to him and moved her head to a more comfortable position on his chest.

Sunrise is coming slowly. The flames have gone out of the fireplace and now only embers remain of what was a roaring blaze. Still awake, he sits listening to the system when he hears Bill Withers' Lovely Day. He slides carefully from under Kathy and goes into the bedroom to find his running gear. He dresses quickly, then tips back through the hall pass the door to the den and on through the dining room, and into the garage. He grabs a set of keys from the rack, and then strolls over to the RENIGADE JEEP.

Kathy is awaken by the roar of the jeep's motor. Running to the window she makes it there in time to see the RENIGADE speeding down the street.

"I hate it when he does that!"

Stroke drives to President Street; a long stretch of nothing. The morning sun forces light through the overcast sky, but he knows that here he will not have a worry about much traffic or anything else.

The run is long and tiresome, but it allows time to think. He started his run just pass the Amoco station, then turned right on Bay street, which will bring him near his destination. The final turn, again to the right pass the Radisson and onto River Street, then forward to the statue of the waving girl. He marks the halfway point of his run by slapping her on the butt and petting her dog on the head.

Sieron and Sajem have just left Shuckers with a special order of oysters and beer for the Deliverance's crew, it was as very costly order, but they did not know of any other place to buy the food they had enjoyed so much, so the cost did not matter for they had promised to bring some for the crew. As they loaded their vehicle. "Look! Sieron! There is Stroke!"

Sieron saw Sajem was correct, they leaped into the car. Sieron whipped the car into the large parking lot behind the Electric Company, after they cruised past Stroke on the street for a positive ID. Then he got out of the car and waited for Stroke.

Stroke had no idea who these two were and he does not recognize them because he didn't give Diddily time to tell him. He picks up the pace as he starts the final leg of his run. He makes the adjustment to run around the men. Sieron grabs him by the arm. If there were a list of things Stroke did not like, well, being grabbed, being disturbed on his run, and stupid people would all be on that list.

He looked at Sieron, who had yet to release his arm, even though Stroke was giving him a peculiar look; stabbing him with his eyes. Then his eyes cast down to Sieron's hand on his arm and he helped him to remove it. But Sieron only grabbed him again and he started to speak.

"I want to talk to you," was what he wanted to say, but Stroke felt it was too late for words and he kicked Sieron square on the jaw, with a round house. While Sieron and falling, Stroke kicked Sajem in the midriff section, pushed him back up, and then delivered another kick to his head. He watched him as he fell slowly to join his friend.

Stroke decided not to stay around for a trophy; he figures they may have some more like them close by. He makes his run back to the jeep as quickly as possible wishing he had not taken such a long run. Short winded like he had just been on a P.T. run, he stepped into the jeep just before Balaam's men came cruising by. He knew he was safe, because he could handle those two again, if he had to. He drives back through the heart of the city to pick up a few pastries from Gottleb's before heading back to Liberty City.

At Quest's beach house, Blaze sits out front in Crystal's 450 SEL Mercedes Benz convertible.

"I really enjoyed last night," said Crystal, as she ran her fingers through his hair.

"Will I see you at the concert this evening?"

"No. But I will see you, sugar."

"Whatever. I'd like to take you to the party afterwards."

"Sounds like fun."

"Come to the stage door, there will be a couple of passes for you and three friends." He pulled her close and kissed her. Blaze opened the door and stepped out, then watched as she drove away. He jogged happily up stairs, chippie as a fourth grader, who had received three A's on his report card. Opening the door Blaze sees the old Boy Scout bugle form troop 56; he picked it up and began to wake the others with his rendition of Reveille.

Rebel turns over in his bed, stretching and yawning. "Damn! You can always tell when he gets laid."

Blaze finished the last few notes. "COME ON, GIRLS! WE'VE GOT A LONG AND VERY BUSY DAY AHEAD OF US. SO I'M GONNA START YOU OFF WITH A WHEATIES BREAKFAST. THE BREAKFAST OF CHAMPIONS. LET'S MOVE IT! RISE AND WASH,…GENTELMEN,…AND YOU TOO, SLEDGE!" He bellowed, as he walked toward the kitchen twirling the bugle.

Rebel walks down the stairs as Blaze enters the kitchen. He stopped at the foot of the stairs and placed his right hand in the pocket of his pale sky blue bathrobe.

"Come now, ol' chap, must we be so bloody cheerful in the mornings?"

Sledge walked to his room door scratching his head. He saw Diddily taking a towel from the linen closet. He moved fast, running up behind Diddily snatching the towel from his shoulder, then slammed the bathroom door in his face. "Come on, Sledge. Damn! I was here first."

"Sorry, kid, you slow, you blow," he said from the other side of the locked bathroom door.

Rebel is seated at the breakfast table. "Man! Do you know it's only nine-thirty?"

He asked, looking angrily at the clock on the kitchen wall. "We don't have to be at the press conference until noon."

"Yeah right, the way you guys move, we will still be late," said Blaze, setting a stack of bowls along with a couple of boxes of cereal on the table. Diddily walked in and settled himself at the table without saying a word to anyone, and he poured himself a bowl of Peanut butter Captain Crunch.

"What's wrong, kid?" asked Blaze, stopping long enough to look concerned. "I thought everyone got taken care of last night."

"It's not what didn't happen last night that made me mad, " he explains while reaching for the milk. " Sledge took my turn in the shower," he said, with a face flushed with anger.

"So now you want to cry about it? Kid, you're gonna have to grow up. Then people will stop taking advantage of you," explains Rebel taking hold of the bowl of cereal Diddily has poured for himself, and then he begins to eat while Diddily watches. Rebel knows what he is thinking. "But this is not a good time to start."

The phone rings. Rebel jumps up from the table, knocking over his chair as he tries to be the first one to the phone. And since there was no one else trying to answer the phone, he succeeds. "Welcome to satisfaction."

"Hello. This is the Mayor. I this 250-20"?"

"Yes it is. Good morning, J.P."

"Rebel?"

"That's right."

"Rebel, you've got to show me that trick you did."

"Next time, J.P."

"Sure deal. Ah, Rebel; I called to find out if Stroke will be able to make the press conference. I'm really looking forward to meeting him and presenting, all five of you, that's all five of you with the key to the city."

"It's sort of hard to say, mayor, I haven't talked with him since yesterday. Stroke is very unpredictable, but I could give you the number. I'm sure if he is feeling better he won't mind you calling."

"Sounds like a good idea. I've heard that he is a very constructive young man."

"More like James Moody if you ask me. So if you want to catch him before he gets out in the new chopper. The number is 250-8280 and we'll see you at the theater, J.P."

"Okay, Rebel, I'll see you young men later."

Rebel hangs up the phone and sees Blaze with something he knows he's not supposed to have. "Yo, dude! You know those Peanut Butter Captain Crunch are strictly for the munchies."

"Don't worry. There is enough for you."

"Good, now pass me a bowl," he said as he returned to the table.

"I see the kid ate my bowl and left."

"Who was on the phone?"

"The Mayor. I gave him Stroke's number…sure hope he's up."

"Yeah," said Blaze slurping his breakfast.

"Didn't your Momma teach you any manners?" Rebel shakes his head, and then begins to make the same slurping sound.

At Solomon's house. Stroke walks into the den wearing a pair of royal blue nylon shorts, with a towel around his neck, as he used a corner to try and finger a bit more water out of his ear.

"System 387 – "9 – 07." He says addressing the house computer.

"System open, access Renegade files. Stroke Tee is in the house," replied the system.

"System, add Que tips to the list."

"In there."

"Now Box one tape reset," he said and the power came on and the reel to reel and it begins to rewind. He kicks his feet up on the coffee table and thinks to himself it was very unfortunate Kathy had already gone by the time he returned.

"Oh well," he reaches for the remote control unit for the television with one hand a smoke with the other. He turns on the television and lights up.

Stroke laughs loudly to himself while watching the game show Press Your Luck and seeing someone press their luck too far and get a Whammy. He sits back, and then takes a toke. "Whammy will fuck you up."

Suddenly he hears the phone ring and he drops the smoke in the ashtray, and then presses the conference button on Southern Bell's addition to the home.

"Elo."

"Hello. This is the mayor. Is Stroke there?"

"Yes, he's here. You're speaking to him. What can I do for you?"

"This is not a business call."

"That's good. I'm very disappointed about not making the party last night."

"No need to explain. I'm sure it can all be very tiring …But, you don't have to trouble yourself. I'm looking forward to meeting you at the press conference. That's if you're feeling better."

"No, I'm not feeling better at all. I had a very restless night. I ran into a little trouble on my way back."

"What sort of trouble?"

He stands and begins to stretch in front of the system. "Nothing really, just a couple of guys trying to get my autograph. But I took good care of them," he started to stretch his legs.

"Listen, I'm going to give you the Chief of police's phone number, so if you run into them, or have any sort of trouble, give him a call just as soon as I hang up with you."

"Thank you, Mayor."

"No problem at all. His job is to serve and to protect; He can solve your problem easily. So remember this before you go taking matters into your own hands. Well, unless you have to."

"Only if you have to."

"By the way don't worry about the press conference. I'll cover for you. Just make sure to let us help, if you have any more problems. We're proud to have you as a citizen of the Low Country and especially of Slovannah. And we will not tolerate any invasions of privacy.… just be on time for the concert."

"Roger that!"

The Mayor gave Stroke the Chief's number and the conversation was ended. Stroke could now do what he was about to do; take a nap. Stroke walks over to the sofa and stretches himself across the length of it. Then he tucks a pillow up under his head and slowly drifts off to slumber land.

International Lunch Time. Quest's first press conference is covered by more of the media than Sledge had expected. Diddily, Blaze, Rebel, and Sledge are awaiting Stroke's arrival. Quietly they remain on stage in the Johnny Mercer Theater. The Mayor enters the theater smiling and shaking hands all the way to the mic stand on the stage. They watch as he prepares to make the presentation without waiting for Stroke.

"Ladies and gentlemen, of the press, television, and media circus. I would like to welcome you to the Johnny Mercer Theater. I'm sure you all know there are five members of Quest, bus as you all can see, one is not present at this time."

"Where did they find him?" whispers a reporter from the Star.

"But, I spoke with him earlier this morning. He is in Slovannah, he's only resting. So at this time I would like to introduce you to Quest."

"It's about time," said Blaze to Sledge using his hand to shield the mic in front of him.

"I will start with the one nearest to my left and ask them to stand, and remain standing until they have all been introduced."

The boys are each dressed in one of their concert outfits; the pants are striped and made of a stretch material, which fits very close to the skin. No glitter or rhinestones, only soft easy on the eye colors. Diddily wears brown, Sledge wears gray, Blaze wears royal blue, and Rebel wears yellow. All of which is heather with black and solid black stripes. The jackets are cut short and are aligned with their waist, textured leather with asymmetrical snap fronts with a stand up collar. There are also zip out sleeves that allow the jackets to convert to vest. Under the jackets they wear rough silk tank top tee shirts to match their chosen colors.

The footwear is just as complimentary; matching soft leather boots which are pulled high and rolled down the leg and allowed to gather around the lower calf and ankle. They strike a stunning appearance as they ready to stand.

The Mayor begins. " Diddily, SLEDGE, BLAZE, AND THE REBEL." As the mayor completes his introduction, a large banner slowly descends from one of the curtain drawers. On the banner are the likenesses of all five members in the same color concert outfit they now have on. And on the banner Stoke wears red. The banner is backed in white with Quest spelled in red letters.

"I would like Diddily the youngest member of the group to come over and accept the key to the city and the hearts of the people of Slovannah."

Diddily walks over from where he was already standing, to move to where the mayor awaits. The Mayor presents to Diddily the key to the city with his left hand and shakes his hand with his right hand, all done while smiling broadly. The flashes go off all through the theater as the photographers capture the event.

"On behalf of the Boys and myself. Well, we would like to say, thank you," Diddily returns to where the Boys are waiting patiently for the real action to begin.

"Now I have taken up enough of your time. So I will turn the floor over to the guys. Then you may begin the questioning with our own local press. After which I will recognize the hands of the others, and you will then address your questions to individuals in the band until they grow tired."

"Hell, I'm tired all ready," whispered Sledge to Blaze.

The Mayor points a finger toward a reporter from the Slovannah News.

"Tom Brown, Slovannah Morning New. My question is for Sledge. How does it fell to be the fastest raising rock and roll band in America?"

"Well, Mister Brown. First of all; we don't play rock and roll. We play metal with soul. So, being the only band in such a category, well, I guess it makes us the biggest band which plays metal soul in the world."

The Mayor recognizes another hand.

"Renee Stone, Musicians Magazines. Blaze, I've listened to album... and I think it's great!"

"Thank you!" They all say at once.

"Even though the sound isn't very heavy on the metal side. It seems to hold or carry a message. Can you explain?"

"Stroke usually comes up with the lyrics. Using all that soul he's always talking about. I guess the best way to describe it is Survival rock. Because we all know survival is what life is all about."

The mayor finds another.

"James Faison. Teen Beat magazine. Rebel, what would you say influenced you, or helped you on the road to success?"

Rebel smiles, then runs his finger through his long blonde hair." Even when I was younger I wanted to have a purpose, and I wanted to do something constructive for people to remember. I also wanted to have a band and able to jam. But, there was always the matter of a serious cash flow, because I didn't have one. But my family and friends always believed in me. Then I met Stroke. We had a part time gig at the same place. I won't mention where, because I don't want to give them any publicity, bad or good. It was a real bad scene. Well we started hanging out together. He had the words, and I had the music. Stroke was not willing to stop until we had something to work with. And, well, you can see how far we have gotten from such a simple beginning, because we have faith."

The mayor is on his job.

"Rufus Mills. Rock and Soul Magazine. Diddily, would you explain the need for the names you have chosen for yourselves."

"We didn't choose the names. Stroke just started calling us nicknames while we were still trying to form. I was the last to join the band. But my name had already been decided for me. Stroke once explained it to me. The Rebel is the rebel, simply because of the definition of the word. Blaze is called blaze, because of his lightning fast moves and balance. Sledge, which is short for sledgehammer. Humh. Well anyway, Stroke said that one time he saw Sledge throw an almost painful move on Blaze, then stop it right under his nose. And I'm called Diddily because of the way I diddle on the neck of that old Gibson I play."

"What about Stroke?" asked Rufus Mills?

Diddily laughed. But tried to cover it up quickly; pretending he was coughing. "I don't know why he calls himself that."

The mayor recognizes another hand. And this question is directed at Rebel. While the questioning and answering is going on Sledge has a question for Diddily. He leans over towards him while covering his mic with his left hand.

"Hey, kid, why didn't you tell that man the truth?"

"What are you talking about?" he asks trying to look innocent.

"The fact that Stroke named himself Stroke because he likes to hear the girls he makes love to giving him directions. This way all he hears is Stroke."

I couldn't say that. It would get printed and Stroke would be pissed."

"Believe me. If you had said it, he would have probably let you hang out with him; at least once."

"I could still tell him."

Sledge looks at him and smiles coldly. "Too late." Then Sledge hears that question repeated because he didn't hear it the first time. Sledge is still smiling as Diddily listens to the question.

"Mike Turner, Mix Master Magazine. Diddily, tell me, how does it feel to be the youngest member of such a popular band?"

Diddily looks down the table at Sledge, Blaze, and The Rebel, and all are smiling.

" WELL RIGHT ABOUT NOW. IT SUCKS!"

The Mayor immediately recognizes another hand. The questions go on until almost every man and woman reporter has had a turn to address at least one of the Boys. At the end of the proceedings the mayor invites the reporters to have refreshments upstairs on the Mezzanine. The Boys begin to rush off stage in order to get their share.

"Where are you rushing off to?"

"Later, Mayor, we want to get there before all the food has been picked over," explains Diddily, while the others wait for him to say the good-byes.

"Why don't you follow me? I know where there are some refreshments that hasn't been touched. Besides you can't go up there, you wouldn't have time to eat for all the questions left unanswered."

The boys follow the Mayor back stage where they find more than enough for them to eat. Before they prepare to leave they made a couple of sandwiches for later. While they busied themselves with stuffing their faces, the Mayor finds an opportunity to tell them what he has been waiting to say all afternoon.

"Listen up! Today when I talked with Stroke, he said he had some trouble with two men harassing him earlier this morning."

The Rebel stops laughing long enough to say, "Don't worry about him, J.P., Stroke is part street and all survivor. He can handle himself, and as a matter of fact, he even gets a big kick out of watching our backs. He knows the street, he has been to college, and he is a veteran. So there isn't much he doesn't know about."

"Well, just the same as a precaution, I have arranged for a security escort to provide protection wherever you wish to go."

"Look, Mr. Mayor, we appreciate the offer," said Blaze, "But as far as we know, there are only two of them and even without Stroke we still outnumber them two-to-one. So if he could handle them, well we would be through if he found out we had the cops following us all over town. So we must decline your offer."

"Okay then I'll pull them. But just be careful."

The Boys decide they should leave before the mayor forced the escort on them.

"Man! Don't you know how screwed up we would have been with cops and cop dogs sniffing around the house finding roaches and joints lying around," said Sledge, walking with Blaze down the aisle toward the lobby.

"Yes. It would have been very uncomfortable. Diddily, make sure you check all the ashtrays and I'll get rid of the stuff," said Rebel.

"Ah, Rebel, I'll give you a hand getting rid of the stuff," said Blaze.

"Thanks, dude, I'm glad I can count on you," added Rebel pushing the door open for Blaze.

They walked quickly toward the Blazer parked in the Civic Center's parking lot. Soon all we loaded and ready for the trip back to the beach house.

Traveling back along Victory Drive, Blaze decided to turn off onto Skidaway Road to the right and drive into the Krispy Kreme Doughnut's parking lot. Blaze becomes philosophical. "Doughnuts are good for you, because they contain sugar. And we all know that sugar gives you energy."

"Dude, I think you have been having too many talks with Stroke. He's really not a Tibetan Monk, you know?" said Sledge holding the door for the other's to enter.

Diddily walks around the store after placing his order; He looks out front and observes two men.

Yes! The Boys are back on their job. He stares at them and does not see the Rebel eased up next to him.

"Blaze spotted them long before we left the Civic Center."

"Why didn't you tell me?"

"Why so you can worry like you're doing now? Check it out…If they try to anything, we will ready." Rebel opens his hand to reveal a four-shot.38 pistol, so small he hides it leisurely in the palm of his hand.

Sledge and Blaze finishes up with their orders and paid for what they got. Diddily was still keeping his eyes on the Olds.

"Here, kid, eat your doughnuts, you're going to need all the energy you can get," said Blaze.

They exit the store and start toward the truck. "SHOTGUN!" Shouts Sledge holding the seat up for Rebel and Diddily to climb in.

"But what about Stroke?" asked Diddily stuffing a doughnut in his mouth?"He can handle himself. Besides we can always arrange one of the mayor's escorts for him even though I really don't think it's going to be necessary. So have another doughnut."

Diddily slowly starts to realize how safe he really was, as they crossed the… Wilmington Island Bridge.

"How about passing me a doughnut?"

Sledge passed Diddily the box with one doughnut inside." You have better enjoy it, kid. That's the last one."

"Last one? What? There is no way you guys could have ate all those doughnuts."

Diddily was right there was no way they could have ate all those doughnuts. But that does not mean that Sledge is about to share any of those he just stashed for a little later. But Sledge had not counted on Rebel spotting his movements as he attempted to shove the bag between the seat and the door. Rebel eases the bag out and finishes his hunch was correct there are doughnuts in the bag. Rebel hands the bag to Diddily, then gestured for him to be quiet and enjoy. Rebel decides he two will enjoy one.

SIX

RENEGADES RUN

THE BLAZER ROLLED INTO DRIVEWAY of the beach house. And as they downloaded their gear, Rebel takes charge.

"We know we're being followed, so that means we gotta do the three S's..."

"Yeah we know; smoke, shower, and street clothes."

"Domino time?" asks Diddily.

"Yeah, that's right. Thirty minutes or less. And, kid, don't forget the ashtrays," added Rebel with a smile, and then he pushed him toward the house. Rebel looks back to see Sledge searching for something in the Blazer. Rebel snatched the bag from under Diddily's jacket and took a doughnut out and gave Diddily half, and then he calls Sledge. "Is this what you're looking for?" He asked holding up the bag, then proceeded to eat the rest of his doughnut.

"I'm gonna tear your tonsils out!" Shouts Sledge running to catch them.

Rebel and Diddily were also running and they managed to reach the door five steps ahead of him. Leaving one pissed off dude locked out of his own place, beating violently on the door while eating a doughnut.

"Where did you get that?"

"Rebel gave it to me to come down and open the door for you. You want a bite?"

"No!" shouts Sledge storming up the stairs.

"I thought you liked doughnuts."

Three: forty-five. Rebel, Diddily, Sledge and Blaze arrive at the Civic center's Liberty Street stage door carrying their bags. The stage manager was hoping they would arrive early and he spots them as they enter the door.

"Hey, am I glad to see you, guys," he said moving over to greet them. "I was hoping to see you before check in time. Where is that cousin of mine? Never mind…I want you to look over some stuff before we arrange the set for the first group."

"That's why we came early, dude," said Blaze giving Bobby a cigarette.

Bobby led the way into the area to show the boys the set up. The crew had been working very hard and Bobby hopes everything will be to their satisfaction. First; he shows the lighting system, then he takes them to the stage for the sound checks. After a full tour the Boys agree that everything is exactly the way they were diagrammed.

"Good work, Bobby, the Boys and I are going to the room to cool out. We don't wish to be disturbed. Understand?"

"Understood."

Five o'clock.

The boys have had more than enough time to relax, sitting about in their smoke filled room.

"What time is it, somebody?" asked Rebel, rubbing his face. Then he saw Sledge lifts up his watch from the counter.

"It's five after five."

"I had better go call Stroke. It's getting close to show time," said Rebel as he reached inside his jacket for his cellular phone.

At Solomon's house. Stroke is still stretched out on the sofa, and he's dreaming the same dream again. But this time he awakens to the ringing of the phone. He reaches blindly for the phone and manages to knock over an unfinished bottle of beer. "Damn!" Stroke recovered on the bottle with one hand while managing to press the intercom button with the index finger of his other. "Hello."

"Well now, how are you doing Mister Superstar? Di you have a nice nap? Is everything alright, Mister Renegade?"

"Rebel, is that you?"

"Yes, it's me. Come on, Stroke, The Mayor can make excuses for you for just about anything except missing your first concert, because the fans will never forgive you."

"Oh man." He tries to rub the familiar soreness from his neck. "What time is it, dude?"

"It's time for you to get the lead out of your ass and shag it down to the arena, homeboy. It's five: thirty. And the show starts in two hours."

"Okay, I'll be there in twenty minutes. Cool?"

"Yes, it's cool. Look, I know you had some trouble with two unusual dudes."

"They were unusual, but they were no factor."

"Yeah right. Well anyway, they followed us around town all day. And my hunch is they're outside Sol's place at this moment."

"BULLSHIT!" said Stroke standing in aggravation, for he knew he had thrashed them sufficiently.

"Why don't you check outside and let me know what you see?"

Stroke strolled out of the den into the living room. And just like Rebel thought, there they were outside, sitting in their car waiting. Stroke peers through the window at them. "I thought those boys had enough."

"Talk louder. I can barely hear you," said Rebel.

" You were right, " he informs him walking back into the den.

"So, ah, what do you plan to do?"

Stroke sees the Police Chief's number on the table as he paced back and forth in frustration.

"I'm going to grab my gear and leave in ten minutes. That should give you enough time to call the Chief of Police and tell him I'm gonna need a little assistance. Two squared cars should be enough."

"Wait a minute, just wait one got dammed minute."

"What's wrong?"

"Everything. First of all; I don't know the Chief."

" If you listen, then I will explain. "

"Okay, I'm listening."

"I have the Chief's private number and it will get you through to him directly, bro."

"How did you pull that off?"

"The mayor gave it to me when we talked this morning. And he has already talked to him about our situation. So now the law is on our side."

"It's hard to believe, but I guess you're right."

"Now, call the chief and tell him I'm bringing Evette and give him a description of Evette. Also tell him he can pick them up on Stiles Avenue for speeding. Right?"

"Right. One more thing."

"What do you need to know that I haven't told you?"

"The phone number."

Stroke gave Rebel the number and he made the call. Stroke can only hope the Chief finds their plan acceptable. He walks through the house to the bedroom, then pulls on his personally designed pair of Renegade jeans; which are a little darker than a robins' egg blue. From his bag he takes out a beige double-breasted shirt and dresses hurriedly.

Stroke brushes his hair, then sits down on the foot of the bed to pull on his banana yellow colored boots that he has owned since high school. He throws his essentials and a few other things since high school. He throws his essentials and a few other things he will need from the house into the bag, then starts back through the hall toward the garage. Suddenly, halfway down the hall, he stops.

"I think I better get a jacket. It will probably get cold tonight," he turns and goes back towards the bedroom. From the closet he takes an old BDU field jacket with all his whoah patches, then he turns to see something which he had absolutely no intentions of leaving; The gold cross Rebel gave him.

He stuffs the jacket through the handle on the top of the bag and pulls the chain down over his head as he walks back through the hall. He checked the time on the Grandfather clock in the foyer as he passed through and continued into the kitchen and opens the refrigerator, to remove a six-pack. A quick glance at the clock on the kitchen wall lets him know; it is time. He grabs the old blue college rucksack from the counter and pulled it up on his left shoulder. Then he starts toward the garden room singing 'Don't Drive Drunk'.

Stroke begins to recall the last time he was alone with Evette. He opened the door that would allow him to enter the garage. Then he saw her. She always looked good in her crimson dress. He decided right then to take her top off. She always looked her best with her top off. Carefully he stroked those secret strokes, which would let her know that, yes, daddy was home.

Evette starts to warm up, and her sensitive voice speaks. "Hi, Stroke, are we going for a ride?"

Stroke starts to speak, and then he smiles. Evette's computer synthesized voice sounds so sweet, and so real. He climbs down onto her and awaits the opening of the automatic garage doors. "Yes, sweetheart, we are gonna take a little ride. Are you ready?"

"Yes, I am. But will you please fasten your seat belt?"

Stroke brings Evette out slowly. The sun beams down hard on her candy apple metallic shell.

The two men immediately spot Stroke. Sieron radios Balaam.

"Balaam, he is leaving."

"Follow him! And do not try anything like you did earlier. These are warriors and you could get hurt!"

"Yes, Balaam, you need not worry," adds Sieron looking over at Sajem's blackened eye.

"I am still with the others and there has been no movement since you left. But time is growing near."

"We will not allow him out of our sights."

Stroke rewinds a cassette tape, as Evette rolled next to their car. "Howdy, boys," he said with his smooth southern accent. "Sorry we met so roughly this morning," he looks at them with all thirty-two showing.

Billy Squire starts to crank what he has long considered his theme song, The Stroke.

"Do you know that you have broken my tooth?"

"Too bad I didn't broken your face," he said no longer smiling. "If you plan to follow me, then you better come on. Say good-bye to Mister Laurel and Mister Hardy, baby."

"Peace," she said.

Stroke burns rubber going down the street west. Their car is facing east. Sajem struggles to turn the car about to chase him, only to have him zoom pass them as Sajem had corrected, or uncorrected the direction they should be heading. Stroke wants this to be a fair chase, even though with the way Sajem was driving, he knows dogging them would be very easy. Stroke stops at the corner to allow his…pursuers time to turn their car around and here they come like a bat out of hell.

Stroke leads the way, and luckily the crowd has not started, so it's easy for Stroke to make a left turn onto Tremont Avenue; a straightaway on which Stroke knows he could lose them with speed alone, but that is not the objective of the game.

"Okay, boys that's the way to hang in there." He watched the car come out of the turn in his rear view mirror. His speedometer shows sixty-five, before he notices that the signal light at the intersection of Tremont and

Mills B. Lane is red and there is traffic proceeding. Perhaps, the light will change.

"Come on, Come on, Come on, baby…SHIT!" He knows the light isn't going to change in time. So he begins to break his speed down; from fifth he goes over to third.

"Owe! Don't do that!…What's wrong with you?"

"The signal light; it's red."

"Stroke why don't you try that new device Diddily installed?"

That was the answer; Diddily was an electronical genius. Stroke had him develop a little gadget to avoid waiting at lights and now was as good a time as any to try it. He stroked the button, which Diddily was cleverly camouflaged as the cigarette lighter. As he touched it, a spark lit up the tip of his finger.

"Damn! There must be a short in this bitch."

"Who are you calling a bitch?" responses Evette as the light changes suddenly.

"Dawggone! Diddily deserves a Christmas bonus." Once again, it's on and Stroke finds the beat. He shifts into fourth as he passed through the intersection; he knew there was no real need to go to fifth. He just wanted to keep a safe controllable speed until the next corner. He switched on the directional lights to let his friends behind him know he was about to turn right.

"Okay, boys, depending on how you make this turn will tell me rather if you're Georgia Boys, or if you are foreigners playing the wrong game." He slows down enough to make the turn safely onto highway seventeen, in order to head east; this route is an extension of the World famous Victory Drive.

With his slowed speed and expert handling, he brings Evette out of the turn without fishtailing all over the road, but the others do not have the same luck. Coming out of the turn they almost run head on into an old Mack truck.

"Defiantly foreigners," he said watching their moves. He looks in Evette's rearview mirror to see if they were too shaken up to follow. They don't look disturbed at all, in fact he is almost sure he sees them laughing. "Well, they aren't homegrown. But where ever they come from they grow some strange weed."

There are two bridges to cross that are less than a mile apart; one is over the Seaboard Coastline Railroad and the other over a turnpike that leads onto Stiles Avenue. After the first bridge Stroke increases his speed to widen the distance between the two cars and by the time he crossed the second, he was so far ahead of them he decided to turn his car around. Actually it was part of the plan.

Sajem was pushing his car hard in order to catch up once they had lost sight of Stroke when he crossed the first bridge. They did not see him again until they crossed the second.

"There he is, Sajem!" Shouts Sieron as they fly pass Stroke parked on the opposite side.

"There they are," Stroke announced to Evette, as he sounded her horn with the use of the foot, while sitting up high on the opening in her roof. He saluted them with a beer. "Come on back, boys, we're having too much fun for you to quit, now."

"Look, he is playing with you! Hurry, you must not lose him."

"Perhaps you wish to take control?" asked Sajem trying to turn the car around.

Stroke turned the beer up, then jumped back down and started driving back toward the west just as they came raising hell behind him. He waited his chance to execute a left turn and the boys were getting closer.

Stroke made the turn onto the hairpin curve with them close behind and the curve straighten as Evette led the way through the tunnel under the bridge. Stroke was now on Stiles Avenue and there was a slight feeling of relief, because he knew the squad cars were waiting there somewhere along the road. They had to be. That was the only way this madness would end.

But now, he and Evette were running for all they were worth and the two behind them were trying so hard to keep up they were not aware of their speed.

At first, he wasn't sure, and then as they drew closer he could see the white of the patrol cars. "Stroke, you are approaching police vehicles. A slower speed is advised."

"Baby the Calvary is waiting."

"Calvary!? Stroke, what are you talking about?"

"The police are with us, and those good old boys back there aren't even wise," Stroke cruised pass the cars sounding Evette's horn. The four patrol cars rolled out onto the road with the blue lights flashing and the sirens blasting.

"I've got to see this," he said as he turned Evette around and parked her facing the excitement. Stroke lit a cigarette, then climbed up through the hole in her roof so he could have a good view of the show. He couldn't help but to recall how the city he loved so much had scarred him with the velvet touch. "Baby, I remember when those same guys had an A.P.B. out on me. Yeah, for twelve dollars and thirteen cents," he stops to think, then takes another drag off his smoke.

"Time brings about changes," he said and continued to watch then the two men pointed toward him.

"Oh no, boys, I've done my time." Stroke jumped back down into Evette, he made a serious u-turn, and then started on his trip to the arena. For Stroke this bit of excitement was over and it was time to move on. He begins to think about his dream. "Why couldn't I see her face?" He asked, but there was no answer. He reached over and ejected the cassette, then turned his radio to a local A.M. station known as the Que. He turned up the volume.

"…More oldies on Que," the announcer informed him. Then started his next selection.

Through the speakers Stroke hears an old Smokey Robinson tune 'Tracks of My Tears'. Smokey sings, "So take a good look at my face, you see my smile looks out of place, but if you look closer it's easy to trace the tracks of my tears."

Stroke shifted up and Evette adjusted herself to another gear.

At the arena the Boys prepare for opening night Quest: The Grand tour. There is a sold out banner over the ticket windows. And the crowd has been prepared for; streets have been secured for speedy access or departures. Stroke sees the crowd as it begins to arrive early. He knows it's the out of town crowd from the out of State plates as he cruises down Montgomery Street.

"Ah, Evette, is the route secured?"

He takes a right on to Gadston, and then sounds his horn at the girls selling dates on the corner. The girls wave as he stops at the stop sign, he waves back and smiles then makes a left turn onto Jefferson. And proceeding north on Jefferson provides a clear shot toward the arena.

The groupies were swarming all about the side door, all hoping for a glimpse of the boys before they came out as Quest. There is one groupie who looks totally out of place. Smoothly cruising through the groupies, and it is Balaam. He presses his way forward pass them all. Then he tries to enter the door, only to be halted by a very huge rent-a-cop.

"No one can get in without a pass."

Balaam reaches inside his robe and removes a leather envelope closed with a twist. "You must give this to Quest now."

The guard takes the envelope, as Keiop approaches Balaam from behind.

"Your Mystic!" A Keiop nod slightly, then continues." Sieron and Sajem have been captured and taken to a cell not far from here."

Balaam turns and faces him.

"The Snookie Brothers will be fine. I'll go get them. I want you to remain here and make sure the ship is ready to land when I call."

"I understand."

Balaam walks between two trucks as he begins to fade himself away. He rematerializes inside the holding tank of the Chatham County Jail. There is another person inside the tank when he enters. Just another hard working citizen caught D.U.I. in the middle of the day, and he looks up at Balaam. The dude is still so heavy with vino, he's not sure if he is asleep or awake. He burps and sits up and begins to watch Balaam.

"This should be interesting," he said.

As soon as the guard saw the car Rebel told him to look for, he opens the garage door, and then draws Stroke's attention toward the opening. Stroke moves around the parking lot carefully, then takes the straight shot in to the back of the arena and deliberately parks the car opposite the spot the cop was pointing at. Rebel walks over toward the car.

"Hey, Rebel, I've got something for you," shouted the guard at the side door. He walked over to give it to him.

"Thanks," he said, then stuffed the envelope down into his left breast pocket, before he continued toward Stroke. "What's hadning?" asked Rebel as he leaned against Evette.

"What's handing?" asked Stroke turning to face Rebel while removing his bag and jacket from the car. "Well, first of all; I've been chased at high rates of speed by two obvious cases of guys who have been eating those, ah, Freakies' Cereal," Rebel laughs.

"Oh so you think that's funny? Well, I don't think it's funny at all."

"...Quest is about to give its first major concert in about...what?" He looks at his watch. "Fifty-five minutes or so," he stops this time to pull at the weight of the bag on his shoulder.

"So?"

"So, that means I've got to get dressed and get buzzed within said time. Then to top all that off I've got this dream that keeps haunting me every time I go to sleep. And then when I wake up, it feels as if someone has hit me in the back of my neck with a crow bar. And you ask what's handing? Well, you tell me."

Rebel said nothing as he slowly digs into his left breast pocket behind the envelope to pull out his Marlboro box, he opens it and hands Stroke a smoke. "Will this help?"

Stroke takes the gift. "It won't hurt." He said, and then started toward the dressing room.

SEVEN

QUEST FOR THE TRUTH

T HE POLICE HAD JUST FINISHED the process paper work on Sieron and Sajem when they placed them in the tank. Balaam stood waiting as they entered the holding tank. "The two of you had better be glad the place they are now is so close to where you are," he explains, then he motions for them to follow him through the wall.

The drunk watched as they walked through the solid concrete and steel. He stands and tries to escape the way they did. But the hole was only opened for them and he bounces off the wall landing on his butt. The police aren't aware that they have gone and they won't get any answers from the one witness, for he is unsure of what he has just witnessed.

Stroke, Diddily, Rebel, Sledge, and Blaze have dressed out in their concert gear and are now waiting for the word. Balaam is at the door still trying to get in without using his powers.

Bobby knocks on the dressing room door and shouts "LETS GET IT ON, BOYS, IT'S SHOW TIME!"

Inside the room they all join hands in a silent prayer.

"Okay, fellas, this is it!" says Blaze, and he is the first to leave the room.

Stroke stops to look in the mirror once more, then he places the gold chain bearing the cross around his neck. He is the last one out and he sees the boys just standing outside the room. "Why are you guys standing here?" Then he looks about and sees Balaam walking towards them.

"Hey, dude, no one is allowed backstage without a pass."

Balaam looks at him and smiles.

"Who is this?" asks Stroke, and then suddenly he realizes that for a concert crowd it is extremely quiet in the arena. "Something is wrong. Diddily, get a guard."

Diddily quickly moved to find a guard.

"There is no need. Come you are needed," explained Balaam, as Sieron and Sajem stand close behind him.

"Stroke, those are the same two cats who…"

"I know, I know," he said before Blaze could finish.

Diddily returns walking swiftly. "This is not good."

"What's wrong, kid? Where is the security guard?" asked Rebel.

"You're not going to believe this, but everyone in here is in some sort of a trance. Frozen. You know, like, someone has stopped time on Bewitch."

"So you would say stopped time. Well, my thoughts were to tell you I had increased your speed greatly. Well, so much for what I was going to tell you. Anyway, you have got a lot of work to do and your time is limited."

"Work? What are you talking about?" asks Rebel.

"You are going to experience more than you are used to on this mission," explained Balaam, before turning to face Sieron. "To the ship. We must journey on," he walks forward as Sieron hold the door open.

The boys all decide without saying a word to the other, that if this man has indeed stopped time or any other way he would care to phrase it, well then he is not one to argue with. They walk towards the door. Outside they see more of the same; everything has been halted, or suspended.

"You must really have some powerful stuff to be able to stop time in a whole city," says Sledge.

Balaam laughs, "A whole city? Why not try this whole system." Balaam points toward Deliverance as it lands. "Diddily, Rebel, Blaze, Sledge, and Stroke, your chariot Deliverance awaits."

This is almost too much for them to comprehend, but they continue to do as Balaam instructs them and they board the ship ahead of Balaam and his men. Then they feel the doors slowly close behind them.

Balaam points to a table where they may sit as he walks through the door, which opens as Keiop, entered from another section of the ship. Keiop placed a bottle on the table along with five octagon shaped glasses.

"What is this poison?" asks Sledge.

"No, this is Bonda Berry Juice from Anemeg. It is a stimulant."

"Stimulant? Just what I need," said Blaze pouring himself a tall glass, while the others watch Keiop walking back toward the door he entered to make his exit.

Suddenly they felt the slight vibration of Deliverance as it moved out of the Earth's atmosphere, and then there was a slight thrust as Deliverance adjusted to a greater speed.

Balaam checks the book to confirm his timing and he finds that he got what he came for at the right time and he was pleased. But now the real work will begin. Balaam must convince the Boys of the true importance of their mission. He decides to talk with Stroke alone and then he can explain the situation to the others.

The boys sat quietly at the table as they waited. Blaze was still trying to get someone to join him in a little drink. "Does anyone wish to join me for a drink?" he asked, There was no answer, so he poured himself yet another.

Balaam enters and begins to walk around the table.

"Man who are you?" asks Diddily.

"My name is Balaam. I know who you all are and I have known for some time now."

"What have you brought us here for?" asked Rebel.

"You will learn in time."

"In time from what?" asked Sledge.

Balaam did not answer, he stopped across the table from Stroke, then he pointed at him, "May I speak to you alone?"

"Whatever you have to say to me you can say in front of everyone."

" I think this you will wish to hear alone."

"What do you think I will find so important that I wouldn't want the boys to hear?"

"I wish to tell you about the dream, your dream. I want to tell you about the girl, the princess."

"Who are you?"

" I told you. I am Balaam, Balaam the Sorcerer."

"Humh. Okay, let's talk."

The boys watched as Stroke got up to follow Balaam. Blaze was probably the only one not concerned as he poured himself another drink.

Stroke walked with Balaam into the section he had seen him enter earlier and he could not help but be impressed by the superior intelligence displayed by the scientific technology he sees aboard. Balaam knows for it shows in Strokes' eyes. So he gestures toward another opening. "Would you like to see the rest of the ship?"

Stroke smiles and shakes his head at the idea of Balaam being so casual. "Look I'm not a rocket scientist, so I really don't care to be taken on the fuckin'scenic route of your ship. So why don't you start talking. I would like to know what the hell you brought us here for."

"You are here to save the princess, my world, your world and probably the entire Universe."

Stroke felt his legs get weak, he had to lend against the wall for support.

"Perhaps you had better sit down while I explain," Balaam showed Stroke that they were not too far from a table which was surrounded by high-backed chairs. And as numb as he felt at that moment even a bed of nails would have been comfortable.

As they settled themselves at the table, Keiop entered the room. "This is Keiop, he is my assistant."

Keiop nodded and Stroke waved slightly.

"If you would care for something Keiop can assist you. Maybe something to ease the situation."

"Yes a drink please."

"Keiop, a bottle of Bonda Berry Juice."

"Listen. Do you have anything stronger than juice? I think I'm gonna need a high alcohol percentage drink, like Thunderbird or some Wild Irish Rose."

"Trust me this will be sufficient," said Balaam watching Keiop pouring the drinks.

Stroke wasted no time throwing down the first one. "WOW! It does have a kick!"

"A kick? I was hoping you would like it."

Stroke shakes his head from left to right. "Well, my nerves are together, so you can start talking."

Balaam turned at an angle with his arm on the back of the chair as he crossed his legs, then he poured Stoke another drink. "Do you remember your dream?"

"Vividly."

"You should, because it was not a dream. You were there with the princess when the Slime Dwellers abducted her. They came at the order of Beezubul and Nud. What you must do; is find Beezubul and free the princess before the end of the two suns. If you fail the Slime Dwellers will be able to up rise and take over Zandoria and then the Universe."

Stroke sits back in his chair. "That's shit!"

"No. That's truth and watch your language."

"If all you have to do is free the princess and kill Beezubul, then why don't you use your powers? Now since that's solved you can turn this ship around and take the boys home and me so we can do our show. Right?"

Balaam shakes his head up and down very slowly. "Wrong. Come let me show you something." He rises from the table and leads Stroke toward a very large book propped on the top of a pedestal, then he points to a section for Stroke to read from.

…A band of five men from a faraway planet called Earth, so that there is no mistake Balaam they are in Slovannah, Georgia. The bands of men together are known as Quest.

Stroke pauses with a curious look on his face as these words now written suddenly appeared on the page. You and your friends shall be the ones to slay the Deacons of Slime and their leaders, Beezubul and Nud the Lord of Slime must die they have gone too far. They wish the power to rule the Universe. And there is already one. The men of Quest are known as Diddily, Sledge, Blaze, and Stroke The Renegade…Oh and The Rebel, too.

Balaam is ready to flip the page when Stroke closes his eyes and places his right hand to his forehead. "I don't believe this is happening to me."

While Stroke stands with his eyes close, Balaam picks up a knife and throws it.

Stroke opens his eyes and ducks…He ducks and the knife zoom over his head. He gets up not looking any longer at the words being written mystically. He heads back toward the chair he had been seated in and stands, he reaches down for his glass and finishes his drink, then pours himself another. Balaam joins him at the table. "What is so special about this girl? And why couldn't I see her face?"

"At the age of ten the princess had to start wearing a scarf on her face at the request of her mother. No man will be allowed to see her face until her twenty-sixth birthday. And that man, the first man to see her face will be the man she has married. But the Slime Dwellers killed Prince Derrag and he was the one she was suppose to marry. Now Beezubul wishes to be the one."

"When is her birthday?"

"The day of the cycle of the eclipse of the two suns will end."

Stroke shakes his head from left to right. "I should have known," he toys momentarily with his glass. "So, unless we help the people of your planet is going to let them take over your world, because Beezubul takes this girl as his wife? What is wrong with you people?"

"There is more to it than you realize. The princess has been surrounded by a mystical aura since birth. Even a simple kiss from her transforms… unbelievable energy. The man who makes love to her for the first time will receive great powers. Power far more superior to what I now possess. This is why you must get the princess away from Beezubul. If he is able to obtain the power, the Universe is doomed. Beezubul will be able to do anything he wishes and stopping time on a small planet would be like, like ahhhh…"

"Like pulling a rabbit out of a hat."

Balaam shakes his head. "That's an old trick. There is something else you should know about Beezubul."

"Oh! So there's more. Well if it ain't one thing it's two or three. Go on."

"Beezubul was once apprentice to an ancient wizard from your plant, his name was Rovalf Alumro. Beezubul would have received all his evil secrets, but he was struck by cupidity and caught by Rovalf as he tried to steal the secrets of the Orb and cross. So Rovalf placed a curse on Beezubul for his treachery. Then used one of the most powerful spells ever conceived to banish him in space."

"What is the curse? Maybe we can use it against him."

"The curse gave him a fraction of the power he wanted. But power just the same."

"Wait a minute! He cursed him with power?"

"Yes. And all merely by accident. And under the curse of the spell, Beezubul has been able to draw his power by absorbing the wills of children. Not all children, only the ones that die young, or stillborn on your planet. From the pain, all the pain felt on your planet he receives power. Broken hearts pain, mental pains, physical pain, disappointment pains, wanting pains, needing pains, hunger pains and pains of adversity. From these he draws his power. And every time you hurt he shines."

"And you expect the boys to go up against something like that?"

"Beezubul's power is not as strong against you, because you have already beat him once by living to the age you are. Just be strong. You are fighting for the will of the Living. You are fighting to ease the pain."

"So you want me to tell the boys they must risk their lives to save a magic virgin or your planet is doomed?"

"No, I want you to tell them they too are doomed. Because if you do not succeed you will never see Earth again. So I suggest you go to them and explain. We have a short time left on this ship. I believe you can find you way back alone. Remember the pain."

As Stroke made his way back, he was worried greatly. "We are but five musicians. What can the band do? Blow their eardrums out with loud music? No. I've got it! We'll just let Rebel bore them to death with his bad jokes. If it doesn't kill them it will definitely drive them insane. Ah hell! Why did I join this band? Why didn't I become a Rapper? Stroke Tee is in the house! Nope I should have become a doctor like my mother wanted. She told me over and over again Boy, hanging with them white boys ain't gonna do nothing but get you in trouble. You were right again mom." He stops and pauses in the corridor.

"I must keep them up…can't go down right now…gotta stay up! This is my entire fault. All right, I gotta take charge, and I gotta be smart and I gotta be smooth for them to understand. Remember the pain." Stroke forms a stupid smile on his face then waits for the door to slide open. He starts toward the table where the boys have been waiting and worrying since he left.

"Stroke!? Hey, dude, you must try some of this stuff. It's great!" said Blaze holding out a glass.

"I've had enough of that for now."

"Been off drinking with the enemy, huh, Stroke?" asks Sledge.

"They are not our enemy, but we do have some and that's why we are here."

"What the hell are you talking about?" asks Rebel.

"Well let me put it like this; I've got some good news and some bad news. So I'm going to tell you the good news first."

"Great! I like it like that," said Blaze slurring his words.

"The good news is; Balaam is on our side and he is going to take us home." The boys are relieved at this news and they ease back off the edge of their seats.

"Now, the bad news?" said Rebel.

While Stroke starts to give them the details concerning the bad news, Balaam has a conversation with Keiop, who is very impressed by the coolness the band has shown so far. But he is still in need of answers to a few questions which he feels should be answered.

"How did it go?"

"About as well as to be expected."

"I think they are reacting well."

"Yes, they are for men forced out through our hatred and driven by their own fears and all under conditions they cannot understand."

"Do you think they will slay Beezubul and free the princess as it is written."

"They are brave men they will do what is right."

"Yes I suppose."

"Besides, what choice do they have?"

"Do you think Beezubul knows we have gone for these men?"

"It does not matter if he knows or not. Stroke will destroy him."

And Keiop is about to ask another question when Balaam cuts him off with, "Don't you have rounds to make and spells to study. Go, leave me! I wish to be alone."

"Of course they will."

But as Keiop exits the room, Balaam softly says, "I hope so, I really do hope so. I would hate to think what would really happen if Beezubul is not defeated."

Balaam moves around behind the pedestal that the Book of Prophecy is on and stands before a sphere shaped object mounted on the wall of the ship. Balaam passes his hand in front of the sphere and an image slowly materializes and it is King Revilo.

"Greetings, Your majesty."

"Greetings, Balaam, I hope you have good news."

"Yes, sire, I have the men. We shall be arriving on Zandoria shortly."

"Good, all went well I presume."

"Yes, sire, they have the strong wills of fighters. We had a little trouble getting them."

"Trouble? What kind of trouble?"

"Nothing that could not be handled. Do not trouble yourself everything is fine."

"Good, very good. I was worried for a minute. Things have not changed since you have been gone."

"Well at least they have not got any worse."

"Which is a good sign."

"Sire, is Cush there in the palace?"

"No he has gone into the city."

"I need him there when I arrive. Have some of the men go find him and bring him to the palace. He will be drunk, but I need him ready to travel when we arrive."

The king fades out slowly and Balaam returns to the table to pour himself a drink. He throws it back as he has seen Stroke do. "Yes, it does have a foot."

Stroke has finished with the bad news and the way things are. So they know where they stand, but it is time of the boys to let him know how they feel about all of this." Okay, let's hear it," Stroke said sitting with his left hand to his temple.

"You want to hear it?" asks Rebel. "This shit has got me all crazy. Right. Let me see if I have this all down correctly, because I don't think something is registering." Rebel slides to the edge of his seat as he looks across the table at Stroke. "Okay now, you mean these assholes, and I use the term loosely here. These assholes believe we are going to risk our lives for some mud duck princess, because we have been described in some book? Bullshit! Stroke, I'll tell you what you have done, Mister I Want To Be a Hero, what you should have done is given them Billy Idols phone number and address. Now we would really get off on something like this. And this Beezubul guy. What do you think he is going to do to us? Didn't you say his power is greater than Balaam's? "

"No I said his powers would be greater if we don't help."

"Well I don't want to fuck with him or no got damn Slime Dwellers either. So you can just count me out, bro, I think I'll take the zero."

"Well what about you, Blaze?"

Blaze looks at Stroke with eyes hazed from Bonda Berry Juice.

"Man, I would fight your grandmother if she told me she was going to take this stuff away," Blaze then drained the last few drops out the bottle straight from the muscle.

"He doesn't know what he is saying. That shit they gave him has got him brain washed, just like you," adds Rebel.

"Sledge," calls Stroke, "You're not drunk or brain washed are you?"

"Of course not!" said Sledge.

"Then how do you feel about this shit?"

Sledge has been quiet through most of this but he will share his opinion. "Well I can only speak for myself when it comes to risking one's life. But in the band we all think as one when it comes to music. That's how we reach decisions and that's how we make great songs. As for this, all I can say is I feel no matter how we go about it we are going to be successful. This is a good cause and we are fortunate to be the ones chosen to fight for such a cause. Think of all the lives your individual efforts will save. Besides we don't have a choice."

Sledge has had his words. Stroke turns to Diddily. "Okay, kid, how do you feel about all this? I know it's all pretty dawgone scary. But you've got to let us know how you feel because your life is on this line too."

Diddily looked up from twiddling his thumbs to listen to him as he was talking, then his eyes looked briefly at the faces of the others. "Yes you're right, it all sounds scary, but since I joined the band you guys have all been like four big brothers. Sure, you call me 'kid', play jokes on me, and give me orders. But every day I learn more from each of you and even with all the bad things you may say or do to me; I know that we are family, and you won't let anything happen to me if you can prevent it. So whatever you decide I'm with you in body and spirit. You've taken care of me and I know you, I mean all of you always will."

The youngest member of the band has spoken and he has made more sense than all of them together. "I'm proud of you, kid, you remembered what we all forgot."

They understand what Stroke is saying and they all know what they must do. They must come together like they do before a big show and feel the magic they give one another, the magic which allows them to go out and make every show better than the first. Blaze attempts to sit up straight as they all turn to look at Rebel. Rebel looks around the table and holds out his right hand.

"So what you gonna do mildew or barbecue?" And just as Rebel has reached out his hand, they all reach out for the strength of the other. Through this bond the vibrations are felt.

Balaam and Keiop enter the room to find the band in their secret bond. Rebel looks up at Balaam. "The Quest has begun."

"I'm glad you decided to join. Otherwise, I would have resorted to force."

"By the way," said Blaze, "Does Joe know what type of work you do for a living?"

"Joe? Joe who?" asks Balaam.

Blaze smiles slightly, "Joe Momma!" The boys enjoy this thoroughly.

"I'm glad you have gotten over the shock. Perhaps you require more to drink?" And instantly another decanter of Bonda Berry juice appears in the up turned palm of his right hand.

"Damn!" said Blaze.

"Watch out David Copperfield." Grinned Rebel.

Balaam walks over to place the bottle on the table. Stroke takes the bottle and pours a round. "Hey, Balaam," calls Stroke with a smile, "Don't worry, if this doesn't work out, well, you can always get a full time gig at Disneyland…You're pretty good with the stuff you use."

"Thank you," He said taking it as a compliment. "But, you better make this drink a short one. We will be arriving on Zandoria within the hour and I do not wish the people to see you overly stimulated."

"Well, in that case, you can take this bottle away. If there is one thing we don't want to do is lower the moral and spirit."

Balaam makes the decanter fade from the table along with the glasses.

"You're good! Now, why don't you try to make a little herb appear," asked Stroke.

"Sure, how much?"

"How about a pound. Since it's free."

"As you wish," Then with a slight movement of his index finger; there it is. One pound of herbs.

"Happy days are here again," sings Stroke reaching for the bag. But Rebel gets his hands on it first. "Hey, bro, there is enough for all of us. No need to try and hog it up. I was planning to share you know."

"I know, I just wanted to check out the quality of the quantity," explains Rebel as he prepares himself to take in the fragrance, which he does and then smiles broadly. "That's okay, Stroke, you can smoke all of this yourself."

Stroke can tell by Rebel smile that there is something wrong. He takes the bag and smells the herb and he knows what it is. He laughs loudly. "Oregano! It's got damned oregano."

"If it's not sufficient, I could give more."

"No. That won't be necessary," says Rebel, "This is where I work a little magic," He reaches into the inside pocket of his jacket with his left hand and pulls out two joints. "Cheeba from the homeland."

"Magic, magic! Ooooh, now it's my turn," exclaimed Blaze as he pulled out a lighter which was tucked across the front of his pants, then he made one of the joints disappear from Rebel's hand and quickly fired it up.

"I see you have been holding out again," said Sledge.

Rebel tries to look innocent. "Who me?"

Balaam turns to see Keiop talking to a member of their crew; he starts over to join the conversation, but the crewman leaves before he can make his way over. Keiop turned to face Balaam. He bowed, and then said.

"There is nothing to worry about. The kind has informed the controller that they have found Cush. He and some of the men will ride into town and announce the new to the people. And they will have everyone at the City docks. This should help to improve the spirits of our heroes."

"Good! At least there was no bad news. But I do not think we need to worry about the spirits of the men," he points back toward Quest as they laugh it up at the table.

On Zandoria, a dark haze has moved over the skies of Talmory. Death and destruction has cursed this land. Now people who were once happy people are no longer happy. There is no one out on Prince Street; a street that is usually crowded with the traffic of wagons, riders, and children playing appears extremely empty.

Suddenly there are riders racing down the street and they seem to have a reason for the disturbance they are causing and the racket they are making as they ride through the city shouting to the people to come out of their homes.

"THEY ARE COMING! COME OUT AND GREET THEM FOR THEY ARE COMING!" Shouts Cush and his men all through the city and on toward the Town criers Platform, where he continues to shout as he stands on his steeds back…in order to jump on the platform to ring the bell.

The people come out of their homes to see what Cush is so excited about.

"THEY ARE COMING, THEY ARE COMING. QUEST IS RETURNING WITH BALAAM."

The people rejoice. They know whom these me are and they know why they are coming. They renewed their thoughts concerning the safe return of the princess when they were told of Balaam's quest for Quest. Now it happens and they have only positive reactions toward Quest's victory over Beezubul and the Deacons of Slime. Cush holds his hand up, so they quiet down to hear what else he has to say."

"Come. Let us go down to the city's dock to give them a big welcome," Cush leaps from the platform onto the back of his ugly steed, He is in front leading the cheering crowd toward the city docks.

Every man and every woman and child in the city is out for a glimpse of these men. And upon reading the docks all turn their eyes toward the sky. And how they wish to see through the thickness of the clouds. But they know when the clouds do break there will be Deliverance.

Aboard the ship, the members of Quest believe they are ready for what is about to happen. Balaam has changed into his usual attire in order to display his authority. "Come, my friends, we are approaching the atmosphere of Zandoria. So prepare to leave the ship!"

If only they could hear the cheers of the people as they see Deliverance cutting through the clouds. Deliverance begins docking procedures and Balaam has already escorted Quest to the door.

"Are you ready?" asked Balaam.

"About as ready as we're going to be," Sledge says as he steps beside him.

There is silence as the people wait. Balaam waves his right hand across the beam to release the door. The door slowly slid open and the people outside push forward, as they try hard to see Quest.

Balaam walks out where he is sure to be seen by all. The people start to cheer once more. Quest remains a few feet behind him. The word begins to travel through the crowd that yes Quest is here. Balaam holds up his hand and the crowd becomes silent.

"THEY ARE HERE! QUEST IS HERE!" He looks back at the boys, "Come on, and step forward." And he calls their names as they step forward one by one. "DIDDILY, BLAZE, SLEDGE, THE REBEL, and STROKE THE RENEGADE! PEOPLE OF TALMORY I GIVE YOU QUEST!" The people begin to shout at the top of their lungs. Balaam starts across the stand telling each of them. "Look at their faces," Then just before descending the stairs he stops and turns. "THEY BELIEVE AND YOU WILL, TOO."

Balaam sees Cush coming toward him as he comes off the last step of the dock.

"Well done, Balaam!"

"I am glad you are pleased," he says with a casual bow of his head. "But we must hurry it is starting to get dark and they must get started. We have wasted enough time. Have the men clear a way through the crowd. I will get them down from the stand."

Cush is off again, to instruct his guards. "MOUNT YOUR STEEDS AND MAKE WAY FOR QUEST TO PASS."

The men mount and carefully make a path though the eager crowd.

Quest is overcome with happy feelings as they listen to the people chant. "QUEST! QUEST! QUEST!"

In this land of despair the people act as if they have known them all their. Balaam calls to them. " Come, we must travel to the palace! " He shouts as he points the way.

The boys walk down off the stand and head in the direction Balaam points. They see there is a path being made for them to walk through the crowd. As they walk no one speaks, they are all too busy trying to see the faces of the people. The group moves quickly through the crowd down Prince Street all the way to the front gate of the palace. Then the guards restrain the people and only those, which are there for the business at hand, are allowed to enter, then the gate is quickly secured.

" I must leave you now. Do not worry you shall see me again shortly, " sais Balaam before he vanished before their eyes.

" That is one strange dude, " said Sledge as they followed Cush through the foyer.

The boys are in awe as they observe the grandeur of the castle. But they know this is not a tour of one of the once famous homes of royalty in London.. No this is live. And they have been brought here to either eliminate or be eliminated. For once they have found something more important than making music and the belief they have seen on the faces of the people has given them even more confidence in their own ability to succeed in their mission and they begin to respond more seriously.

Balaam stands waiting for them as they near the throne room. " King Revilo awaits you. " He said, then turned to the guards at the huge bronze double doors and waved his hand for them to open them. Balaam entered first and Quest followed him in. He begins to speak while walking toward the throne where the king sat.

" Sire, I give you Quest. These men have traveled a long way to defeat Beezubul and they will do what is necessary to return the Princess Reikciv home safely. "

The king stares at them as they approach, and then he stands. " WHAT IS THIS YOU BRING? THESE ARE NOT MEN, THEY ARE BUT BOYS. AND THESE BOYS ARE NOT WARRIORS. BALAAM YOU HAD ME BELIEVING YOU, BECAUSE OF A FEW WORDS WRITTEN IN A BOOK. " The king stops to shake his head from left to right in frustration. " WHY DO YOU BRING FECES LIKE THIS TO ME AND CALL THEM OUR HOPE? "

Balaam is about to speak in their defense. But Stroke steps ahead of him." FIRST OF ALL: YOUR HIGH AND MIGHTYNESS, HAD IT BEEN LEFT UP TO US, WE WOULD PROBALY STILL BE AT HOME. SO I DON'T KNOW WHAT TYPE OF DRUGS YOU AND YOUR BOY BALAAM HERE ARE ON... NO YOU MUST BE ON SHIT, BECAUSE DOPE DOESN'T MAKE YOU THAT CRAZY. AND AS FAR AS I'M CONCERN BEEZUBUL CAN HAVE YOUR NUTS FOR BREAKFAST. "

The king is amused for men have been put to death for much less. And Stroke is not finished.

" JUST LOOK AT YOU SELF ACTING LIKE A FRIGHTEN LITTLE BITCH WITH HER TAIL BETWEEN HER LEGS NOT DOING ANYTHING EXCEPT SITTING UP ALL HIGH AND PROPER ON YOUR THRONE! IF YOU THINK YOU CAN HANDLE THIS WITHOUT US, THEN BE MY GUEST. YOUR THOUGHTS WERE RIGHT, EVEN IF YOUR WORDS WERE WRONG. WE ARE NOT MEN WHO GO AROUND FROM PLANET TO PLANET SAVING THEM FROM UTTER DESTRUCTION ON A DAILY BASES, BUT AT LEAST WE WERE WILLING TO TRY. SO DON'T YOU EVER ADDRESS ME AND MY FRIENDS HERE AS FECES LIKE THAT. YOU DIG? YO! DUDES LETS ROLL. PEACE AND WE'RE OUTTA HERE. "

Stroke turns and leads the way out as the others follow close behind. The king watched as they moved from their abreast positions and started out of the room, He holds up his hands, and his guards block their exit.

" YOU THERE! WAIT! COME BACK YOU ARE RIGHT I WAS NOT CORRECT FOR WHAT I SAID. "

Rebel looks back at the king. " YEAH! NOW TELL US SOMETHING WE DON'T KNOW. "

" You are our only hope. "

Balaam is eased; he will speak now before there is a change. " Your Majesty, I would like to present to you; Blaze, Diddily, Sledge, Stoke, whom you have already met, and last but not least The Rebel.

The king looks them over once more, and this time with mere amazement. " You are good men and I believe. " He says as he nods his head. " Now! I have gifts for you to use on your journey, " The king claps his hands three times. " BRING THEM WEAPONS! "

" O weapons. Well personally I think that's down right considerate of you, to consider the situation and give us a few toys to take, 'said Blaze as he lends against Diddily.

Two men roll in two long tables, which are both, covered with assorted weaponry and as they are being assisted with their gear, the king wishes to give them a bit of advice. " First we must start with the facts; which one fact being they have more men than you and even more power t. But you must be arrogant, you must be courageous and ruthless, you must have fidelity added with inner strength. Then after you have all of these you must remember anger. " The king lets his eyes flow from one face to the other while he speaks. " Beezubul will use all he has against you and he will not think twice about who must suffer in order for him to hold onto the princess until the seventh day. "

Cush enters ready to travel with Quest. " I am ready to go. "

" Cush will be your anger. He will also serve as your guide for he knows many areas on our planet and he is the best I have to give in support of your campaign." King Revilo turns to walk back to his throne. " Now will you be in need of anything else? " he asks taking seat on his throne.

" I know what I need, " said Blaze, " How about some more of that Bonda Berry juice? "

" That is an excellent suggestion, Blaze, " said the king, " BRING SOME BONDA BERRY JUICE! " He shouts.

While they wait for the porter to return with the Juice. Diddily wishes to satisfy and as a few questions about their weapons, which make for a strange combination to him, because they have been given a sword and a laser pistol; equipped with scope. " Balaam, why do we have these two weapons?"

" Yes you will enjoy these. " He says, and then he turns. " Blaze, and Rebel draw your blades. "

Blaze and Rebel draw their blades in confusion and await Balaam's next request.

" Now strike the blades...go on strike the blades. "

Rebel sneers at Blaze and he sneers back, then the blades clash causing a loud thunder like noise and red and blue sparks dance in the air.

" Damn that was better than Star Wars, " said Blaze.

" Just small addition to aid in your appearance an illusion which might add to your defense and save your life. "

Blaze tries to sneak Rebel with an overhead blow. Rebel sees it coming and he grips his sword firmly and blocks the offense. " Come on, bro! Stop playing so I can hear. "

Balaam continues. " The laser is for power and usually not used, well, except for long range fighting. You find that most warriors use swords instead of laser, because of the high pitched sound it makes when it is activated and also the fact that it is illegal to carry lasers openly in some sectors, but these are times of renegades. So you have the kings' permission to use as you see fit. And another thing about these pistols; they only fire six shots, then it must be turned off to recharge itself. So do not waste your shots. "

The Bonda Berry juice is served and the king wishes to present a toast for their success. They all hold up their goblets. " MAY YOU HAVE THE STRENGTH OF A THOUSAND MEN AND THE SPEED OF A RODAGON. AND LET US HOPE THAT WE ALL LIVE TO TELL OUR GRAND CHILDREN ABOUT THIS. "

Balaam steps forward after the toast. " Your first journey will be to the Land of Soul. " said Balaam.

" The Land of Soul? " asks Sledge.

" This is where you will find the maps of Zandoria. Cush will be able to determine the grid co ordinance of Mount Seficul, which is the mountain where Nud and the Deacons of Slime have made their fortress. I know you are thinking that we should know all of this...Right? Well there are many areas most people here will not travel for where they are is all they know which is all they need. But there was once a great explorer by the name of Taerg Rugus, who traveled this whole planet before his death and the maps he made are protected by his descendants, and the protectors in a castle in the Land of Soul. "

Rebel smiles, " This sounds like a nice place to visit. "

" No not really, because the protectors will try to kill you. The only way they can be stopped is to separate their heads from their bodies, or to remove the talisman from around their necks. "

" You said stopped. Why didn't you say killed? " Inquires Blaze.

" Because you can not kill what is already dead? Do not forget what I have told you. Stroke and all the rest of you must remember the pain! "

" What happens once we know where Mount Seficul is? " asks Sledge.

" Cush will help you'll you have to do is try to keep a level head, so you can follow your instincts which will be enough to take you as far as you need to go and back safely. "

" Okay, I think they know all they need to know. What I want to know is can they shoot and can they fight? '

" Dude, you don't have to worry about that. We all had BB guns. But when my life is on the line, I want to know everything there is to know. If that's alright with you? " Said Rebel.

" Well, if there are no more questions, " said Balaam rubbing his hands together. " I suggest you prepare to travel. "

" I have a question, " said Stroke as he adjusted the weight of his utility belt. " Where is the Land of Soul? And how long will it take to get there? "

Balaam walks over toward the throne. " Draw your lasers and turn them on," he instructs while walking with his back turned to them, then he turns to face them, " The journey will or should I say would take days of travel, but you will be there in seconds. "

" O, I see you can use your magic to sap us there. SO why don't you just zap on us on over to Mount Seficul? " Asked Stroke.

" Because there are things you must do before you are ready to face Beezubul and that's the way the book is writing it. " Balaam lifts his left hand up to the level of his chest, then downward to his stomach and out as he brings it up again, as if he were drawing a half circle.

Stroke begins to speak. " O boy, now we get to the real shit. " he starts to say standing there in front of the king, but before he can finish , he finds that his surroundings have changed.

EIGHT

LAND OF SOUL

BLAZE SEES A RAGGED MORTIFIED body running toward him. " WHAT THE HELL IS THAT? " He shouts.

Cush turns, " That, my friend, is a female protector, and if you do not do this, " said Cush firing his laser, causing fragments of what was once a skill to fly everywhere and what was left of the protector dropped to the floor as well. " It will be all over you. "Cush tells them this, then drops two more the way he did the first.

It is said 'that a word to the wise should be sufficient '. Quest demonstrates along with everything else they also are wise. And as the protectors pour out at them from all angles the boys prove them selves to be really good shots and soon there are thirty four protectors piled on the floor. Cush has already started to use his sword on the heads and arms of the protectors to slow them as he rips talismans from around the necks of the protectors.

" How do you like this for fun? " asked Cush looking back at Rebel, as he too must draw his blade.

" Yeah, this is real fun. Auuuuuugh! " he grunts kicking off a protector.

" Almost as much fun as being the only trout at a fish fry. "

" Well I don't think this is fun at all! " shouts Blaze. " This is too much for a man to take. Just a few short hours ago I was dressing for my first big concert, Augh! " He added with a grunt as he whacked off another. " A concert to make people happy. Now here I stand in the Land of Soul, seeking a map to find a... guy named Beezubul," again his breath is shorten by the weight of the sword, " Who has stolen a magic virgin. Think about this shit if you would. Here I am trying to stop something, which is already dead. I tell you this is worse than a Frankenstein movie. "

"Stop sniveling!" said Sledge with an arm wrapped around the neck of one protector, while he fights off two others, "...and give me a hand! "

Diddily is really enjoying this, he feels like Errol Flynn. " How are you doing, kid? " asks Stroke.

"I'm fine! This is more fun than Joust. It's the real thing! " Said Diddily as he forgets the instructions on how the Protectors are to be stopped during the excitement and he sends his sword through one about midriff.

"Okay, kid, just be careful and don't get soft, " said Stroke as he placed a foot on the chest of one and takes hold of the talisman as he kicks the shell backwards to watch it crumble to the floor. He then looked back toward Diddily to see the kid did get cocky. The Protector, which Diddily so carelessly cut in half is about to split him, down the middle. Stroke moves and moves fast. Diddily feels the Protector pulling at his leg and goes into a semi – state of shock, the protector raised its sword in order to strike, but Stroke used his own sword to block the offense before he reached down to rip the talisman from around its neck.

" You okay, kid? " asks Stroke grabbing Diddily by the arm.

" I'm straight! "

" Just pay attention. You're doing great. And don't let anymore-stupid shit happen. " LOOK OUT BEHIND YOU, KID! "

Diddily turned and showed Stroke that he was alright as he fended off another protector.

Stroke starts toward a protector, one that has the same thing for him he has for it; a long, cold and very sharp blade. Only one must be more aggressive and that is what will make the difference. Another protector falls.

The clutter of remains on the floor has forced the boys to widen out as they swing their swords in mad frenzies. Then suddenly the protectors stop coming and those there cease in their attack as if they were shut off. The boys stand around looking at one another.

" Man, that was some freaky shit! " Rebel says bending over to catch his breath.

" You aint never lied, " said Diddily reaching for his water can.

Stroke looks at Rebel and they start to laugh. Soon all join in but no one knows exactly what the joke is. But whatever it is they find it very funny and begin to walk through the wave of bodies until they are close together, forming a small circle. " You were scared half to death," says Rebel pointing at Stroke.

" No way, dude! I was diesel. You know, hard like a Mack truck. If anyone was scared, it was Kidd Ace here! " Said Stroke turning to point Diddily out. " Look! There he goes again, Look! There he goes again, look at his face! "

Diddily has an askew look on his face, he tries to speak, but all he can do is point behind them.

" What are you pointing at, kid, another protector? I'll get him, " said Rebel turning to stop it cold, but what he sees is a rather attractive woman wearing a dark green gown laced with gold embroidery.

" Ecinaj! " explains Cush.

" You know her? Damn, she's fine! " Said Stroke.

" This is not the time for your pretty boy bullshit, Renegade! " said Sledge.

The woman has not yet spoken a word; She stands cautiously looking them over.

" If she is Ecinah, then she is a daughter of Ragus and the person we are here to see, " said Cush in answer to Stroke's question.

" She is gorgeous, " said Blaze.

" Yeah, about as gorgeous as a case of herpes, " says Rebel, " And you don't play games with that shit either. "

She moves toward them. " Who are you? I am sure you know who I am. But who are you, and what do you seek here? For all you will find here has no purpose to exist. Cush steps forward. " I am Cush and these men are Quest. We wish to see your father's maps of Zandoria. "

" Why should I let you see them? Look what you have done here. "

The Rebel is in no mood for games, " Look Bitch! It's like you've got a choice: Either let us see the maps so we can find Beezubul or there will be nothing here at all. Well maybe a pile of rocks where your castle stood. "

" I am not your bitch! I can't believe Beezubul is still trying for anarchy. "

" Yes an he will be unstoppable if we do not get to Mount Seficul. " explains Cush.

" Mount Seficul? Beezubul is using his curse to link forces with Nud and Deacons of Slime. This could prove to be an interesting and dangerous combination, " she paces the floor, " Come, follow me. "

She leads them the way down a dimly lit corridor.

" Tell me, Ecinaj, where did you find those Protectors? " asks Rebel.

" I do not find them, they find me. They are people whose last thought before death revolved around the fact they had died without serving any particular purpose, or they lived their life in fear of doing what they wanted to do, or being what they wanted to be. "

" And now? "

" Now, they have only one conscious thought which is to defend the castle. But your attack has caused many to fail once again. " She stops at a huge wooden door, then points at two torches in the wall. " We will need those. "

Blaze and Stroke grab the torches as Rebel helps her to pull open the huge door. They enter and begin to walk along the musty hall until arriving at another door and this one is locked. She quickly produces a very thick chain which was hung about her neck. The door is opened and it is obvious that this room has not been cleaned or aired for many years. And as the tainted moldy air rushes pass them they all have words of disagreement.

" Got damn! It smells like O.G.G.S. in here. " said Blaze.

" OGGS? What is that? " asks Cush holding his nose.

"Onion Garlic Gorilla Shit, " said Blasé.

Their complaints do not make the situation any better, but they cannot make them worse. They follow Ecinaj down a long flight of stairs, which lead into a very large room. Ecinag takes one of the torches and lights the ones already propped in the walls, then she pulls out several rolls of paper from a concealed section in the wall, which she exposed by using the strangely shaped key she wears about her neck. She holds the rolls across her arms to transport them over to a table in the center of the room, where she begins to sort through them.

" I believe Mount Seficul is in the thirteenth sector, " She says as they look on. " Yes, here it is... Mount Seficul. First; you must travel to the River Syng and cross it, then travel through the Land of Exile and journey on ward to the Land of Desolation and there you will find Mount Seficul. It will be a two-day journey walking through the Land of desolation, if you could survive the Desert of Sufferance. You had better hope that Maiko gives you Rodagons when you get there and that will cut your time. "

" Get where? " asks Diddily.

" The Den of Thieves, " Said Cush.

Rebel looks at Stroke, " Sounds like some of your homies, Stroke. "

" Are we trying to be funny? "

" We don't plan to stop there, " said Sledge, " And if we decide to sleep over we'll check into a Days Inn."

" This is not a choice passing through Maiko's land he will find you. "

" Anyway. How do we find the River Syng? " Asks Cush.

" When you leave I will point you in the direction you must travel. "

Out side the castle the Boys stand at the foot of the castles stairs.

" This is East, " she said pointing. " Travel straight from here and you will reach the River Syng by morning. "

" Thank you for all your help, " said Stroke, " But tell me why you changed your mind when you found out we were going after Beezubul? "

She knows this man has seen her reasons for wanting them to succeed.

" Because he killed my father and the only man I ever loved. "

" They will be revenged. "

" I want you to have something, it will bring you luck and protect you, " she said as she removed a ring from her index finger.

Stroke took the ring and placed it on his right pinkie finger, " Thank you, I can use all the help I can get. "

" Good blessings to you all. " she said watching Stroke running to catch up with the others as they had already started toward the river.

As Stroke Followed he picked up rear security. Rebel falls back to see what had taken him so long. " Hey, Stroke, what happened? "

" Nothing."

" I guess it's hard getting laid so far from home turf, Hunh? "

" Wrong! She wanted me to rock the boots, but you know, never mix business with pleasure. Ah, anyway, she gave me this little token of her esteem; just to let me know how much she wanted this body, " Stoke holds up his hand and shows off the silver ring, which bears a blood red stone and embedded in the stone there was a bolt of lightening, which seemed to glow as Rebel looked at it.

" Yo! Stroke, seems like I've under estimated you again. "

" Yeah ya did! " He says with a smile, " But ah, she really gave it to me for luck. "

" So, why tell the truth after such a good lie? "

" If this ring will really bring me any good luck, then I don't want to jinx it by telling a lie. "

" Why didn't she give us all a little something for good luck? " asks Rebel with an evil glare in his eyes.

Stroke tries to play off his own thoughts along the same line by giving Rebel a look which would say, you are a poor specimen of anything.

Then he continues to tell him why he was give the ring. " Look! I promised to take care of something for her when I see Beezubul. "

" Man, don't tell me you have gone and gotten yourself involved in some one's personal shit. "

" You want to know something? "

" No, but I know you're going to tell me anyway. "

" Revenge is sweet. "

" No, Stroke revenge is a mutherfucker! And don't you forget it. "

During their journey Cush wishes to ease his curiosity, " What is your planet like? "

"That's sort of hard to answer, " said Rebel, " Because, sometimes it can be very beautiful, then people with askew ideas make if very ugly. "

" What do you mean? "

"You see, our planet is much like yours, except for one difference; Racism. "

" Racism? I've never heard the word before. Will you explain it to me?
"

" No, my friend, it's a terrible word and the way it effects some people they would rather be dead than face the injustice. You and your people are better off not knowing the word, or a lot of terrible others which go along with it. "

" But, " interrupts Blaze, " We can teach you about Rock n Roll!"

" Sounds interesting. "

" You're right, it is. We were about to throw down for a lot of people when Balaam so rudely interrupted us, " said Diddily walking backwards to face Cush.

" Will you roll some rocks for me? There are plenty here. And I am sure you must be good if people wanted to see you do it. "

They look at you and laugh. They forgot he would not understand.

" No, Cush! We don't roll rocks. It's a style of music, which really turns people on. You know, let them get their groove off, you know what I'm saying, and on. " Said Stroke.

" Just have a good time., " said Rebel.

" Yeah! And you can usually tell a lot about a person simply by the form of music they like, " said Blaze, " Take Beezubul for example; He would probably get off on some of that acid rock, the type Rebel usually listens to, right? " Blaze smiles then continues. "But we like Metal, Soul, Rock, Country, Classical and Jazz, and basically any type of music with a meaning, or something to make you think. Which is why we write our own material. "

" Wait I do no understand. You are talking too fast. Now explain again please. "

" I've got a better idea, we can just do a couple of tunes. But first we need a dobbie, " Said Stroke, hinting for Rebel to respond, which he does and produces a nice fat doob. Blaze fills in his position with a lighter as usual; Rebel holds it out for Stroke.

" Let me explain how this little device works. Strokes prepare this joint for action. "

Stroke takes the joint and holds it pointed up straight, then sticks it in his mouth.

" Next you need some fire. "

Blaze showed a blaze to Cush and then to Stroke.

Stroke took a drag and held it as well as Cush's full attention.

" Then you must hold the smoke with your chest for as long as you can without dying, or turning blue, which ever comes first. Now watch. And when it comes around you do the same thing you see them do, right? "

" Right! " said Cush, waiting his turn.

Rebel takes a drag, and then he starts the opening for 'There She Goes Again' Stroke whips out his mouth harp and begins to blow like he would on stage.

There She Goes Again
Oooooo, there she goes again
Looking better than she ever did
And I, I see her in the night
And she's looking so right
Girl I want you can't you see
Girl I need you next to me
Unhunh

The first half of the lyrics are done by Rebel and where he ends Stroke begins.

Ooooo, there she goes again
That girl used to be a real close friend
And I, I see her everywhere
And she looks at me like she don't care
Girl I want you can't you see
Girl I need you next to me
Unhunh
Then as the rhythm picks up Rebel takes over again,
Now now is when I make my move
To go get her and forget
All about you
Stroke comes back to add the finishing touches.
Girl I want you to know
That I think of you no more
Unhunh – unhunh

While trying to show that he can hold a toke and talk as well as any one of them, Cush finds himself attacked by a series of very violent coughs from his attempts, but still he manages to say, " I like it! "

" Yeah, it did sound pretty dawg gon' good, " said Diddily, still snapping his fingers.

" Yeah it did. I just wish we had music like they do in the movies, " added Rebel.

" I wish we had something my bottle besides water, " bitched blaze.

" You have water in both? That is not correct. Have you checked the bottles? "

" There are two bottles? " asked Blaze as he looked about his belt and found there were two. " Alright, this one has water. What's in the other one? "

" Check and see. " said Cush as he removed his and pressed the bottle to his lips.

Blaze took hold of his bottle and removed the top, and then he inhaled the aroma. A big smile traced across his lips. But he said nothing else until he had let some of that sweet Bonda berry juice run down his throat.

" Ahh, this is almost like being home., " said Blaze, and the boys nodded and agreed as they all took one straight from the muscle. Stroke watched them as he maintained rear security.

After a couple of rounds they are more than happy to sang another song for Cush and maybe even more on their long walk to the River Syng. The good time they are having has put them at ease, but they were still all very much alert and ready for any surprises.

Cush was having the best time of his life. Then he asked the magic question. " What type of women do you have? What are the girls like on your planet? "

" They are the best in the whole universe, " bragged Sledge. " Surely you jest, " said Cush, " I bet you don't have special virgins on your planet who can give you powers like you have never imagined."

" Wow! " said Diddily, all excited.

The boys had to stop for a moment to pause and look at him, because they know the kid always has a hard time when it comes to sex.

" No we don't, " said Rebel, " But I know a few girls who can make you feel like king for a day. "

" See! You do not have the best in the universe. "

" But how many virgins around here have the same power the princess has? " asked Stroke.

Cush looked at his left hand as if to add up a few more he knows of in the area, then he looked up. " There is only one that I know of. Ricki is the only one. "

" Well the princess may have the best pussy in the universe the first time, but what about the second, the third, fourth, fifth and so on, jack. Yo! That is the question. " Said Stroke with a big grin. " And If I'm here long enough, well I do plan to find out for my self. Lets just hope Beezubul hasn't solved his own curiosity. "

" Man you'll make love to any thing. One of these days you're going to stick your dick in some dark path that has been traveled before, and your dick is going to drop off. " Said Rebel, joining in with the laughter of the others.

" Well, until that time, might I suggest you keep an eye on your favorite girl, " Stroke meant what he said.

If they were to walk at the rate of speed their mouths were traveling they would reach the River Syng in no time at all.

The stars about Zandoria seemed exceptionally bright, but one galaxy is somewhat dimmer than usual, that galaxy of the Milky Way.

Brunch time, the boys have watched the two suns rise during their journey. They have had no rest, but their night was filled with adventure, song, conversation and a whole lot of Bonda berry juice from Zandoria and Red buds from Earth. Traveling the night, they had walked twenty-four long miles to reach the River Syng.

Now as they stood looking at the river the thin line on the paper is now as wide and as rough as Broad River in Beaufort, South Carolina. Yet the Land of Exile lies on the other side and that is where they must be. And the river is too wide too swim and too deep to wade. Even if they tried to swim across, her current would probably carry them for miles. Helplessly they stand looking at the river.

" We' re here! " informs Blaze.

" Yes we are. But as you can see we don't have a boat, " says Sledge. " It's like; driving to a concert in another state and when you get there you find that the last ticket was sold five minutes before you got there. "

" So, what now? " asks Rebel looking at Stroke.

" Why are you looking at me? " asks Stroke. " Here is the man you should be asking, " he said turning to Cush, and as he did he saw some thing he could use.

" Hey, dude! Where did you get these muthers from? " He asked as he removed the object from Cush's eyes to place them over his own.

" Glarebreakers. All of you should have a pair in your belt. Check the pouch on the left, " advised Cush, taking his from Stroke's face to return to his own.

" Have mercy! Will you have a little mercy? " Asked Rebel, as he removed the glarebreakers from the pouch on his belt.

" Well, as I was saying, " starts Stroke now wearing his dark lens, black metal rimmed glarebreakers. "Guide, why don't you lead the way? " Stroke used his right hand to show Cush he had the floor.

Cush looked up the river, then down the other way. He drew his sword and threw it high towards the sky and waited for it to return. Then he stood over it and pointed in the direction of the blade, it was pointing down river. " We will travel in this direction, " Cush picked up his sword and returned it home as he started in his chosen direction.

Rebel watched Cush, as he strolled along the shore singing There She Goes Again. He turned to look at Stroke. " Well, Mister Renegade, any more bright ideas? "

" Personally, I don't think that shit was called for. " said Stroke.

They laughed as Stroke started behind them.

The walk seemed as if it would have no end and the river has shown no sign of slacking in current or slacking in depth anytime soon.

Sledge is not pleased at all. He decides to release his frustration and Cush will be his target, " Well, Cush, what do we do now? "

Cush slows his pace, then stops and looks across the river. " I do not know, but I know I am about to sit down and rest a while before I take another step, " he said then he found him self a spot along the river and sat down.

"That's the best idea I've heard all day. Besides, I could use a bite to eat," said Rebel as he took a spot next to Cush. " Hey, there wouldn't be a Pizza inn or Pizza Palace around here that delivers would there? "

" A Piece of Palace? " asked Cush.

" No a Pizza Palace, " Rebel explained, " Ah, just forget it!

Cush still didn't understand, but he did wants to hear more about a Pizza Palace. So, while the others used the time to rest; Rebel described to Cush the wonderful cuisine of Italian cooking.

Stroke knows that he too should rest, but if they do not find a way across the river; they will have all the rest they need through death.

" I'm going further. This thing has got to thin out somewhere. You guys can catch up later. "

NINE

DEN OF THIEVES

The shoreline along the river is strange and hard to predict. Some areas are grassy, and then there are bluffs, which peak high above the river. Other areas gradually become rough and very rocky.

Stroke has walked along the river for close to a mile and a half. He continued as it made it's way around a bend, and now he stands almost ten feet above the river's shore at a point where the bluffs reach out over the water. He hopes this will edge his advantage against the terrain. And it did! He sees a large object beached on the shore. With his thoughts trying to make out the object, the glarebreakers give him a current reading then they begin to zoom in and stop at a selected viewing distance. With this help Stroke is sure now what the object is and it's a boat.

" Dawggone'! " Stroke shouts as he turned to start his run back to tell the others what he has discovered. Since he has seen no one around, he tells himself, 'the owners won't mind if I borrow it for a little while, besides they can have it back once we reach the other side of the river. '

In his excitement, he wishes to move fast, but the load he carries makes it difficult and maintaining his sword makes it awkward. He tries to steady them as he runs. Running down the bluff he discovers that it climbed steeper than he had remembered and he falls flat on his face. But he allows himself one quick tumble and he is back on his feet. And sure this time he will not fall again he begins to run even faster as he crossed the rough and rocky terrain and even faster as he ran through the grassy area toward where he had last seen the boys.

" Something's wrong, " he stops to catch his wind, and then he notices footprints leading toward a sand dune in front of where he stands. He takes the sand dune with all he has left, calling to them as he neared the top.

" Rebel, Sledge, Blaze, Diddily, Cush, I found a boat. I found a boat! " He reached the top and finds them all, but they are not alone. He has ran straight back into an ambush. He finds several lasers pointed directly at him.

" What's hadnin'? " asked Rebel, with his hands behind his neck.

Stroke puts his hands up behind his neck, as he sees the others have been told to do.

A giant of a man looks at Stroke and begins to smile. " Come down and join your friends, " says the man. " I guess the boat you found is our craft. And you were going to borrow it? "

Stroke has already started a slow walk down.

" All you had to do was ask we would have been more than happy to give you a ride across. Besides did you not know that you should not take things, which do not belong to you especially when what you are planning to take belongs to a Thief? " The Thieves begin to laugh. " You came back at a good time we were just about to leave and now we can all leave together. Unless there are more of you. "

No one answers.

" You can not talk? Now I am troubled, because, you were shouting not too long ago about the boat you had found, " once again he and his men enjoy a good laugh. " Good! Lets not hear a word from you until you are in front of the king. He will make you talk. Move them to the craft. "

Stroke finds himself being taken back the way he had just hurried from with such enthusiasm, but they are not as happy as he thought they would be to have a ride across the river.

The Thieves run at a pretty steady pace back along the shore. The men move quickly; lifting the boat from the shore and placing it in the water.

" Excuse me, please, I have been very rude to our guest. " says the giant of a man, " I am called Ayogia, " he leaps aboard the boat, as four of his men steady it by holding ropes on the shore. While the rest of his men stand guard over their captives. " Come, join me on the boat you were going to borrow. "

Soon all are aboard and the men holding the ropes on the shore move quickly to get aboard, as the current has already begun to drag the boat.

Ayogia looks them over carefully and decides they may need a few words, because they look as if they are traveling post - haste. " Move forward toward the bow, " he tells them, " I know what you are thinking, you are thinking ' we still have our weapons and his men are busy rowing, so why not kill them and take the ship. Do not try it! Look around you, you see the river she is very angry. If I wanted to I could have thrown you to her a long time ago and I still can. But you look like you may be good for something; maybe even a ransom, or perhaps you can use those fancy new weapons you have. " He smiles, " But serious, who knows where Beezubul will strike next. I still can no t believe he attacked King Revilo in Talmory, " he shook his head.

" Well as long as we are in the open like this, you may prove yourself. So you will live for now, or at least until we get to the Den. " he finished and faced the front, as if he had seen a picture of George Washington crossing the Delaware.

The craft is swift as a racer; the trip across the river is short. Soon they are on the other shore and running again. Ayogia no longer considered them to be a threat and they were allowed to travel as a part of their strangely modified rifle...

Squad, and for the most part they are the frontal security. They travel for close to an hour toward a series of mountains, which are surrounding an even larger one located in the center of a ring of smaller ones.

They enter a cave, which appears to have been cut into the solid rock of the mountain very crudely. They exit the cave to find themselves in a large forest. A forest where the trees are very tall and grow so close together they cut off the sunlight.

The journey continues, until suddenly without warning they stop. One of Ayogia's men walks up to him. " Do you smell it? " he asks.

" Yes, but I can not tell if it is in front or behind. Prepare a flare, " he orders.

One of the men holds up the flare to show he is ready.

The boys were not close enough to hear what they were discussing.

" Do you think this is where they plan to kill us? " asks Diddily. " Do not worry, " said Cush, trying again for the fragrance, "They will not hurt us. They are only puppets. Maiko decides everything. Even when, where and what they steal. Then the take is always brought back to the Den of Thieves. "

" Okay, in other words, these guys don't have the sense to pour piss out of a boot with the instructions on the side, " says Sledge and they laugh loudly.

" Quiet! Said Ayogia, and they became silent to try and hear what he was listening for.

Suddenly one of the men in the rear lets out a scream of shock as a huge wade of mucus wrapped around his ankle, then his scream of shock became one of pain as a huge claw was shoved through his shoulder as he was lifted up toward the mouth, of the Mucus (Booger) slinging Barunzee.

" Barunzee! " Shouts Ayogia. " Rozig, the flare! "

A loud swoosh is heard as the flare is launched it makes a loud pop before it lights up a very wide sector of the forest. They see the Barunzeies are everywhere; some running, some sitting under trees digging in their nose, and some hunting as another glob of mucus was hurled toward them. And blood gushes from the headless body of a thief who had held the line as they boarded the boat.

The Barunzee continues to crunch down on the mans head, then it swallows and takes another bite of what is left of the body as it still kicks violently from the severed nerves another Barunzee comes up to split the meat.

It happens all to fast. So fast, they almost didn't hear Ayogia shouting. " This way, quickly. Sound the alarm. "

Rozig, while running like everyone else placed his hands to his mouth and makes a weird, yet, musical sound which is returned by the identical sound from the direction they are running towards.

Running blindly through the woods as fast as their legs will carry them with more and more flares giving them a very eerie light. Sledge runs wide and Blaze runs into what he ran wide to avoid; A Rodagon. Blaze stumbles backwards and almost fell, but he managed to maintain his balance and drew his blade.

" There will be no need for that now, " said Ayogia, who was standing next to the creature.

Cush and the rest of the boys have not stopped running and they do not until they reach a stream in a clearing in the woods and there they notice they were the only ones still running.

Blaze watched the Rodagon as it chased a Barunzee off through the woods he heard loud roars as it caught it.

Wait a minute. Let me tell you a few things you need to know: The Barunzee;

A Barunzee has four limbs like most land creatures. It can walk upright or on all fours, which it seems to prefer. In height it can grow any where between twelve and fifteen feet tall. There have been reports of some which where as tall as thirty feet. But finding a Barunzee that tall has been found to be a very bad move. Barunzeies also spend a great deal of time digging in their noses, which often the mucus extracted has been used to subdue their victims. They look like a cross between a lion and a golden Northern Grizzly bear. Their claws grow longer than seven inches. Yet still the Barunzee would be handsome if compare to the Rodagon.

The Rodagon;

A Rodagon, which looks like, it sounds. It has the body of a very large rat and a head liken that of an alligator. In measurements from its snout to the tip of its long thick tail it would measure fifteen feet.

The Rodagon is quite ugly yes, but Blaze thought it was the most beautiful creature he had ever seen as he watched it chase off the Baronesses. But when it galloped back toward them, he thought it would be better for him if he had joined back up with the others. Where ever they were.

Ayogia rubbed the Rodagon under its chin as it brushed playfully against him. " Good baby. Pretty baby. "

A man approached as Ayogia soothed the Rodagon. " Come, Ayogia. I have sent Foabe to inform Maiko of your return, " Said Komn, who had been responsible for bringing out the Rodagons. " Who are the men you have brought with you? "

" These are men who were going to steal my boat. "

" My kind of people. " He said as he led the Rodagons.

Cush, Diddily, Stroke, Rebel and Sledge were waiting for them to catch up, while they tried to catch their breath.

Blaze wanted to keep his eye on the Rodagon, because he was not sure if any thing so ugly could be trusted walking behind him in the dark. But since Ayogia appeared to be on such good terms with the creature, then Blaze decides to walk between him and the Rodagon, you know, just in case.

" How are you doing? " Asks Ayogia.

" I guess you can say I'm doing fine for a man who was almost ate by a Barunzee and a Rodagon. "

" No, my friend you are wrong you were almost ate by a Barunzee. Rodagons are gentle creatures. If you show them love and kindness, then they return love and kindness, " he stroked the Rodagons fur.

" Well, why don't you kill the Barunzee. "?

" Kill the Barunzee? We could never destroy the Barunzee! They have been here as long as the trees. The forest belongs to them. We come and go, but the Barunzee is always here. We lose one and sometimes two men, but a man ate by a Barunzee is not soon forgotten. And they usually feed on intruders and other harmful creatures of the forest. The Barunzeies care for the woods as much as we do. And we have nothing to fear from them as long as there is a Rodagon about. Rodagons are the only creature that the Barunzee fears. "

Blaze has heard the reason way and he understands for many creatures no longer exist on Earth because man could not learn to live in harmony with them as these men have learned to maintain a balance in order to live with the Barunzee. Even though it did seem like a strange sort of balance. But What the hell!

He was from Slovannah Georgia.

Blaze only hoped he would not be the next man honored by being ate by a Barunzee.

The woods begin to thin as they neared the stream. Blaze could see the others waiting. The boys were glad to see he was still breathing and not a snack.

" Blaze! Man, am I glad to see that thing didn't eat you, " said Sledge as he walked up to shake his hand.

Blaze will use what he has learned. " I have no need to fear a Barunzee, when there is a Rodagon around and look at you. The way you ran out of there, "

Blaze shakes his head from left to right " It was embarrassing for me. "

" Well excuse me! I embarrassed you. Well in this I' d rather be embarrassing, than dead and have you be proud of me. Especially if my head is to be eating by a Barunzee, " said Rebel following the troops as they walked against the flow of the stream.

The water roughens; reason being the waterfall flowing from the side of the mountain.

" A water fall! " shouts Diddily in excitement.

" Keen observation, Doctor Diddily, " said Sledge. " I' d like to thank you for enlightening the rest of us on that subject. "

" But you don't understand. I have never seen a waterfall before... Well except on television in those Ol'Tarzan movies. You know, and almost every time there was a secret passage, which had been hidden from the world, and Tarzan was the only one who knew where it was. "

" Yeah and all the natives were stupid, " said Stroke.

" Hell that would make one hell of a back door for the brothers, " said Blaze hanging from Stroke's shoulder.

The group walks straight toward the waterfall, and then eases carefully along the side, walking cautiously on the slippery rocks along the stream. They are led around the back of the waterfall into a passage to the Den of Thieves.

" I told you! Didn't I tell ya? " Diddily looking about the cave in excitement.

" Okay, kid, you can be Tarzan, " said Rebel almost slipping off a slimy rock.

Diddily does his imitation of Tarzan as he lends towards Stroke. " Me, Tarzan. You, Boy. Him, Cheetah. "

" Who you callin' boy? " Asks Stroke holding back a smile.

" Sorry, Stroke, I forget."

Stroke can hold no longer." Don't worry about it, kid. "

The only light in the passageway is the light from behind them. The Thieves have traveled this way so many times they need no light. Soon they see a bright light just ahead of them, this is a huge hollow point with stairs, which go down about forty feet into another section, which is damp and very moldy smelling. There are big stone-faced arched openings to the left and right of the bottom of the stairs.

The boys are taken through the doorway on the right while Ayogia's men follow Foabe to the left. Traveling down a long hallway the once narrow passage of the Den has changed from the natural texture and begins to show signs of a well-guarded palace with all the trimmings. They are led through a maze of twisting halls. Soon they begin to hear noises. The closer they come the clearer the noises become; and they can tell that there is conversation and laughter.

The double doors at the end of the hall are pushed open by the two

large men, as they approach. They enter into the dining hall of the Den of
Thieves. Only they find it to be more than just a den.

It is luxury. This place shows the sign of a very successful organization
and the people here are carefree in all aspects.

As they enter through the doors the boys could see a group of men
sitting at a long table to the left of them, at the far end of the extremely
large room.

Ayogia steps lively, as he leads the way. He grabs a bottle from a table as
he passed and turned it up without losing his pace, he wipes his mouth with
his arm and smiles. " King Maiko, I have brought guest for you. "

The men at the table change their facial expressions. Then suddenly one
of them stands, while holding his hands up to silence Ayogia. Everyone in
the room becomes instantly silent. He draws his sword then uses it to push
the setting in front of him slowly to one side. He then climbs up on the
table.

" Ayo, sometimes you amaze me, but this time you have shown that
even a Rodag has more brains than you! "

Ayogia stops about three meters away from the table.

" Why did you bring this man here? " He asked pointing the sword at
Cush. "Draw you blade! " He shouts at Cush, and then he leaps from the
table.

Cush released his blade and they begin to stalk one another moving
in circles like two big cats closing in for the kill. The boys also drew their
blades, but they are out numbered. Chairs and tables are toppled over as
the Thieves stand to draw their blades. Ayogia gestures for Quest to return
their swords, they do not.

" Out of the frying pan... " States Blaze.

The way Cush and Maiko are looking at each other, tells them all things
are about to peak. They both lunge at the same time. Maiko grabbed Cush's
hand and he Maiko's then they embrace.

Everyone watching this is very much puzzled. First they act as if they
are going to cut one another's' heart out. And just as quickly as they started,
they suddenly act like long lost brothers.

The boys continue to watch, not exactly sure what is going on. But at
least there will be no bloodshed, for now anyway. The swords are returned
home.

TEN

THE THIEF WHO COULD NOT STEAL

I T HAS BEEN A LONG TIME, MY BROTHER, " With his arm about Maiko 's shoulder." TOO LONG, MUCH TOO LONG. "

Blaze drops his sword into the sheath. There is something he can no t resist saying. " It is a small world after all. "

" Shut up! " said Rebel, folding his arms across his chest.

" Why did you tell me to shut up? That's not nice. If you don't wish to hear what someone has to say, well then you should ask them to be quiet. "

" Would you shut up? "

" You both need to cut the shit! " said Stroke stepping between them.

While these three start in with their childish game, Cush walks Maiko over toward them. " Come, I would like for you to meet my new friends. Quest. "

" You always did like being adventuresome. "

" You are one to speak. "

Maiko laughed. " They are different, " he added smiling at the way they were dressed.

" They are like no men you have met before. They have traveled here from a faraway planet called Earth. They will tell you about Earth and you will like their stories. "

Sledge looks back at the three still playing the shut up game. " Shut up! They are coming, " he says and he gets away with it.

Cush makes the introductions as quickly as possibly so that they can get down to business.

Maiko is impressed. " Your names are peculiar, but they seem to fit you perfectly. Come, my friends and join us we were just about to dine before all of this excitement. You will all sit at my table, " He opens his arms to welcome them.

" Bring food for our guest, " orders the king as he walks toward the table. And the men seated there make room for the guest.

The thought of food has already over excited them. Quest has forgotten that they are far away from home on another planet; A planet with different creatures. But the aroma grabs their noses before the food is placed on the table.

Luckily for them the children had already been fed. So now Maiko will make sure his guest are fed even if he doesn't eat. But there are no shortages and there has not been any in a long time.

Soon as the food is placed on the table they forget all manners and dive in. The women surveying them giggle at the appetite of their handsome guest and hope the will desire a little more later to cure their hunger.

Maybe it is the fact that they have not ate since they left Earth, or it could be the way the food has been prepared. But what ever it is, they find the food delicious.

Sledge takes a bite of what looks like beef, but doesn't have the beefy taste. " Man, this is great, " said Sledge, nudging Blaze in the side. " I wonder what it is. "

" Yeah, you're right, it is good and I'm not going to spoil it by asking what it is. So eat up and shut up. " Said Blaze.

With that understood, they can enjoy seconds, after two large helpings they must decline Maiko's offer for them to have more.

" Well, if everyone has been satisfied by their meals, then I would like to know about your planet. "

" Before they do, Maiko, let me tell you why they are here on Zandoria, " said Cush resting his elbows on the table.

" Please do. I have a feeling this will be more interesting than hearing about Earth. For now anyway, " Maiko inter locked his fingers across his full stomach.

" I am sure you know by now that Beezubul has joined forces with Nud and they are planning to hold the Princess until the Seventh day and this is the fourth day. "

Maiko nodded.

"Now Maiko do you know what will happen if he keeps her until the Seventh day? "

" Of course I know. Beezubul will get some of the best in the universe, " said Maiko, causing laughter to break the air around them.

Yet Cush maintained a straight face.

" Maiko thinks like you, Stroke, " said Diddily.

" Yeah, kid, you're right. Kinda scary isn't it? "

" I am glad you understand, " said Cush, " Now what we need is your Help. Quest and I must travel to Mount Seficul to find the Princess and slay Beezubul. "

'' Well, my friend, what ever you wish of me I will do. "

" Maiko, you know the Land of Exile better than I do and you could lead us straight to Mount Seficul and show us how to enter undetected. "

" You' re right, Cush I do know the area better than you, and I could get you in side Mount Seficul undetected. But you are wrong if you think that I am going to."

Cush could not believe that his friend has lied to him. " Maiko, You said what ever I wish. "

" But you forget, my friend, I am a Thief, " he said as he turned more to face Cu sh. " Not only am I a Thief, but I am king of Thieves. Have you not been told before, a man who will s teal will also lie. So, I lied. "

" No! " Shouts Cush. " Something is wrong. You have never lied to me before and I know you would not turn down a challenge like this. Especially, when all you talked about when you were Prince of Thieves was an opportunity to steal the Slime Dwellers Treasure. Your eyes would light with excitement as you told the story. Do you remember? "

" Yes, I remember. I also remember the fact that I was much younger then. My friend now I have a thriving business training Rodagons. And the business is so good that Thieves are being respected as they were during the times of great treasures. But if you must go, then I will give you anything you need, food, Rodagons, more weapons. Name it. Anything you want."

Cush looks him straight in the eyes. "What I want is for you to tell the truth to an old friend. We once called each other brothers for life. Do you remember? "

Maiko is taken by this even a Thief must be loyal to someone and he is surrounded by a room full of his men. And as Cush has said, the man he has called his brother. " O Kay, Cush, you want the truth. "

" When E. F. talks people listen, " said Blaze.

" Can't you be serious? " asked Sledge.

" Sure and you can be Roebuck. "

Maiko is ready to begin. " Do you remember when my father, the Great King Malik died and I had to return home? "

" Yes. "

" Well I tried my first big steal to prove that I was worth of his throne. It was an attempt on the Slime Dwellers treasure. There were twelve of us on the steal. Everything we did was perfect. We used Rodagons to get there and they would have been used to bring back the take. We endured the changing weather of the Desert of Sufferance without a problem. By the time we made camp it was dark. More perfect, for the darkness covered our dismounted approach. We were able to enter the Slime Dwellers fortress totally undetected. Once inside, we had a brief encounter with a few of the guards, but they were easily disposed. It was not hard to find the treasury for we had a Thief with us, who had once been a Deacon of Slime. Hurriedly, we loaded our bags. There was more than we imagined some of our bags burst when we tried to lift them. We had as much as we could carry out of there. The men and I were leaving, heading home, back to the Den. But the deacons were waiting for us to leave the room," Maiko paused briefly.

" It was like a game for them to catch us that way. There was nothing we could do, but being the one in charge I spoke up for my men. I asked Nud if he would release them, then he could do what ever he wished with me. He refused and then he asked me how I found out about their treasure. I told him I had heard through conversations, " Maiko lifted his left hand, in order to touch the left side of his head, and then he decided not to.

"He said I had heard too much and I would hear less with one ear. With those words he drew his sword, " Maiko lifted his left hand once more to pull back his long black hair to expose the spot where his left ear once was. " And to stop the bleeding he had one of his men slap a hot blade against the side of my head. Then I was tied to a post while still agonizing in pain. I had no choice but to watch eleven of my men brutally molested and tortured to death. The next day Nud decided he would spare my life, I guess he said he had done almost all he could do to a man. Then he told me if I ever had the thought to come back, he would cut my head off. So I would not think too much. His next move was the last in the game. " He paused.

"Nud told them to release me, but not before he personally split open the heads of those eleven dead men and removed their brains which he placed in one of the sacks we had brought with us. Nud had this sack tied to my back. He said, I did not have enough brains. I was carried down the Mount where I was left with my hands still tied and the sack of brains still on my back. I was left to either make the journey home or die. It seemed as if my journey would have no end. I walked back through the Desert and through the Land of Desolation. I was delirious from the heat, the cold and the smell of the brains, " Maiko held his head down.

" I started wishing that I had died like the others. Even now I do not remember all, which happened to me after I reached the desert. Men found me three days later from the Den, who had been out looking for our party. They brought me back here and no one ever asked what had happened. I tried to forget, but still I am haunted by their screams in my dreams. Very vivid dreams. Dreams, which wake me in the middle of the night. I took those eleven men to die. It is worse still for one of those men was my younger brother, Chive. "

King Maiko has shared a very painful secret. His sad story has touched everyone. He sits still and silent at the table clinching his face in his hands while all in the Den are shocked and speechless.

Anyway, Stroke stands, he walks around the table to the middle of the floor where he stands and faces the king. He clears his throat and calls the king.

" Sire! Your Majesty! It took a lot of heart to tell your story. And I want you to know that I understand your pain and I know about being haunted by a dream, for I am haunted by one, now. But ignoring a problem never helps and it doesn't make it go away. Right now, we have a very serious problem. "

Maiko looked up at Stroke for the first time, he tries to understand what he is saying to him.

" After the pain and the suffering at the hands of Nud and the Slime Dwellers at least you could go home where it is safe, " He motioned at the band for them to walk down and join him. " Come on, dudes, help me out, " He waited until they were all facing Maiko before he continued.

" We were taken from our home and brought here against our wishes. And we have been told to kill Beezubul and other men, whom we have never been personally, threaten by. Yet, we are being forced to kill people we don't even know. But they are a proven threat to you and your people and your world, so if we just do nothing, just sit back and let Beezubul get the power he is trying to obtain. Then he just might bring down disaster upon the entire universe and Nud will be right there beside him all the way. Still alive and living it up and s till doing to others what he has done to you. And unlike when you failed we will no t have the safety of home, the pain will be everywhere. "

Opening his arms as he turned to remind Maiko of all he has, " There will be no where to hide, or seek shelter. We need your help. If you don't do it for us, then do it for Chive. But if you decide not to go all together. Then we will have to go at it blindly."

King Maiko looks at these men, he admires their show of courage. This display of bravery was not expected. He stands and smiles slightly. " Today I have met the bravest men in the universe. Each one as brave as five. We go together. "

His people begin to cheer.

" But now we celebrate! "

" What is there to celebrate? " asked Diddily.

Maiko strolled around the table to Diddily, who is about the same age as Chive would be. Maiko placed his hand on Diddily's shoulder, " You, my little brother, and how you are going to make me richer than I already am! " He hugs Diddily and then laughs loudly. "THEY ARE TO BE GIVEN ANYTHING THEY WANT. THESE MEN ARE MY BROTHERS. THEY ARE ALL PRINCES AMONG THIEVES. " Maiko goes to them all and hugs them like family.

The servants hurry the preparations for the celebration. Barrels of liqueur and ale are brought in. Cush talks Quest into singing for Maiko, and he enjoys their songs. They all laugh and enjoy, even though tomorrow they are to face death once more.

But tonight Maiko's entertainment makes them forget. The mood has been changed. Stroke is coerced by Blaze to recite Dolomite. The Thieves find his story very fascinating. Soon they are telling a few stories of their own. They continue all evening and late into the night.

Some people believe drinking will make you forget, but the more Stroke drank the more he realized that his memory was being enhanced. Causing him to remember the dream and the look on the face of the people. He remembered the men he must kill and his words to Maiko. And all he wanted to do was get back to what he knew. He tries to hide his pain with his usual act of being content with the way things are, using the phony smile he has used before, when he was not pleased with a situation.

King Maiko does not see pass the smile, he does not know. What he knows is that he would like to hear another one of Stroke's stories.

" You know Rudy Ray Moore wrote Dolomite, I didn't. "

" I am sure Rudy Ray Moore would not mind you sharing his stories with others so far away. "

" You know, Maiko, I've been thinking. "

" Do not think so much. It will only make you mad. Relax let's talk."

" Not now, Maiko, I feel closed in. I'm not use to surroundings like this. I like to be able to see the outside and breath fresh air whenever I want to. But that seems difficult, since we are trapped inside this mountain. "

" Follow me, Stroke, " said Maiko rising. " I know where you will feel comfortable and I could use a little air myself. "

Stroke follows Maiko through the hall having to weave around drunken bodies stretched out on the floor. Once they are out the dining hall and in the corridor Maiko resumes the conversation.

" Your planet is it a very beautiful planet? "

" Yes, at times. "

" Are you a king on your planet? "

He laughs loudly. " No, I'm not a king there are few kings on our planet. Earth is similar to Zandoria in many ways, but different just the same. There are sections, which are called nations, and most of the nations are ruled by a person, who has been elected by the people of said nation. Other rulers dominate the people, and limit their freedom and sometimes their thoughts. It's all hard to explain and I' m sure you find it even harder to understand. "

" Then you must be important, because you understand. "

" That's where you're wrong, because sometimes I don't understand. "

Maiko is confused. " Then your people should elect someone like you."

" That's another thing all together. You see, others have set the basic standard of what an ideal American citizen should be, therefore a majority of the people think that people like me aren't capable of doing anything at all, or at least anything of significance. Because of their standards we are often looked down on because of the way we live and think. "

Their walk has carried them to the top of a flight of stairs. Maiko opens the doors, which leads to the terrace. Stroke takes in a deep breath, and then yawns as he releases it.

" Come with me, I would like to show you where we keep the Rodagons."

He follows Maiko, even though he does not care to visit the strange looking creatures. Maiko is very convincing and he shows him how gentle the Rodagons really are. He points out to Stroke a few of his favorites; favorite because their colours will bring higher prices. He continues through patting others on the head playfully. By the time they were have way through the stables he had talked Stroke into petting them, and there was even talk of Stroke buying one.

Stroke was amazed how such ugly creatures could be so tame. "Yo, dude, I haven't seen so many weird, yet contented creatures since I left Slovannah State College. "

" Slovannah State College? What is that, my brother? "

" Just the place where I accumulated most of my knowledge, " he passed behind Maiko with his eyes glazed by a substance as he thinks of the memories of his college years.

Maiko can feel his sadness he turns and follows. " These Rodagons are a good trade, but they have peculiar appetites. For one; they like to eat Barunzeies, as you know. They also like the bush of the Bonda Berry, " Maiko lifts up a hand full of the Bonda Berry bush for Stroke to see.

And Stroke is shocked by what he sees, he can not believe that they are feeding the Rodagons a plant which looks like, smells like, and will probably smoke like cannabis sativa. " Where did you get this? " he asks holding up a hand full.

" Where else? We steal it from Anemeg after the Bonda Berry harvest. Anemagaians usually burn it all off during the festival, " said Maiko not understanding Stroke's concern.

But Stroke knew, and he also knew why they had a festival when they burned off the bushes.

" Come, Stroke, follow me and I will show you where we keep the new arrivals. "

Stroke stuffs a couple handfuls of the bush into his jacket, so that he may analyze it later. " The new arrivals? "

" Yes. The babies, the Rodags, " Maiko shows him all the new arrivals to the herd and points out one Rodag in particular.

" This little one has had a rough time. Its mother died during the birth and none of the females will adopt it. So it has been attended to by my children. "

The Rodag makes a whining sound. Stroke releases the latch, which secured the door to the lonely Rodag's pen, "Come on, now, " he says as if he were calling a puppy dog. The Rodag runs happily up to Stroke and brushes against his leg.

" You have made yet another friend. That one is yours my brother. "

The Rodag takes to Stroke and follows him foot to foot all around the corral. And he has gotten over his unfamiliarity and he does not mind his Rodag tail him about as he prepare s to leave the corral. Maiko leads him over to the edge of the terrace.

" I think it is time we return, " he said stretching and yawning. " I could use another drink, " he said turning his glass upside down to show that it was very much empty. " What about you, my brother, are you thirsty? "

" Not really. If you don't mind going back without me, I think that I would like to stay a little longer, " said Stroke as he eased himself down to rest his back against a boulder and he was joined by the little Rodag.

" I will send something for you in a while. "

" That won't be necessary. I just need to be alone for a while. But, thank you anyway. "

" As you wish, " said Maiko, and then he turned to walk toward the door.

He begins to gaze toward the stars, not sure, which is his solar system. He tries to battle sleep in fear of being haunted by the dream again. Then he begins to fumble through his pocket for something, while observing a strange mixture of purple and white clay. He pulled out the Blount cigar he was looking for and prepared to sample a little of the Rodag's food. He slipped the baby Rodag a little to chomp on as he blazed up.

Suddenly the Rodag senses something behind them.

" What is it, Gail? " he asked the Rodag and he turned to see Balaam. " What do you want? "

" I have come to see how you are getting along. "

" Why didn't you just read your book? "

" I did and it said I was supposed to be here now. "

" Cool "

" So how are you doing? "

" I was doing fine until I saw your ugly face, " he said scratching the Rodag 's wings.

" You must be strong. I know this is not easy for you. But you must continue as you have been doing and not lose your confidence, because you will succeed. The well being of the Princess depends on you all. "

" Don't worry about me, dude. This ain't shit; I'm a well-trained soldier. I only wish that I knew she was not being harmed. "

" Would you like to see how she is doing? "

" Can you do that? " he asked with excitement.

" No, but you can. "

" How can I? I have no powers."

" When you have all of the right forces behind you, anything is possible. You are stronger than you know. Just close your eyes and she will come to you. "

" All I have to do is close my eyes and she will come to me? "

" Yes. "

" Do I have to click my heels three times and all that shit? "

" No and I asked you to watch your language. "

" Forget it. Just tell me how I can see the Princess. "

" Close your eyes and she will come to you. "

Stroke will waste no more time with his sarcastic remarks. If all he has to do to see the princess is close his eyes, then he will. And he tries hard to make the images appear.

Slowly the images begin to appear. He sees a mountain as he approaches from the sky, he does not recognize the mountain, yet the sight of it stirs him inside. The mountain is Mount Seficul. His thoughts ring him further inside to the chambers of the Princess.

He hears the muffled sound of someone crying. He advanced further to find out where the sobbing was coming from and found the Princess sitting to a bureau with her head pillowed on her arms, as she rested them on the counter. He moved closer, trying not to be heard, but the awkward weight of his weapons make it hard for him not to be detected.

The Princess holds her head up and sees him in the looking glass. Her eyes are red from all of the crying she has done. Stroke is close enough to touch her and he does, letting his hands feel the soft silkiness of her hair down to her shoulders, as his eyes hold contact with hers in the mirror. She turns to hold him around his waist.

He is not sure whether he is holding the princess to comfort her, or to comfort him, yet, he is glad to hold her just the same. He lifts the princess to her feet and uses his thumb to gently wipe the tears from under her eyes.

ELEVEN

DEFIANCE

CUSH IS TRYING TO WAKE Stroke by shaking him, " Stroke! Stroke, wake up! "

Stroke wakes like a combat veteran, suffering from flash backs of a bad skirmish. The Rodag is unhappy he moved the leg it was sleeping on.

"Man, don't you ever do that shit again, " he said using the boulder to get to his feet. He reached down to rub the Rodag on the head when it brushed against his leg.

" Stroke, it is time to leave and you must get your own gear. We have a long journey ahead of us. "

" Ah man! I really had too much to drink last night. How can they party like that? Hunh, tell me, " Stroke cracked his neck. " Are the boys ready? " He asked as he walked toward the doorway leading to the stairs.

Cush did not answer, because he had a question of his own. "What is this?"

Stroke turns to see the Rodag following him and when he stopped, it stopped right between his feet and sat down. " That, my friend is a Rodag. "

" I know what it is. What I want to know is what is it doing following you? "

" I guess... it is following me...because it likes me. "

" Stroke, you do not have time to nurse a Rodag. We have got to go!"

" Yeah, yeah, yeah! Just chill out, dude. I can handle this. Besides, I like the little Rodag, " he said as he reached down to rub its head.

" It reminds me of Gale; a freak I knew in college. So leave it alone. Come on, Gale, Uncle Cush has got a feather up his ass this morning. " He walked pass Cush on his way to the stairs and Gale was close behind.

Maiko is trying to make them understand the need for the tactical gear he is making them pack. He takes control like an Officer in Charge. As he points out each device and explains it in quick details. "Okay, you all know our journey will take over half a days travel and you know you will be in need of covering better than you know have. The seamstress made new coverings especially for this mission during the night. We will need them once we reach the Desert of Sufferance. The weather is terrible there, " he informs as he paces the floor nervously in front of them. " We should arrive at Seficul just before dark. We will eat; feed the Rodags and water them down then hide them inside a boxed canyon. From there we shall continue the rest of our journey on foot, " He smiles and points at the rucks. " Of course, we will be carrying those on our back. Then we will do what we have to do in order to enter undetected, or I will handle anything, which turns up. "

Rebel enters as Maiko finished. He had just returned from relieving himself and he was still having trouble fastening his belts.

Maiko signals for him to move over and join the others. " You will have no need for those old lasers the king gave you, " he said pointing out the new ones on the table. " We have others, which have been modified. They shoot twice as many shots and the shots are as silent as smoke. I have another surprise for you, " adds Maiko as he lifted a light weight headphone set with a mic attached. " These will help us communicate easier. So if there are no questions I want you to grab your gear and I will see you all on the terrace, " Maiko grabbed a pack and the others did like wise. Then each one made sure he picked up one of the new lasers.

" What's hadning? " said Rebel, " Where is Stroke? "

"I don't know. Cush was suppose to have been going to get him. " Said Diddily picking up his pack.

" That's alright. I see him coming now, " he said watching Cush and Stroke enters the hall.

The Rodag still follows Stroke in every direction he turns and he is enjoying having it tail him about. Rebel is trying to understand how he could let such an ugly little creature follow him. He continued to watch as Stroke feed the Rodag something from his pocket.

" What do you think you are doing? "

" I'm feeding Gale. "

" I can't believe you gave that thing a name, " said Rebel shaking his head.

" Your Momma gave you a name. I saw you baby pictures. You weren't Mister Cutes. "

" Why name it Gale? "

" I'm not sure if it's a boy or a girl and I didn't want to look, " he said with a big grin. " So I figured Gale was a name, which could go either way. "

" Well, just keep that thing away from me. I hate those mothers. "

Stroke shakes his head and walks toward the table, where Blaze tried to briefly explain to him all he had missed. He had to walk near Rebel in order to pick up his ruck and the Rodag was right under his feet.

" I told you to keep that thing away from me, dude, " said Rebel.

" I don't care if I never see another Rodagon again, " he added as he started on his way down the hall.

" It seems to me that you have got yourself a problem. "

" And what do you mean by that? "

" You'll see. Come on, Gale. "

Rebel followed Stroke and Gale up the stairs still trying to make Stroke explain his last statement. But Stroke knew he would find out soon as they reached the terrace.

Rebel walked through the doors to the terrace and what he saw were seven Rodagons saddled and ready to travel. " Oh hell no! O hell no! I'm not riding on one of those things. And that's that. I quit! "

" Fine. Then we will just have to go without you, " said Stroke.

Maiko notices the Rodag still following Stroke foot to foot. " Stroke, you must return the little one and have one of the men tie it up in the corral. Otherwise she will follow you all the way to Seficul. "

He nodded, and then started toward the corral, knowing that Gale would follow.

The Rebel continues to voice his complaints to Blaze, " I don't want to ride one of those things. I'd rather get slapped off my surfboard from another thirteen-foot wave down at Cocoa Beach. "

" What's wrong with you? You know we can't leave without you. Now stop acting like a pussy and take your ass over there and mount that Rodagon before I kick your shit! "

" Man they couldn't melt you in a glass and pour you on me. "

" What if he had some help? " asked Sledge.

Rebel looked behind him and found that he was a bit out numbered, well about five to one. So he smiles. " Can't you dudes take a joke? Dawg gone! You boys know I wouldn't miss this. Not even for a brand new multi coloured Washburn. "

He eased pass them toward his Rodag. "So I guess I'm on this one over here, " he said keeping up the front. But while placing his pack securely on the Rodag he mummered to himself " Those filthy bastards are going to remember this shit. Dirty Mutherfuckers. "

Stroke walked over to see Rebel had already mounted his Rodagon.

" How did you guys get Rebel on that Rodag? "

" How do you get Rebel to do anything he says he is not going to do? " asked Blaze.

" Why didn't you dudes wait for me? I like it when he wants the physical stuff to help make up his mind. " Said Stroke rubbing his knuckles as he looked at Rebel.

" O yeah, and what do you think you would have done? You're nobody!
"

" Nobody?! I'm Stroke the Mutherfuckin' Renegade. And don't you forget it. "

" Here, Stroke, stroke this!" says Rebel holding his balls for him to understand what he is talking about.

Stroke is ready to reply.

" Get mounted! We must be on our way, " shouts Cush.

" Stroke did you have one of the men tie off the little one? " asked Maiko.

" Don't worry, I took care of it personally, " said Stroke as he mounted.

"Okay, my brothers, on to Mount Seficul " shouts Maiko galloping his Rodagon toward the edge of the cliff.

The Rodagon takes to the air as it approached the last few feet of the terrace.

" Airborne! " Shouts Stroke.

" Airborne! " shouts Sledge.

" No way, " said Rebel, who took one look at this and decided that even if they beat him close to death he was not about to ride this beast off a cliff. Blaze saw the hesitation on his face, he moved over toward the Rodagon and slapped it sharply on the rump; causing it to gallop toward the edge with Rebel struggling hard to maintain some sort of control.

He has a difficult time, but the others find their beast easier to handle. Gale watched them leaving and she tried hard to fly behind them, but the rope was restraining her from doing so. Still determined to get free Gale begins to chew through the rope.

The boys are soon handling their Rodagons like they have been riding them all their lives. Rebel has relaxed and is enjoying his ride. Maiko is pleased at the way they have easily adapted to the s kills of flying Rodagons. He decides to show them a few flight maneuvers for training, which they are more than ready to attempt.

Maiko spotted a few Barunzeies and swooped down to make them run frantically, like a herd of wild animals would dodge an air plane on the open fields of Africa. The Barunzeies retreat to the protection of the forest, screaming and digging in their noses as they run. And as they watched, it seemed strange to see a creature run with the thought of such a shaking fear, for they were seated on the backs of the animals they feared.

The suns find their spot directly overhead. It is midday.

" We will stop and rest here briefly. Soon we will exit the Land of Exilo and enter the Land of Desolation, We shall break here and then continue. "

Maiko leads them down toward the ground.

The men eat, then each on sees to their animals; watering them and checking the straps before time comes for them to continue their journey.

" Okay, my brothers, this would be a good time for you to try on your covers. Remember, no matter what happens you will not remove them until I tell you, " he warns, looking to see if all are doing as he has instructed.

Gale has chewed through the rope and she wastes no time taking to the air in hope of catching Stroke.

The Land of Desolation. Nothing lives here; no trees, no animals and no people. Even the ground looks dead, with its hard cracks and crevices. The Rodagons begin to react very strangely to their environment as they pass over the area.

In this land, there are many strange and unusual things, which could completely baffle even the greatest minds on Earth. And the Desert of Sufferance would probably be the most confusing. The mystical effects of the weather on the travelers is one that no Climatologist has been able to explain. There is scorching heat and the freezing cold, which come at will.

They have been warned and now they will experience.

" Damn it's hotter than forty Hoe's in a Volkswagen, " complained Diddily.

" You know what you were told, kid! So keep that coat on, " ordered Sledge.

" The heat is nothing, for the cold comes just as suddenly. So remember to keep those covers on, " insisted Maiko.

The cold tries to overcome Blaze, but Rebel feels the heat. It is like this for all of the men; some are hot, while others are cold at the same moment.

" We should not have to put up with this much longer. " explained Maiko, " There, over the horizon, look you can see the peaks of the Mountains. Mount Seficul is within walking distance from those series of Mountains. We will leave the animals there. " He pointed toward a canyon,

" From there we will continue on foot. "

" Sounds good to me. I don't mind walking, just as long as I don't have to put up with this freaky weather, " said Blaze.

Gale is trying hard to maintain her balance to fly as fast as she can. Even though the little Rodag is hungry and tired it will not be detoured. She is determined to find Stroke.

" Down there, " points Maiko. " We will make camp down there. " Maiko guided his animal toward the ground.

" Man! If I never ride through there again it will be too soon, " said Sledge as he followed Maiko's lead.

Maiko showed them where to leave the animals. " Walk your animals inside here. Do not worry about tying them off, these have been thief trained. They will be here when we return. " Maiko drops his ruck on the ground.

" I will start a fire and one of you can water the animals... This is a good time to check your equipment before we leave. "

" Diddily, water the animals, " orders Sledge, " I'll carry your pack over to the fire and check your gear. "

" Roger that! "

Quietly, they sit around the fire eating what they know could be there last meal. Maiko notices the ring on Stroke's right hand.

" What a beautiful ring you have there, my brother. "

" Yes, I like it too. "

" Do you think you could let me have a closer look at it? "

" I don't wish to take it off, " said Stroke, as he twisted the ring tighter on his finger. " It was a gift from Ecinaj; she gave it to me when we visited her in the Land of Soul. She said it will bring me luck. And I need all the help I can get. So don't try and steal it. "

" I understand, " said Maiko. " Well, it is time for us to leave. You can remove all excess food from your bags. But keep those coverings on. "

They do as Maiko instructs. Cush kicks out the fire they had used to warm their dinners. The animals have been fed and watered and were left there in the canyon. There was no more to be done there so they began their journey once more.

The suns begin to settle in for their nap. There will be no sunshine tomorrow. And when next the light is shown they must have freed the Princess and Beezubul must be dead.

Mount Seficul is easily visible from where the men are on their journey. Usually a mountain so majestic would leave them in awe, but the sight of this one only fills their heart with anger, each man's as intense as the next.

Stroke was not surprised to see that Mount Seficul looked exactly like the mountain from his vision, He only hopes the princess has not given up hope.

Inside mount Seficul, Princess Reikciv slides a fork around her plate. She did not feel like eating and if she was hungry, then sitting at the same table with Nud and Beezubul has removed her appetite. But these two do not care if she eats or not she eats, if she does not then so be it. They have more important matters to consider at the moment.

" It appears all is going better than we had expected, " brags Nud, sipping from his goblet.

" Yes and it worries me. It has been a bit too easy, " says Beezubul.

His statement draws the attention of the Princess and she glares down the t able at him. " There is no need to worry, Beezubul, you know you are going to die for what you have done. "

" Princess, power does not die, it only fades away. And you shall feel my rod long before it fades, " said Beezubul.

Nud laughing draws the attention of Beezubul. " Save it, Nud. Guards! Escort the princess back to her chambers. She does not seem to be very hungry this evening. "

The guards moved from their post in front of the door and walked up behind Reikciv's chair. She slid her plate forward and her chair back, and then stood slowly.

" Not even if I were starving would I sit and eat at the same table with you and your mindless friend. Nor will I be cooperative for someone, who smells like a Rodagon! "

Nud and Beezubul stand, as she turns to leave.

" Thank you for the complaints, " adds Nud, " And may you be as happy on your next menstruation. " He bows, " Only women bleed."

Beezubul walks away from the table to think and Nud sits back down to finish his meal.

" Nud, I want you to put more men on all post and possible entrances. In case we have any unexpected guest this evening. "

" I will take care of it just as soon as I am finished. " said Nud, not bothering to look up from his plate. I want you to handle it, now! " Shouted Beezubul, as he pointed a finger at his plate, causing it to slide across the table.

" What is wrong with you? " asked Nud coming to his feet. " How many times have I told you not to use it on me! "

" I'm sorry, my friend, but we can not afford to waste time. "

Nud had already started away from the table, but he has not finished with Beezubul. " You should try some of that on the princess. Then, maybe you will not have to get up in the middle of the night. "

" Do not concern yourself. Soon she will be with me all through the night, doing what ever I command. "

Beezubul's words are wasted for Nud has left the room.

At the base of mount Seficul. The darkness has begun and so has the assault. The boys stand looking up at the mountain they must climb.

" Are you sure this is the right spot? " asked Rebel as he looked up at the mountain.

" Do Thieves steal? " said Maiko, " Look, my brother, do you see the ledge sticking out up there? " He asked as he pointed toward the ledge.

" Yes, I see it. "

" That, my brother, is Deacons Lip and there is an entrance a short climb from there. "

Inside Mount Seficul it appears that it may not be as easy as Maiko has said it will. At that very moment there were squadrons of Slime Dwellers moving through the cathedral to the lower sections inside the mount their mission is to double the guards at the main entrance, as well as to cover all other possible points which could be accessed by land or air.

The boys have unloaded their climbing gear and Maiko stands at the base ready to show them how to place their lines in the deacon's lip.

" My brothers, watch and the rest you can learn as we go a long, " he said sliding a metal stud down into what looked like a rocket launcher, and then he extended it with the press of a button. The fifteen-inch stud was attached to about eight hundred feet of rope. " First; I need to pick a spot to secure this line, then.. "

Maiko held the cannon up on his right shoulder and pulled the trigger. The metal stud was launched so far by the force of the cannon that most of the rope had untwined before it was lodged securely in Deacon's Lip.

" Make sure you use your utility belt to secure yourself to the rope and for those who have not already done so, this would be a good time to put on your... gloves, " Maiko tells them this as he searched through his ruck for another one of his special toys. He held it up for them to see. " This will help to make the climb with ease, " he walked over toward the rope and secured his belt and the small machine to the line.

"Okay, my brothers, see you at the next stage, " Maiko squeezed on the pulley and up the side of the mount he flew with the machine doing all the work.

They each found their pulley, and then waited their turn to do as they had seen Maiko do before them. Up they went carrying their rucks on their backs.

Cush saw something flying overhead. " Maiko, there is a scout flying up there."

" Where? I see nothing. "

" He is circling the mountain. Just keep watching, he will be back around."

Maiko sees it and he knows it is too small to be a scout. Even at the height it is flying. " Do not worry. It is only a Rodag, " said Maiko, as he continued on the climb.

" Why would the Slime Dwellers have a Rodag out like that?" asked Blaze.

" I do not know, but what ever their reason is we will not let it concern us. Keep coming. "

Six hundred feet above ground Maiko is waiting on Deacons Lip for the boys to arrive one by one they make their way.

" From here, we shall climb by hand up another three hundred feet. Continues up at an angle, which will make it easy to climb. But just the same, be very careful not to try and pull your self up by a loose rock, " said Maiko starting up.

" Well damn, don't we get a breather? Shit! I haven't done this type of shit in years, " complained Stroke.

" Ah is the little renegade getting tired? " asked Blaze following Cush up behind Maiko.

" Don't worry, I have a feeling that this mutherfuckin' renegade is going to have to save your butt before this is all over, " he said grinning as he pulled himself up behind Blaze.

Maiko feels his way up expertly for without the use of a life line it would only take one wrong move and he would be splattered all over the foot of the mount. There is no room for errors.

He makes his way to a perch, about four feet below the ledge of the entrance. He removed his pack and tucked it behind a pile of rocks. Then pulled himself up in order to make sure the way was clear. What he saw was two guards standing outside the entrance. Quickly, he dropped back down to wait for the others.

" Be very quiet. There are guards just above us, " he tells each man as he helps them onto the perch.

Stroke peeped over the edge carefully, so as not to be seen. He knew what he saw would only cause a greater complication.

It was Gale, the little one, which he thought, he had tied up securely. She was landing and he was sure she had seen him as well. And if she did, then she would lead the guards straight to them.

" What guards? " asked Blaze, " You said there would be no guards. I knew this was a bad idea. "

" I also said I would handle any difficulties. Now watch my smoke. "

Maiko reached into a small pouch with his right hand. The pouch was attached to weapons belt and out of that bag he removed two well balanced five inch throwing knives, which were both pointed at either end.

Stroke dropped back down after watching to see how fast things would develop. "We have a small problem. Ah, Gale is here and she is leading the guards this way. "

" Do not fret, my brother, I was just about to take care of them. "

On that note he stands, not caring if he is seen or not, because before they can react, he has lodged a knife in the chest of each of the guards. Then he finds a very happy little Rodag in his arms. He gets rid of it by dropping it quickly down on Stroke.

" I believe this is looking for you, " He said before leaping up onto the terrace of the entrance.

One of the guards is not done yet; he presses an emergency button on his belt, which caused a heavy metal door to be released, securing the passageway.

Stroke lifts Gale back up on the ledge, and then pulls himself up. The others are right behind. " Well, Maiko, it would seem that they had a surprise of their own. "

Maiko only smiled, as he reached into another pouch on his belt. He brought forth something, which looked at first like a slice of pizza. He pressed a button on top of it, which forced it to fan out into the shape of a world class Frisbee.

" Get down! " he shouted and with that he flung the object toward the door and he watched as it hovered there in front of the door.

" Perfect, " he said, and then he got down into a prone position.

A very loud explosion was the sound they heard. When they looked again there was a nice big hole in the door.

Maiko pushed himself up from the ground and brushed some of the dirt from his clothes. " Shall we? " he asked, as he walked toward the door.

" You can not take her with us, " insisted Cush walking up behind Stroke.

" Be quiet, dude, we can't afford to waste time. So she will just have to travel as a part of the group, " he said as they walked cautiously behind Maiko, who was about to pass through the entrance.

" Looks like we will be kicking some ass soon, " said Maiko grabbing Rebel by the arm.

" You learn fast and you're right it's going to be like taking candy from a baby. "

" I would never take candy from a baby. "

They made their way through being casually cautious, as they strolled through the room, which was obviously a storage place of sorts. There were barrels and boxes stacked all over. Yet still, the walk way was wide enough for them to walk abreast. But this is a combat situation, so they form a staggered column and continue.

" Hurry, there is a door just a head on left, " said Maiko turning the corner.

" I am glad you know your way about this place, " said Cush. As they rounded the corner they were stunned by the sight of Nud seated in middle of the now wider section of the aisle and there were seven men standing next to him with their laser pointed in their direction.

" Welcome. It is so nice of you to pay us a visit. It is not often we receive guest. So I must apologize for not being able to provide a proper reception. But this was the best I could do on such short notice, " he lifts his left hand.

Twenty more Deacons stood high above them on stacks of crates, boxes, and barrels. And the width of the path makes them very easy targets. They know there is no need to fight, they must wait another chance. If it comes.

For now they stand motionless while Nud stands as the seven next to him move forward. Nud begins to smile.

" I hope what we have here is enough, " he said, then he recognized a former visitor. " Maiko! I did not know they were with you, " he said as he stepped forward a little more. " And I see you have brought more of your men for me to play with. Do you remember what I told you the last time you were here? Wait what is this I see? Is that a little Rodag I see? " Nud sees the little Rodag as it peeps around from behind Stroke.

" Maiko, you should not have done all of this for me. But do not worry they will all get the same treatment as the others. "

With those words Nud felt a warm sensation. No not in his frozen heart, but lower. Nud looked down to see what was causing the warm feeling and there was Gale relieving herself on his leg.

Maiko and the boys found this very amusing, especially in their situation. But Nud does not share their laughter. He gives Gale a taste of his boot; sending it sliding across the floor.

She cried out from pain.

Stroke is not pleased with this, he starts toward him, but Rebel and Maiko quickly restrain him. " You sick slimy little bastard. I'm going to smoke your ass! "

Nud knows he has the upper hand. He released his whip from where it was secured to his belt, he snaps it once in order to make sure it was fully uncoiled, then again, this time it wrapped itself around Stroke's neck.

" Now, what was it, you said? " he laughs, " I think you have got things confused, but maybe a taste of this will help to dear it all up. "

He adjusted the whip in his hand to better his grip in order to give the whip a good hard jerk. Rebel grabbed a hold of the whip with his left hand as he drew his sword with his right; bringing it out in one upward motion, he cut the whip from around Stroke's neck just as he starts to pull. This caused Nud to stumble backwards, then fall to the floor.

Stroke removed the piece of whip, which was left around his neck and threw it toward Nud, as His men hurried to help to his feet.

" For your actions you will be the first to die, " he said pointing a finger at Rebel.

" Having you try to kill me would be an honor, douche bag! "

" So be it! Take these men to the Hold. There they will stay until I think of an interesting way to kill them. I have a feeling they will prove themselves to be very entertaining when they start to beg for their lives. Delop, get the Rodag and follow me. I already have plans for it. "

Nud exits but the Deacon assigned the task of removing Gale finds her to be very unagreeable, having to be separated from Stroke once again. She snaps viciously at Delop, who finally must use his weapons belt to drag her in the opposite direction from which the boys are taken.

The boys seem a bit more agreeable, as they find themselves disarmed. " Do you think we pissed him off? " asked Sledge.

" Hah, he's just so happy to see us he does not know how to act, that's all, " Said Blaze. And they share a laugh before they are hit in the ribs, as they are lead to the Hold.

TWELVE

STRANGE WEED

THE WALK TO THE HOLD is a long one. They are escorted through the lower sections of the mount; traveling down well lit halls. Finally they halt at a very large wooden door, but just long enough for the jailer to unlock the door from the inside.

" Yeah what do you want? " Asked the jailer.

" We have some very important guest for you. And uh, give them the best accommodations. But be advised, keep a very close eye on them, " explains the Deacon in charge of the guards which escorted them down to the Hold.

The man he is addressing is a short, rat looking man, who grins fiendishly at his new occupants. " It is so nice to have distinguished ones pay us lower ones a visit every now and again, " he is broken off by a series of violent coughs, which rattle his body severely. The attack ceased and he wiped his nose with a very grimy rag.

" I have the perfect room for you. It has plenty of space for this happy little family. Come, follow me, " he turns and walks down the stairs to show them where they will be staying.

The boys enter the Hold. Stroke takes up a spot in a corner of the four walls, sitting on a bottom bunk.

" Here are their weapons. You know what to do with them, " he added.

" Odak, are you trying to tell me how to run my place? "

" If you let them escape you will answer to Nud. "

" Yes, and if you do not leave, you will find yourself locked away in one of my private rooms. "

" Move out, Deacons! Our work is done here, " said Odak and his men followed him out of the Hold.

Once again their mission has been halted and this time it appears that things are a bit worse than they had been before. Seven men awaiting death and some are a bit more depressed than others.

" Do you think he will be all right? " asked Cush, sitting down on Rebel 's bunk.

Rebel looked over toward Stroke, who had been in retreat in the corner since they had entered the cell.

" You need not worry about him, he's just pissed off. He has been locked up before and he hates it."

" Maybe you should talk to him. "

" About what? How we are going to get out of here? I don't think that's a good idea. He can be very hard to deal with once he goes inside himself and starts tripping on the magic and shit. The best thing to do is just wait until he comes of it. "

" Well. I think if someone to talk to him, he would probably feel better."

" Listen, Cush! I knew that man when he was a boy. And I know when he doesn't want or need to be bothered, and so do the rest of the boys. Just take my word for it and don't fuck with him. You dig? "

Rebel starts to dig in to the inside pocket of his jacket. " Here, I've got something for you, " said Rebel, then he looked over toward Blaze. " Watch this, Cush... Hey, Blaze! " Said Rebel holding up the joint for him to see. " Look at what I've got. "

" Fire it up, dude, we might as well have ourselves a little party. So lets get stoned, " He said as he moved over to join them. He recovered his lighter from where it was tucked securely in front of his pants.

Nud had to make sure the Rodag was properly prepared before he personally delivered the news to Beezubul about the intruders. And with all taken care of, he joyfully made his way through the palace toward Beezubul's chamber.

Beezubul really digs his privacy and as he sat alone in his room about to receive relief from the Orgasm ball, which was floating directly in front of him.

The Orgasm ball is a very unique device, for with a little concentration it can make the user feel as if they are actually making love to the person of their desire.

And the one Beezubul is concentrating on is the princess Reikciv. Deeper and deeper, he plunges into the trance. He is full into the act when Nud rushes through the door of his chambers. Forcing him to break his concentration. The ball falls onto its rest.

" Why have you disturbed me? " shouts Beezubul as he closes his robe. "I was in the middle of very important business. "

" Yes. Half a ball can give you a headache, " said Nud, with a smile. "But you will not need that for I have something I am sure you will find more stimulating. "

" How many times have I told you, I am not interested, nor do I wish to participate in any of your sex games. "

Nud can only smile at the thought of getting in Beezubul's pants. And he does remember all of the time s he has offered his body to Beezubul only to be rejected.

" Where have you been? I sent you to increase the guard long ago and you just now return. "

" I had a few matters to take care of before I could return. Remember I work with you, not for you. " He said without a smile. " I have returned to tell you that I have captured Maiko and a small band of his Thieves, who were trying to steal my treasure. I am sure you will find these seven men very entertaining. "

" Thieves!? This time of year? You fool! They are not here to steal your treasure. What they wish to take is the Princess. Where are these men? "

" I had them taken to the Hold. "

" Picture this! The king still tries to foil me and his men were stopped by you. To the Pain! Now, maybe the princess will be more agreeable after she has had a look at her would be saviors locked up in my cells. "

" What do you mean your cells? This is still my cathedral. "

" Yes, my friend, for a second I lost my bearings. Will you have a couple of your guards bring the princess to my chambers, and then I will join you shortly in the main hall. I wish to speak to the princess. Ah, there should be enough time in there for you to wash and change your clothes. You, my friend smells like Rodagon urine.

The princess sits in her chambers, not really sure if anyone will rescue her, but all she can do is hope and w ait. Suddenly, there is a forceful knock at her chamber door, as if someone has an urgent need. Then two females guards enter without a reply from the princess.

" Come, " said the taller of the two, " Beezubul wishes to see you in his chambers. "

The princess moves without a word. She is escorted through the halls of the palace toward Beezubul's chamber.

Beezubul's door is open when they arrive. The Deaconess show her in, but they do not enter with her, they take up their post outside the door. Beezubul stands looking at himself in the mirror and he sees her enter the room.

" How nice of you to comply and come so promptly. I have something you will be interested in seeing. " Beezubul moves from the mirror over toward his cloak lying on the bed.

" Nothing you have will ever interest me. "

" That is where you are wrong, my dear, come we are going to meet Nud in the main hall. He should be just about ready now. After me, princess, " he said walking out the room first.

The walk to the main hall does not take long and they find Nud waiting for them. He is sitting in the hall fingering back his long black hair as they enter the hall. Nud greeted Beezubul and the princess and they continued on toward the Hold.

Diddily had his arms hanging casually through the bars of the cell when he noticed a few prisoners in the cell across from theirs. " Hey! You there. What are you in for? "

The dark haired man he was addressing looked toward him, " My name is Boo-gee Woo-gee, I am from Wasugie on Trimelva. "

" Who is that you're talking to? " asked Sledge.

" Do not worry, they are allies, " said Maiko, " They are from Trimelva, the planet of sound; where noise is an art. But they know the game. Ask them what they are about to do. "

" What are you about to do? " Asked Diddily.

" We are getting ready to escape, " said Boo-gee. Suddenly, the jailer becomes alert and Diddily sees why.

" Hey, you guys had better come check this out. "

They all crowd toward the front of the cell, all except Stroke. But the others stand there trying to see what is happening.

" Here they come. I knew it would not be long, " said Maiko.

Beezubul approached the cell door and stood looking them all over ever so carefully. Then he laughs as if he has just remembered something very funny, which happened long ago.

" So you are the would be heroes, who thought you could defeat Beezubul?"

Rebel has never liked being taken as a joke. " If it ain't the head Slime Dweller himself. Can't say that I'm glad to see you without your balls dangling from the end of my blade. "

Beezubul is not pleased, for he is not accustomed to being spoken to in such a manner. " Then you shall have your chance to have your blade in your hand in the arena. "

" No, Beezubul, I wish to have the pleasure of killing this one myself, " said Nud.

As Nud, Beezubul and the jailer stood staring through the bars of the cell at the men, Reikciv sees something lying on the table unsecured. She knows it is something the boys could desperately use. So she carefully lifted it from the table and tucked it under her robe quickly.

Nud notices that they have not touched the meals he had prepared especially for them. " I see none of you wanted your dinner. You should have taken advantage of your last meal. O well, that is too bad, for I have heard Rodag can be very tasty and I am sure your little Rodag would have tasted excellent. "

Nud walked away from the cell laughing loudly, for he found his revenge on the little Rodag to be very sweet and amusing.

Diddily found it to be sickening to his stomach and bent over in a corner to throw up.

Stroke looked up for the first time since they had entered. He was biting down hard on his lower lip, so hard he drew blood.

Beezubul had one more thing to say. " Oh, and by the way the princess would like to convey her sympathy, " Then he turned to hurry and join stride with Nud.

" Did I not tell you they would be entertaining? "

" To the pain! " said Beezubul, as he started up the stairs. " But tell me why did you cook their Rodag? " he asked between his short-winded laugh.

The princess was whispering something to Cush as Stroke made his way to the cell door, he succeeded just as she finished talking to Cush and he walked away. He sees the same smiling eyes he has seen only in the form of a vision. Her eyes take him with the same overwhelming effect they did when he first saw them.

" Who are you? " she asked observing the way he looked at her. " You came to me the night I was abducted by the Slime Dwellers. I thought they had taken you. Then, you came to me again last night and I knew you were alive. But you never say a word. Not even to tell me your name. Can you speak? "

" Yes, but my name is not important, " he said.

" I have not given up hope, I know you will save me, " she said as a tear fell from the corner of her left eye.

He had his hand on the bars of the cell. She placed her hand on his. He wished to hold her, but that was impossible at the moment. But he must say something to make her feel a little more at ease.

" Don't worry, princess, I have not come this far to fail. You shall be free. "

She believes his words. But she has a strong urge to cry, she released her hold on his hand and ran toward the stairs, she did not want him to see her cry.

He watched her leave, then he drifted sadly back to his spot in the corner. He thinks of his words to the princess, and he starts to feel as if his words were wasted for he is still locked up with no immediate plans of how to get himself free, furthermore; her rescue.

Cush had been watching it all and he saw that the pressure from all the changes was really getting the best of him. He moved over to where Stroke was sitting on the bunk.

" You really like Reikciv. Am I right? "

He could not deny it. " Yes, you' re right. But I have no way of helping her locked up in here. "

" I think you are wrong. "

" Yeah and what do you know? "

" I know how to get out of here. "

" Okay, slick, why don't you tell me. "

" You use the key, " Cush held out his left hand, then revealed his up turned palm exposing the key.

He took the key from Cush's hand. The sight of the key renewed his hope, but most important his anger had shifted from himself back toward Beezubul. He begins to think more clearly. Sledge walks over to join in the conversation.

" Stroke, when it comes to women, you never cease to amaze me. One quick conversation with a pretty girl and you act as if you have the key to success."

" But I do, " he said, showing Sledge the key.

" Is that what I think it is? "

" You bet your sweet ass it is, " said Cush.

" He really learns fast, doesn't he. " said Stroke.

" Yes, he does. But what do we do now? I mean, like, when do we get the hell outta here? ! "

" Just as soon as we think of a way to distract the guards out there long enough to un-tick the lock and get our weapons. But, right now it appears that we'll have to do all the work. Everyone else is too high to be alert, " explains Stroke.

Sledge leans against the wall, thinking about what he had just said. Then he realized that he had said the magic word. He smiles to himself, as he thinks of his flawless plan.

" Stroke, look at Blaze and Rebel. Then tell me what you see. "

He looked them over and saw that they about to finish off a roach and Rebel was digging in his pocket in order to pull out another joint.

" What I see there are two guys doing what they do best and that's get stoned. "

Sledge smiles, then points his thumb toward the cell door, " Right! They are about to get high. "

He knows what is going on inside of Sledge's head and he likes it. So he eased across the room toward where Blaze and Rebel were sitting and grabbed hold of Blaze's hand just as he was about to light the joint.

" What's hadning, dude? If you want to hit it, you should wait until its been flamed. "

" Just be cool for a minute, " said Stroke, " Look, we've got the key that opens the cell, but we must have this to buy some time. You dig? "

" No. How do you plan to use a joint to buy time? " Asked Rebel.

" Watch this little bit of acting and you can follow my lead from there, you dig? " He held out his hand for Blaze to pass him his lighter, and then he walked over to the cell door and stretched his arms out through the bars.

His act begins with the loud sound of him clearing his throat. Which he did in order to draw their attention? Once they were looking his way. He makes his next move. He flips the joint into the air by smacking his right with his left hand and it pops into his mouth. The jailers looked at each other, then back toward Stroke, as he lights up they continue to observe.

" You there what do you think you're doing? " Asked the man who showed them in.

He inhales, and then starts to explain. " I'm just trying to have a little fun before I die, " He takes another drag, after which he laughs very loud. The jailer rises from the table where he and the other Deacon have been watching Stroke's actions. He walks over to the cell and slams his stick on the bars.

" Are you laughing at me? "

" No, man, don't be stupid. I'm laughing at that torch. "

The jailer turns to look at the torch. " I see nothing funny about that torch. "

" This is what makes it all happen. Here try some. "

" No. I do not want it, " he walks away.

It did not work. Wait! The other Deacon stands up andwalks toward the cell do.

" I would like to try some, " said the younger looking deacon. Stroke smiled and passed him the joint. He did as he had seen Stroke do.

" Yes, this is good. "

" You're right. Good pot isn't suppose to make you cough. "

The deacon takes the joint and walks away thinking he is one up on Stroke. On his way back to the table he begins to laugh loudly.

" What is wrong with you? "

" What is wrong with me? " he said in a very psychotic manner while still walking toward the table. " Nothing is wrong with me. I never felt better in my life, " he said as he sat down.

" Give me that! " Said the older deacon, as he snatched the joint away from him. He smelled it and he liked what he smelled. He placed it to his lips

The plan has worked. The guards have allowed their curiosity to dig their graves. They have allowed their alertness to be altered by the intoxicating effects of the strange weed. Soon they begin to find everything surrounding them very amusing.

Stroke inserts the key and gives it a quick turn. The door opened and the weapons were found unsecured down the hall. The jailers pay no attention to the men, as they sneak about not far behind them.

Cush has his weapons, he walks up behind the men just as they are about to pass what is left of the joint between them and he makes an interception.

" I think I'd like a little of that. If you don't mind? " He said with his pistol pointed at them.

The deacons looked up to find Cush and the others had gotten out of their cell. But they do not care if they want to come out and join the party, well it is all right. So they begin to laugh.

Blaze walked up to Cush. " Yeap, that reminds me of the first time I got stoned; everything was funny. I bet he'll find this funny, too. " Blaze used the handle of his laser pistol to knock the older deacon unconscious.

He was right, because the younger one seemed to find this even funnier than anything else, which has happened so far.

" What the hell are you laughing at? " said Rebel, strapping on his weapons belt. " Pick him up and take him to the cell. "

The jailer does as he is told. He gets up still laughing and drags his friend by the shanks of his boots down to the same cell the boys were locked in. He takes time after dragging his friend inside to return and slam the door shut.

" The key? " said Boo-gee as Stroke passed.

" I thought you were going to escape. "

" We all are. The key, please. "

Stroke tossed him the keys, and then pointed his pistol, "After we leave. Deal?"

" Deal."

" We must not waste time, " said Maiko, leading the way to the stairs. He draws his sword as he enters the hall and the others do like wise.

They travel through the hall as a whole; seven men all being as Maiko had stated, 'as quiet as smoke as they take to the hall working their way through the fortress.

Soon they enter a hall where they can no longer go forward; to continue they must make a choice to go either left or right.

" Okay, which way do we go?" asks Stroke, " Maiko, it's your call. What do we do? "

" I say we split here. Half in one direction and the rest in the other. That way if we get into any heavy trouble they will not be able to take us all. "

" Stroke, you take the kid and go with Maiko to the left and the rest of us will go to the right, " said Rebel.

" We're going to turn this muther out, " said Blaze.

Carefully they moved down the long corridor; each of the two groups in their chosen direction. Suddenly Rebel and the others are face to face with a squadron of about twelve deacons.

Stroke, Diddily and Maiko are returning to help, together they could defeat the small group of men. They begin the long run back, but as they do, they see that the deacons are being reinforced by more of their own.

Rebel makes the call. He knows that the deacons would only capture them all again. "No! Go back the other way! " He said across the mic. " Go get help! We will hold them off as long as we can."

Rebel pulled down a huge drape in an attempt slow them down, which was enough for they found themselves temporarily entangled. But the deacons behind the bundle still made their way forward by stepping on their fellow deacons in order to continue the attack.

Maiko grabbed Stroke's arm.

" We can't leave them like this! " Stroke shouted.

" Get the hell out of here! " said Blaze, as he held his ground against two. " If it were me I would leave you! Now go! "

" Go ahead! Leave now that is the lonely way you can help us, " said Cush.

" Get the hell out of here, kid! " shouted Sledge, throwing a torch at the deacons.

Diddily pulled on Stroke's arm in an attempt to force him down the hall, but he only jerked hi arm away. Maiko and Diddily start down the hall without him.

Stroke has seen enough, so while they continue to hold the Slime Dwellers back he runs down the hall to catch up with Maiko and Diddily. He was returning his sword as he did, but he was quick to draw his laser. He plans to be prepared for any more unexpected visits from the deacons.

" This way ordered," Maiko " We must make one quick stop before we can leave. "

"Lead the way, Maiko, we are right behind you. Kid, put away the blade and ready your pistol. If we are going to get out of here, we're gonna have to blow some mutherfuckers away."

" Yeah! For the boys! " Said Diddily.

" That's right, kid, for the boys! "

Diddily did as he was advised. Maiko turned the corner to the sound of four-laser blast and he still had his sword drawn. Stroke's laser was ready and he fired three shots; dropping two deacons.

But one of the remaining two shoots and hits Diddily in the shoulder. His pistol is ready as well, he fires two shots; dropping both of the deacons as he fell up against the wall for support.

Stroke walks over to help Diddily. " Are you alright, kid? "

" Sure, I'm fine. I get shot in the arm with lasers all the time. Remember?
"

" Don't worry, smart ass, I still remember a little of that bullshit combat medic stuff the army taught me, " He quickly rips off a piece of the drape from behind him, then applied it to Diddily's wound. Then he made use of another strip in order to secure the dressing.

"How's that? "

" Can we go home, now? "

" Yo! Lets get the hell outta here, " he helps Diddily up to his feet.

" Damn! Now where in the hell did Maiko go? "

" He ducked when the shoo ting started. "

" Where to? "

" Into that room. "

" Shit! He's probably looking for something to steal. " He helped Diddily over toward the room Maiko had entered.

Stroke was right, Maiko was looking for something to steal and what he had found was the Slime Dwellers treasure. Stroke and Diddily stood in awe of what they saw scattered all over the floor. There was enough silver, gold and jewels to ransom five kings and their sons. There was such a brilliant glare from the treasure they had to place on their glarebreakers.

" Well, my brothers, is this enough to make you happy? "

" Me and the boys, " said Stroke, as he lifts a nice gold bangle to put on his wrist.

" Look at it! Is it not beautiful? It will all be mine. "

" Not if we don't get the hell out of here. So quit bullshitting and lets pop smoke. "

" Just a minute. I must take something to show my men. They will fight like mad men to be rich. "

" Can you believe this shit? I'm bleeding to death and he wants to collect a few souvenirs for the family. "

" Hurry it up, Maiko! The kid is badly hurt. We must get back to the den. "

" Alright, we will be out of here in no time. "

" Good because that's what we have, no time. "

" Let me help you with the kid. "

" I've got him! Just move out. You're going to be point man and use that pistol. "

Maiko moves out and draws his pistol as he enters the hall. They are on the move.

There is one chance; they must exit the way they came in. Even though they are more than positive the area has been re-secured.

They approach the hall, which will lead them to the deacons who stand between them and freedom. They halt around the corner in order to prepare a plan, Maiko peers around the corner to see how many they will have to answer, and then he eases back to tell the others what he has seen.

" There looks to be about four, two on either side of the door. Stroke, you and I should be able to take them. Are you well enough to shoot, kid? We are going to need you to fire security shots just in case they try to take cover. Do you think you can handle it? "

" You bet! As long as I can stand on my feet I won't let a little pain get me down. I'm ready when you are. "

" Roger that, kid. Now stand on this side of the wall. And try firing down the middle of the hall. We don't want any friendly fire," said Stroke, with a grin.

" Don't worry, I got it "

" Be strong, kid, this will all be over soon . " he said, then he walked back over toward Maiko.

" Move fast and stay low. Do not allow them to take cover, or we will be here all night, " said Maiko.

" Lets do it, dude. "

Maiko looks away, and then he runs across to the other side of the hall, and then remains completely still, pressing his back hard against the wall. He held his breath as Stroke peeped around the corner to make sure he had not been seen and he was . . . not. Maiko releases his breath.

Stroke moved his lips in order to form a word Maiko should understand.

" Ready? "

" Ready! " shouts Maiko, as he came off the wall.

Stroke takes the middle of the hall and Diddily stands ready to fire any security shots needed. But the silenced shots from the lasers catch them by surprise. They need not worry what Nud will be doing to them for letting these men escape. As a matter of fact, they have nothing at all to worry about.

" We must move quick! Stroke, help the kid out to the terrace and I will make sure no one else is coming. "

" Don't worry about that, if someone is coming they will catch us anyway. The kid can't make the climb back down. "

" Sorry, kid, I forgot. "

" I can do it, " said Diddily.

Maiko has another idea. " I know a better and faster way down, " Maiko walks through the storage room, then out onto the perch to search through the rucksacks they had left there earlier.

" Man, you've got all sorts of shit, " said Diddily as he watched Maiko going through the bags.

" A good Thief has many tools and many secrets he will only share with a few, " he said, removing rope and a stud similar to the one they had used earlier to secure the line for the climb. He takes the stud, which is about seven inches long and he crams it down in his laser pistol.

" We are going to rappel down this mount. Once we secure these two ropes. We should be able to reach the bottom. "

Maiko pointed his laser toward the mount, when the sparks cleared the stud was lodged securely in the solid rock. He worked fast, making sure he tied the rope tightly to the stud.

"Okay, Stroke, throw the rope out as far as you can. It has got to uncoil. "

Stroke tossed the rope out as far as he could; causing both sections to go sailing from the perch.

" Good job. I will go firs t in order to see how far we can rappel down using this rope for if we have to change over before we hit bottom, then someone will have to be there to help the kid make the change over to the other rope. "

Maiko removed his sword, still encased and fastened the rope where his sword had been. " Drop your sword and lock the rope in your halt to make it easier. Use your hand as a break like this, " He said as he maneuvered himself over the edge. He pressed a button on his leather wristband and a light came on which was shaped like a Rodagon. The Rodagons have been alerted and are on their way. " See you at the bottom. " was the last thing he said before he dropped into his rappel. He was cruising down about fifty feet every five seconds, or less. Then he would kick off the side of the mount and drop a little further. It took him several kicks to reach the end of the rope, where it stopped short about ten feet away from the base. He jumps for it, tucking and rolling as he hit the ground.

Diddily has already secured the rope to his utility belt.

" Okay, kid takes it slow and easy. Don't force yourself to do more than your arm will let you. Remember, Air assault. "

" Don't worry, if I need help, I'll let you know, "

Diddily pushed himself away from the mount, he made a few short kicks, and then he let it all hang out. He was hamming it up as he hot-dogged all the way down the side of the mount. He looked good, almost too good. Sliding down the rope as if he was not injured. He tucked and rolled to his right in order to avoid causing any more pain to himself.

" You did good, kid, " said Maiko as he helps him to his feet. Diddily does not object to him calling him kid after all they have been through so far. Back up there on the ledge. Stroke hurried to fasten the rope to his belt and he decided not to leave the sword that had save his life so far. He chow slung it across his body where it would stay tied to his back.

'' Man I sure wish this place had an elevator, " he said as he lowered himself over the side, then he went into a couple of short kicks. He felt confidant, so he committed his first big kick; dropping about sixty feet. He felt even better as he kicked off for his second big one; this time ninety, then another eighty feet on his third.

The stud slipped. The weight from Diddily and Maiko rappelling on the same line before him has loosened the rock. Nope, then it must be the two deacons beating on the stud with their weapons.

" What the hell? " said Stroke.

Boo-gee Woo-gee and his men come up behind the two guards and they take them out.

Stroke felt another twang and this time the stud is free of the rock. He starts to drop. Free falling to his left; he dropped about thirty feet still clawing at the wall with his hands and arms in an attempt to slow his fall. He can no longer reach the wall to slow his fall and he falls freely for another fifteen feet before he slammed into Deacons Lip.

The force from the contact caused him to turn and he started falling headfirst. He reaches blindly as he falls, his hand feels the rope. It is the hand, which he wears the ring he received from Ecinaj. The stone within the ring begins to glow brightly.

Any way, he had grabbed a hold of the line they had used earlier and he held tight. He hurried to use his free hand to release the dead line from his belt and secure himself to the other line.

Maiko and Diddily both released the breath they drew when he started his fall. Stroke finished his rappel.

Boo-gee Woo-gee and his men needed no ropes for they had wings of their own, so they flew away.

" Are you alright? " Asked Diddily running up to the foot of the mount.

" Yeah. But I ruined my jacket. And now we both have sore shoulders, " He said as he rubbed his side.

" I am glad you did not die, my brother, " said Maiko.

" So am I, " added Stroke.

" We must hurry, now. There will be no rest tonight for our brothers need us and we have a long way to travel. "

The Rodagons land in front of them as Maiko speaks. And soon they are on the backs of their Rodagons flying high and fast to the Den of Thieves. They are accompanied by four Rodagons without riders.

THIRTEEN

MENTALLY WASTED

REBEL, CUSH, BLAZE AND SLEDGE are forced to stand in the throne room of the Lord of Slime. Now they wait the new sentencing for their attempts, as Nud and Beezubul interrogate the jailers.

" You fools! How could you allow them to get out of the hold? " Shouts Nud.

" They tricked us with some sort of smoke stick. We were only curious. We will never let it happen again, your greatness. "

" Never again. You should not have allowed it to happen to start. And about you being curious, someone should have told you that curiosity kills people. " Nud said as he pointed his finger at the jailer.

" You are right about never letting it happen again. Because the both of you will die. Oh and this is not a trick! " Nud looked over toward Beezubul, who was sitting with an unconcerned look on his face.

" Take them away, " Nud shouted then he looked toward the others.

" Step forward!" he stroked his chin, as he looked them over carefully. "It seems that I underestimated you. But no matter, for you are very unfortunate not to have escaped with the others. But you will not receive another chance to trick some one. "

Beezubul feels a strong urge to interrupt. " What Nud means is, you will have no need to try again, because we find you no threat. But one of you will be chosen to fight for the lives of the others. If he wins. . . Which I doubt. All of you will be allowed to go free in the event of such a victory. Now, since you, my friend, " Beezubul pointed a finger toward Rebel. ". . . Wanted to have a blade in your hand, then you shall be the one. "

Rebel nodded his approval.

" Take these men to the arena and ready this man for battle. "

They escorted the boys out of the throne room as Nud and Beezubul watched.

Nud approached Beezubul with a puzzled look on his face. " Ah, Beezubul, why do you promise these men freedom? They will only cause more trouble. "

" There will be no more trouble, especially from the one with no respect, once he has met Eyaf. Besides I'm bored. This is supposed to be a party. Come on lets have some enjoyments. TO THE PAIN! "

Nud smiles in agreement. " Too bad that man must die, he would have made an excellent Slime Dweller. "

" Yes, he would at that. Guards! " He shouts, " Bring the Princess to the arena. " He turned to the right and smiled at Nud. " She may as well have some fun, too. " Beezubul just had to add a wink. " And the sight of blood and death would make anyone happy. "

" Especially, if they are not the bleeder. "

Beezubul, Nud and The Princess sit in their reserve box high above the other spectators, as the remains of the two jailers are dragged from the middle of the arena floor. Eyaf has fought the two men and he has killed them both without even perspiring.

" Well done, Eyaf! We have only one more battle for you this evening. And I'm sure it could be as brief as the first. But, do try and make it more interesting."

Nud quickly held up his hand to quiet the cheer of the crowd.

" Bring in the prisoner! "

The Princess, Cush, Sledge and Blaze all cheer The Rebel onward, as he walked toward the center of the arena. But their cheers are drowned out by the hissing boos of The Slime Dwellers.

Once again, Nud holds up his hand to quiet the deacons.

Beezubul stands to speak. " My friend, as I said. If you win, then you and your friends go free. So . . . TO THE PAIN! "

Rebel looked across at Eyaf, and the man is a giant compared to Rebel.

Eyaf stands facing Rebel with the blood of the two men he has unjustly killed smeared all over himself, and his sword is still dripping.

A bell sounds. Eyaf charges Rebel with his sword high above his head ready to slice him in half. Rebel moves quicker than Eyaf had anticipated. He rolls under his legs causing him to fall flat on his face.

The Rebel is back on his feet. He will take advantage of Eyaf being down, he brings down crashing blows. Rebel will use his sword on Eyaf the way he had planned to use his on him.

Eyaf rolled over quickly to his back and used his sword to block Rebel's offense.

Rebel tries to cut Eyaf on the left side swinging his sword from his right and again it is blocked.

Before Rebel can try another angle, Eyaf kicks him hard in his left side. Rebel stumbles off and as he did Eyaf found his way to his feet.

Eyaf has turned aggressor once more. Rebel has been weakened by the force of the kick, but he sucks in the pain and is ready to go again. No time for pain.

But Eyaf is skilled in his attack and he has been told to make this one a little more interesting.

All Rebel could think about was all of those Errol Flynn and Tyrone Powell flicks he had stayed up late so many nights to see. They were all now paying off, for every move Eyaf had, he had one of his own.

Stroke, Maiko, and Diddily ride the Rodagons as fast as they will go, but it did not appear fast enough. Diddily's wound had long since stopped bleeding, but the pain remained. He doesn't know if he can make it much longer at the hard pace and the flight over the Desert of Sufferance is not making it any easier.

" Hang in there, kid! We should be there shortly. Just be strong. Don't let this win and you will survive, " You know who said all that. " He will be alright, once we reach the Den, my brother. "

" Yes, I know. I just hope the others are doing better than we are. "

What? . . . Be for real Stroke. At least you are out of there. But back there, well, it was not a pretty picture. The arena floor has gotten very bloody and most of the blood on the sand belonged to Rebel.

Eyaf knows he has him weakened almost to the point of submission. Rebel knows there will be no mercy in this court; he continues to use all he has in attempts to fend off Eyaf's mighty blows. Blows, which seem to have grown stronger and stronger. Suddenly Eyaf changed the direction of the next blow Rebel was anticipating and he caught him far off guard.

His sword goes sailing through the air and lands half w ay across the Arena. The princess draws a breath of life for the Rebel.

Eyaf smiles down at Rebel, Rebel smiles back as Eyaf prepared to bring down one last overhead blow. Rebel reached deep down and I mean as deep as he could reach to pull up all he could. Then he kicked him between the legs so damn hard.

" Right in the balls. " said Rebel.

Eyaf made a very high pitched sound for a man his size, as he crumbled to the floor.

Rebel turned to leave; he was seeing only blackness in a room filled with light. But he walked away, slowly walked away. He tripped slightly over something at his feet, but just the thought of it being Eyaf gave him a quick adrenaline rush, But it was only his sword, He bent over to recover it from the dust and dropped to his knees there where it rested.

Eyaf forced himself to stand. He was grunting and growling all the time. The madness of this man was shown in his eyes, as he started his run, with his sword high over his head. It was not hard to determine his desire.

Rebel had his back turned, he could not see Eyaf in his charging rage.

" Behind you, Rebel! " Shouted Sledge, " He is coming behind you! " And as he finished, he received the backhand of a deacon's fist.

Rebel turned not really having the strength to stand; he made use of his sword as a prop and remained where he was. He lifted his head and he could see the rage in Eyaf's eyes. And as Eyaf came closer he did not move. Then just when Eyaf was close enough to start bring down his sword Rebel lifted his sword and the force from Eyaf charge knocked him over.

Motionless they both laid there in the sand. Rebel looked over toward where Eyaf's lifeless form lied in the sand only a few feet from him and he looked at his sword sticking out of Eyaf's back and he knew he was through.

The Rebel pushed himself to his feet. His friends ran out to stand next to him for he has won their freedom. He struggles to stand under his own power, as he faces Beezubul and Nud.

" My friend, you have won. As I said, you will go free. So go! " Shouts Beezubul.

Rebel wipes some of the blood from the corner of his mouth. " Don't call me your friend, " he turned, to lead the others out.

The Slime Dwellers were furious. They expressed their anger by throwing trash and shouting insults at the group as they proceeded to leave.

" You can not allow them to leave. You cannot allow that man to live, " said Nud pointing at the men.

" Ah yes, to the pain, " Beezubul lifts his laser and shoots Rebel in the back.

The Slime Dwellers exult at the sight of the smoke coming from the Rebel's back, as he lies face down in the sand.

" Take them back to the Hold! " orders Nud.

The deacons continue to cheer Beezubul's actions as they watch the boys carrying their friend back to the Hold, with an escort of guards.

" Nud? "

" Yes. "

" So what do you have planned next? "

" Perhaps something to drink. "

" Sounds good, I do feel a bit dry, " He said as he stood and stretched his arms over his head.

" You know what, Beezubul. "

" What? "

" I am going to miss Eyaf. He was a good fighter. "

" Sure! I know what you are going to miss and it is not his fighting. "

" Yes, he was good at that, too. Oh well! Deacons take the princess back to her chambers, " ordered Nud, as he walked pass the guards at the doorway.

The princess sits in shock of what she had seen. She can do nothing but try and hold back her emotions. Yet still a tear rolls down her cheek, as the guards step up behind her chair.

Blaze and Sledge lay Rebel on the bunk in the corner of the cell. They know he will not survive the wound, for he has lost too much blood. But they cannot let him know.

" Take it easy, dude, you are going to be fine. Do not try to speak, " said Cush.

" Don't try to bull shit me, Cush. All I want you to do is tell Stroke to get Beezubul. I want you to tell him to do it for me, " Rebel begins to cough violently. " I want you to tell him to keep it in the bond. "

Cush walks to the other side of the room. He will not stand there and watch his friend die. Rebel coughs up blood and it forms in his mouth. He turned his head to one side to spit the blood on the floor.

" Blaze, Sledge, was are you? Come on; let me talk to you, " he said.

They were not as far as he thought. He opened his eyes. " Why are you looking like that? The Grim Reaper is not knocking at your door. "

They find no humor in his jokes, even though they have laughed with him many times before.

Blaze laughs slightly and Sledge nudges him in the side.

" Come on, you guys. That was a good one, " he said trying to get them to smile, " O yeah! Tell Diddily that he can have my yellow Washburn when you get back home, " Rebel only realized what he had said, after he had said it, " Home.. . Home . . . Hooooommmmmmmm . . . " Rebel will say no more his time has ended on this strange faraway planet.

At the Den of Thieves, Stroke, Diddily, and Maiko have made the journey.

" Hurry, help these men! " shouts Maiko wearing the new crown he had stolen from the Slime Dwellers treasure along with a few other items Stroke nor Diddily had seen him taken, he was truly the king of Thieves.

" Turecoi, go tell the healing one; the king has returned and his brothers are in need of attention. Bozar, gather all my Thieves and tell them to adorn their battle dress uniforms, tell them to ready to travel as soon as possible. Tonight we declare war!"

The King of Thieves had spoken and it began. It is not long before everyone in the Den is up and active; all working to ready for battle against the Slime Dwellers.

Diddily is resting. Maiko had been looking for Stroke ever since he finished briefing his men the operation order. He located Stroke sitting outside on the terrace.

" My brother, why do you sit here when you should be resting? "

" There is no way I can sleep when I know that evil bastard has my friends. I feel that something terrible has happened, and I don't like this feeling, man!

I don't like it. It's too strong. I know he is doing them harm even at this moment. He has probably killed them all," He shakes his head.

" Diddily is young, he shouldn't have to go through this. If they aren't dead and I pray that they aren't, then they will be expecting me to return and help them. And I ask you, how can I? I've tried my best. Beezubul is just too damn strong.

" That's right you have tried. Now you must try harder. Stop feeling guilty, because you are here, instead of locked up in the Hold with them. I know they would feel the same way if the situations were reversed. But you need to keep your head. Do not let this make you insane. They are counting on you and that is all they have to keep them going. "

" Yes, if they aren't dead and I pray that they aren't or Beezubul will pay."

" That is right. Now direct your anger elsewhere, at anything other than yourself and do not forget that anger tomorrow. But for now, you must rest, or you will be no good to neither yourself nor me and most importantly to the men who are depending on you. Do not forget what you told the kid, ' Be Strong'. "

" You' re right. I must be strong, that is the only way. "

" Now you have got it. But now, you must be strong enough to get some rest, but even if you do not sleep, then go lie down. "

" Okay, but first; I want to see Diddily, so I can assure myself that he is doing better. I need to tell him something. " Stroke starts toward the doors to the stairs.

" What is that? "

" Well, I think it would be better if he didn't go back. "

" I do not think it will work. "

Maiko leads Stroke to the place where Diddily is resting. He takes him through to the heart of the Den in a motorized cart. Maiko drives to the royal sleeping quarters. He stops the cart and motions for Stroke to follow him through the high arched doorway, from the doorway Stroke could see Diddily lying comfortably on a large silver bed.

" Dawgone, kid! You look like the Mummy, " said Stroke on seeing Diddily's shoulder wrapped in the bandaging.

" Stroke! " calls Diddily, as he tried to prop himself up on the bed. " Am I glad to see you. "

He walked over closer to the bed. " What's wrong, kid? "

" Will you explain to me what in the hell is going on? This shit ain't fun no more. My arm really hurts! "

" Look, kid it's like this; the only things that matters are papers and power and the more I think about it the more it seems like a fiction novel. You see, a rich little princess has been taken from her happy little home and her father is a king with enough power to control the whole scene, " he said, as he paced back and forth.

" Now even though, those two suckers can't actually match his power, he sends for us and here we are. Trying to save our own skin... And the way things look right now, it doesn't appear as if we're doing a good job. The way I see it, kid, it's like, a game. But the stakes are high and only the best will survive. So, what are you, kid? " He said, then he sat at the foot of the bed.

" I am between a rock and a hard place. "

" I guess that's right. "

Diddily looks at Stroke's eyes and notices that one of his pupils has changed colours. " What happened to your eye? "

" Nerves, kid, I've got bad nerves and high blood. "

" Then why aren't you resting, Stroke? The both of you need to go some rest. "

" You know I couldn't go to sleep with out checking to see if you were doing better. "

"As you can see, I'm doing just fine, " Diddily lifted his head toward a pretty young maiden coming toward the bed to sponge him down. " And if you get out of here, you could make it possible for me to do even better. "

Stroke stands, then walks around the foot of the bed, smiling "At least I know that you are better than you were earlier, because you' re not sniveling any more. "

" You came pretty close to being a fallen angel yourself. So don't try it! Tomorrow I will be better prepared for those Slime Dweller. "

" Ahhhh, look, kid, " said Stroke, as he walked from the foot of the bed and talked with his back turned to Diddily." That's another thing I've been thinking about, you know, since you're injured and all, well, I decided it would be better if you stayed here. "

Diddily is shocked; confused and hurt that Stroke would even consider it. How can Stroke think to keep him away when he knows his brothers need him.

" No way! The guys are counting on us to return. We are all they have. You can't expect me to stay behind, not when my brothers need me. "

Stroke looks toward Maiko for support. It is plain to see whose side Maiko is on. This is one argument He will not win. " Okay, kid I don't think that I could leave without you anyway. So, you better save your strength, " He used his eye to point toward the young lady seated next to Diddily's bed. Diddily understands and he winks at him.

" I'll try to have enough strength to keep your back covered and slay much Slime dwellers. So why don't you two nurse maids get some rest. "

" Did you hear that? He is talking like he had to protect us all day, " said Maiko.

" Yes, I heard him. But at least I don't have a laser burn in my favorite shirt, with a burnt shoulder to match, " said Stroke walking along side Maiko, as he exits the room.

Maiko is ready to show Stroke to his room, " Climb aboard, your chamber is just down the hall from here. "

Stroke jumps aboard and the little cart makes a swift trip through to the other side of the royal chambers. And by the time they arrived Stroke was looking forward to the bed he had been promised.

After Maiko had showed him in, he did not bother to remove his clothes, but slowly laid himself down onto the bed very carefully, so as not to trouble his shoulder, his ribs, his back, his arm, his legs, and oh yeah, his head any more than they already were. He stares up at the ceiling hoping he will receive another visit from Balaam. He lies on his back with his eyes close. But every eye close, ain't shut.

He sees Balaam standing near the foot of the bed. " I thought you would show up, there sooner or later. "

" I see you have met Beezubul. "

" Yes, I have met the princess as well and my friends are still there. Can you tell me if they are alright. "

Balaam draws a blank expression. But he changed the look with a quick smile.

" Do not worry, Stroke, everything is going to be as written in the book."

" That's not the answer to my question. Is It? "

Balaam knows he must get his mind off of that subject " Here, Stroke, I have something for you, " Balaam held up a red eye patch.

Stroke used his elbow to prop himself up on the bed, as he stared at the patch. Then he held out his hand to receive it. He tied it around his head over his left eye.

" How did you know that I had lost a contact? "

" The same way I know everything will be alright; Thee book. "

" Thank you! " He yawned. " Now, if I could get to sleep without being haunted by the dream, " He said as he laid back on the bed.

" It will go away after your success, " said Balaam as he extinguished the light.

" Leave it on! I don't want it out. "

Balaam made the light come back on, and then he slowly fades himself from the spot he is standing. Stroke began to drift off into a very uneasy sleep.

The Sixth Day:

The darkness covers Zandoria. Even though the night is over and morning has come. The eclipse of the two suns has begun and they know that time is not on their side. Maiko's army of Thieves has been working all through the night to reach this point; they are ready to travel to Mount Seficul. Diddily and Stroke will ride lead along side Maiko.

" Diddily, Stroke are you ready? " shouts Maiko, as he prepares to mount Rodagon.

Stroke looked over toward the corral where Maiko had taken him, then he looked over toward the boulder where he had spent his first night. A cold chill covered him as he thought of Gale. Then, there on the ground he saw something.

So he knelt to dip his finger in a little of the purple clay, then a little of the white clay and he applied it to his face; like war paint. " Whowahhh! " he shouted and walked to his mount.

" WE ARE READY WHEN YOU ARE!" shouts Diddily.

Maiko kicked his Rodagon off to a galloping pace and it leaped from edge of the cliff with its wings doing the work.

Stroke and Diddily were close behind him; the army of Thieves will follow. Soon the sky is filled by Maiko's Calvary and mounted infantry. Thousands of Rodagons with riders and wagons loaded with hundreds more. The Quest has been reinforced.

Inside Mount Seficul there is total chaos Beezubul stands in the Nave, he has been inspecting the final arrangements of the set where he plans to marry the princess and he finds it not to be as he ordered.

" Is there anyone here who can understand a simple command without having to be told a second time, what they should have understood the first time. Who is in charge of these anal orifices? " He shouts daring one of them to come forward and claim responsibility.

" I am, " said a deacon with a very feminine voice and he steps forward where Beezubul can see him clearly.

When Beezubul sees who the man is, he smiles and runs his finger through his hair.

" Do you know that seeing this has made me quite ill ? "

" I'm sorry to hear that perhaps you need something to settle your stomach. "

" Do not worry about my stomach. Do you remember what I ordered in here ? "

" Well you know that I remember your orders. But I thought you would like it better standing under the stairs to the windows. It would have given your wardrobe such a nice effect, with the lighting I have planned and all. "

" You had second thoughts about an order I gave? " said Beezubul as he moved his hands together very slowly; as if he held an object between them.

Suddenly, the man grabs his head as if he feels great pain.

" Auuuuuggggghhhh! Why are you doing this to me? " He asked as he fell to his knees.

" You have done a very bad thing and I am seeing to it that you never do it again, " Slowly, he brings his hand closer together as the man's skull begins to crack from the pressure Beezubul's magic is putting on it.

" BEEZUBUL RELEASE HIM AT ONCE! " shouts Nud as he enters the room.

Beezubul stops what he is doing and bows toward Nud.

" What do you think you are doing? No one tortures my men without my permission. "

" Then your men should learn to follow my orders better. Zeneb, come here, " he calls and the deacon did not waste time but, he ran over.

" You are now in charge. So I will explain this to you and there will be no second's thoughts. "

Zeneb bows.

"I do not want the alter at this end of the hall for the simple reason that the suns always rise from the west and when the light from the suns shine through those windows, " Beezubul points toward the windows over his head, and the deacon nods that he understands.

" I want it to shine on me as I hold the princess in my arms. Since you know why. Go over there and move everything where I told him to place them to begin with and I want those windows patrolled. Is that understood? " Beezubul turned and exited the room smoothly.

Nud looks about at his men. " You heard what he said, now do it! "

Nud walks swiftly through the hall in his attempt to catch up with Beezubul.

" You certainly are busy for one soon to be wed. "

" If it were not for the incompetence of your men, I would not have to check behind them all the time. But, that will soon change. "

" And what do you mean by that? "

" Do not worry, my friend, you will always be my right hand man. If not in body, the in spirit. "

Nud is not thrilled by what Beezubul has probably said as a joke. For he knows once Beezubul has the power, he could easily do away with him.

" Nud shall we sample some of the refreshments? "

Nud joins Beezubul for the journey to the entertainment hall.

" What do you wish to do with the ones we still have locked in the Hold?" Asked Beezubul.

" I plan to leave them there without food or water. Maybe they will take advantage of their friend for a little fresh meat to keep from starving to death. If they do not die from the stench of the rotting carcass first. "

" Well, I thought we could use them to entertain our parishioners, " he said as he made a table slide from one side of the hall to another. " They would enjoy a show of my power before the ceremonies. "

" I do not think that would prove a very entertaining event. And they understand what is happening. From the beginning, they knew that you were the one. But, now they are ready for the fruit, " He said, as they passed through the doors opened by Beezubul's power.

" You are probably right. Maybe it would be more fun to watch them devour their friend and be converted to the lowest form of animal they can be, all out of the need to survive. "

Nud walks over to table and removes two goblets and one barrel of Bonda Berry Juice; while Beezubul sits himself down at the long table.

" Will this be enough? "

" Yes, for now. But we shall indulge ourselves, since we do not have to worry about any more attempts to rescue the princess, " He said nudging Nud in the ribs.

" Yes, those others are probably still trying to get out the Desert of Sufferance, " said Nud, then he sipped from his cup. " This is good. "

" Yes, it is... But, do not thank me I do not deserve the credit. This came straight from the cellars of King Revilo. "

" Okay, to King Revilo, who se life will end as quickly as my first cup of Bonda Berry juice. "

" I will drink to that, " said Beezubul, to let Nud know he was in full agreement and he decided to add a little toast of his own. " To the princess Reikciv! May the glow in her eyes be out shined only by her performance on the groin? "

" Yes! TO THE PAIN! " He said emptying his goblet, only to fill it and do the same again.

Rebel's body has been covered with a blanket by his friends in the Hold and they all sit in silence. Not knowing whether Stroke, Diddily, and Maiko actually made their way back to the Den for help and if they did, will they make it back before Nud and Beezubul decide to entertain themselves by having their blood spilled all over the arena floor.

But they truly are not worried about their own lives when the Rebel lies there dead, and his death has filled their hearts with anger. But there is nothing they can do except waits and hope that the others will return.

Blaze knows what they need is more than hope, what they need is a good prayer.

" Dear heavenly father GOD of all things great and small. I am not sure if this strange world is of your dominion, even though I am almost certain that it is. But please hear me dear father and send us a blessing for we sure could use your help. In Jesus name. Amen. "

FOURTEEN

EKTENE

MIDDAY HAS LONG SINCE PASSED. The darkness remains and the stars are the only source of light in the heavens. The princess watches the stars as they twinkle and she feels that they too are trying to tell her she will soon be as free to shine in her glory as they are. She has been gazing at the stars so long that every one seems to have the same glow as Stroke's smile. Her imagination has grown so intense she begins to see images of his face.

" Please, come back. Please, try one more time. I know you felt it. You must try again. "

At that moment four women entered her chambers, " We are here to ready you for your wedding, " said a very masculine looking woman as she displayed the long gold satin gown with mutton sleeves open front and a black body suit to go underneath which the garments were being held by the other women.

" I am not going to wear it! " she said and turned her back to the intruders.

" Good! Then we really get to help you into your gown, I was hoping to kick your royal anus around in here and your refusal has made it possible. "

She turned slowly, " Come on. Do what you have to do. "

She sheds what she knows will be the last tear she cries before their return.

The army of Thieves pushes their Rodagons hard; there will be no time for rest or water. The foam from the saliva mixed with the sweat of the Rodagons has covered both the Rodagons and rider.

Stroke hopes his animal does not die before he reaches Mount Seficul. There has been a change; Stroke has a completely new attitude. For now this is a battle he has not been forced to enter, but one he has entered of his own free will. It is now his battle and the battle, which must end the war.

Anger drives He and Diddily on. But, cupidity forces the army of Thieves on. Yet all will fight as strong as the next; until they have satisfied their urges.

" Be on the watch for Warner's! There should be Scouts securing the outer region of Mount Seficul. As soon as we spot them they must be stopped before they can report us, " Orders Maiko, over the command network and his orders are then echoed over the net until heard by all.

Beezubul stands facing his reflection. This is a product even a mother would have a problem loving. But for Beezubul it is all he needs. He has changed his clothing and now wears red loose fitting slacks and a white over sized shirt with gold embroidery. He straps on his gold coloured sword and laser, then sneers at himself in the mirror, before he walks from the mirror over toward where his animal skin cape has been laid. The full-length red fur cape seems to add even more enhancement to his outfit.

Nud enters Beezubul's chambers and he has also changed his clothing.

He is we a ring something more suitable for the occasion. And he thinks basic black is more suitable draped with chains and weapons; all silver and chrome.

" Have all the guest arrived? " asked Beezubul.

" All those who were ordered to appear. "

" Fine. Have you secured the area? In case King Revilo has another surprise for us? "

" I have done better than that. My gift to you as a wedding present shall be King Revilo and Queen Sesma's head. I sent a company of my men out earlier to bring them back for the reception. They should arrive before the end of the ceremonies."

" You and I are going to make a great team evil and sin, side by side. Together we will bring the universe to its knees. "

" Anything to please. "

" Shall we greet our guest? " asked Beezubul showing Nud that he will grace him with the lead way out. But Nud allows him the privilege, so he may keep an eye on his own back.

Beezubul walks quickly even with the weight of his weapons. Nud catches up to his pace and the usually long walk takes no time; confidence is their speed.

The waiting room is crowded with various faces. Only Nud and Beezubul could wish to have people such as these for friends. Their guests were busy entertaining themselves with their own company when their host entered the room.

" WELCOME! FROM WHAT I CAN SEE, NO ONE DARED TO DEFY MY REQUEST TO APPEAR. THAT IS GOOD! ENJOY THE DRINKS. WHEN THE TIME COMES, THE DEACONS WILL ESCORT YOU TO THE NAVE WHERE THE CEREMONY WILL TAKE PLACE SHORTLY, "

Beezubul stops to remove a goblet from the tray of a passing servant girl.

" OH YES! AFTER THE CEREMONY, WE ARE EXPECTING A VISIT FROM KING REVILO AND QUEEN SESMA. "

This group does not party with that sort of crowd and they wish they would just stay away. So their reaction is snarls.

" DO NOT FRET, MY FRIENDS, YOU WILL FIND THEM VERY COOPERATIVE, AND MOST ENTERTAINING. NUD HAS SOMETHING SPECIAL PLANNED FOR THEM. "

They applaud for they know Nud's warped sense of humor. So what ever he has planned will please them more than the king and queen.

Maiko's army nears closer to Mount Seficul and the lights from the Slime Dwellers fortress calls them on. Diddily sees a campfire below.

" Down there! Down there, Maiko, I see a camp. "

" Spotted them a while ago, kid, " said Maiko.

The Warner 's have seen them as well and the large mass has frighten them. The Warner's rush to mount their Rodagons in order to race the army of Thieves to Mount Seficul.

" STOP THEM! " shouts Maiko, ordering a squadron of his men to break off from the main attack group. Forcing their Rodagons into a dive.

The Warner's are no longer on the ground, they have taken to the air and their Rodagons are not tired. They will be able to out race them easily.

A blast and a Warner falls. Quickly, the Warner's ascend higher, as they return a few shots at the Thieves.

The Thieves handle their animals expertly, but the Rodagons are tired and a Warner succeeds with a shot, which causes it to sway in the path of another Thief, knocking him from his mount. The well-trained Rodagon is aware of the lost of its rider and it swoops down and catches the Thief on its back. While the injured Rodagon goes into a spin and the Thief on its back holds tight to the raines trying to maintain balance to make a very unorthodox landing.

The other Thieves are still on case and they have the chase advantage. The Warner 's try to avoid them, yet to no avail. The Thieves do not cease their attack until the last of the Warner's has been blasted from his Rodagon.

The army of Thieves has flown closer to Mount Seficul under the cover of darkness, rain and fortunately an eerie mist, or other wise they would have been detected long before the point they have reached. Snow flurries begin to mix in with the freezing rain.

Beezubul has mingled with his guest, who all seem to be about as low life as he is. In other words; just freaks. No one need tell him for he knows he has spent too much time with these people because he has actually started to listen to what they have to say. So as he is not really interested in the conversation of the tones, which are surrounding him, he walks away while they are still talking to him.

Nud stands enjoying the chance to impress a few women with the details of his share of the dirty work in all the events, which have occurred, and what their team has in store for the future.

Beezubul can hear that his own share of the work is being under minded by Nud, who is totally unaware that Beezubul is approaching, as he continued his story.

" Of course if it were not for me none of this would have been possible."

" Really? " said one of the women.

" O yes! I have been the real key behind the success of the whole operation. You know, my place, my deacons, my everything. I have even thought of moving to Talmory when this is all over. "

Beezubul placed his right arm over Nud's shoulders. Nud is shocked to find that he was so close. He now plans to toy with Nud.

" Yes, yes, If it were not for Nud, well, I do not know what I would have done. If you do not mind, I need to find out what he plans to do next, " He used his arm to guide Nud away where they may speak alone. "

" Beezubul, what do you need to know? "

" Do not be a fool all your life! Have your men bring the princess and move the guest to the nave. Our time approaches. "

" No problem. I will personally escort the princess to the nave and on my way there I shall order the guards to show the guest to the nave. "

" I will take my place after a short visit with our friends the heroes, " he said as he exits the hall.

Nud made his way out. " Zeneb, show the guest to the nave, " he said, before he entered the hall and traveled the opposite direction of Beezubul.

In the Hold they sit still waiting the return of their friends. Beezubul enters unnoticed and smiles as he leers through the bars of the cell.

" I would like to invite you to the ceremony, " he said, " But you Look too comfortable to disturb. "

They all hold their heads up after hearing his voice. Sledge looks at him with death in his eyes. His anger has waited a chance to speak " Go suck ass! Your time will come soon. "

" Sooner than you think, for my time is now…Ah, if you decide join us, please bring your friend back there. He as if he could use something to liven him up, " he does not try to conceal his laughter.

Blaze leaps from where he is sitting and grabs hold of the bars of the cell door. He tries to use physical strength to force his way out for the pleasure of ripping Beezubul's heart out. But he is halted in his rage by the new jailer, who uses a bucket filled with urine and feces to calm him. Then he joins Beezubul in his laughter. Then he strides with Beezubul as he struts out of the Hold.

Blaze is sickened by the smell and the thought of what has happened. His body goes limp and he slides down, pressing his face against the bars. Sledge walks over to Blaze and squats down beside him, he can see that Blaze is about to let go. Sledge places his arm about his shoulder.

" Have faith, Blaze. You know he won't let Beezubul win without another try. "

" This shit doesn't make any sense and I don't want to play anymore, " he said still pressing his head against the bars.

" But you must remember the Rebel. You must try to keep yourself together, so that when the time comes you can be ready. But the way you are now, you will be no use to no one. And Beezubul will have won. "

Blaze understands what Sledge is saying, but he can form no words. Sledge moved his arm around Blazes' shoulder and used his hands to turn his head where he could view Rebel's body. " He was my friend, too. "

Blaze takes one look at Rebel and he regains his composure. He grabbed Sledge strongly, so that he could feel his renewed strength. He will be ready when the time comes.

Outside the fortress; there is silenced darkness. Through the mist there is a faint sound of the stirring swish of Rodagons' wings and the muffled sound of several thousand hearts beating with a strong rhythm. The adrenaline pumps savagely through their veins. The fog about them begins to thin as they push forward. They are now in full view of the watch deacon in the tower as he peers through the snow flurries and frozen rain; their numbers startles him.

" O feces! O feces! " He shouts, as he reaches for the bell.

The princess stands at the base of the alter facing the conjugation and Beezubul, as he starts the distance down the aisle. His flowing cape adds the exact effect he wanted. Nud paces himself a few steps behind him trying not to step on his cape, again.

Suddenly the bell sounds with a continuous ringing to alert the deacons. Beezubul call s Nud up to walk beside him and he grabs his arm.

" Go find out what is going on, " he said with a whisper. " Make sure you handle the problem before you return. "

Nud walks swiftly back down the aisles, as the sound of the bell seems to intensify.

" We have been seen! Kill the one ringing the bell!" Shouts Ayogia, as he rode up next to Maiko.

" Do not kill him. Let him ring his bell. They are not ready for what we have here. Maybe their confusion will work in our favor. "

So now it all comes together, everyone knows what they have to do.

The beat quickens.

Maiko knows there is no room for error. " MOVE FAST, MY THIEVES, BUT GIVE THE FIRST ASSAULT GROUP TIME TO CLEAR BEFORE ANY MORE SUPPORT LANDS, " Maiko has given the first order.

" STROKE, AND DIDDILY, YOU WILL FOLLOW ME IN FOR THE FIRST ATTACK. ARE YOU READY? "

" IS WATER WET? " asked Diddily, holding the raines in one hand and drawing his laser with his other.

" OKAY, MAIKO, WHAT YOU GONNA DO; MILDEW OR BARBECUE? " asked Stroke, doing the same as Diddily.

" BARBECUE!" Shouts Maiko leading them in, only a hundred feet away from the entrance and closing in fast.

The sounding bell of the watch deacon has caused the Slime Dwellers to add support to various entrances and they take up their positions in order to blast at the army of Thieves. The Thieves make easy targets in their large numbers.

Maiko dispatched more of his men to assault those areas with laser and cannon blasts. They begin to attack the Mount from all angles. Stroke and Diddily continue to blast at the terrace of the entrance, which they plan to walk through. Stroke knows that as long as they are on the backs of the Rodagons, they will remain easy pickings.

" Hold back! Pull back! " He orders the first group. They pull back on the raines of their mounts. " I have a plan. "

No one is sure what he has planned as he fires one shot over the heads of the Slime Dwellers, then another and another; until the loose debris of the falling rocks, forces the deacons back far enough for the first group to land safely.

" COME ON, DIDDILY, LETS SHOW THESE HERE BOYS HOW TO PLAY THE GAME. "

No sooner had the words left his mouth, he saw Diddily force his animal into a dive; heading straight for the plateau. Diddily dismounted and rushed into the scattered thickness of the Slime Dwellers without waiting for support from He or Maiko, who were both close behind him.

" Damn fool ass kid! " said Stroke.

But he sees he has no reason to fret, as Diddily used his sword to cut his way through. He was not worried about Diddily's safety after he saw his actions. He only hoped that Diddily would save some for him.

But he and Maiko will both have the opportunity to quench their thirst for Slime Dwellers blood long before what is left of this night is through.

The ceremony had begun. Beezubul has no idea of what is going on. He shows this by his broad smile of confidence as he stands forcing Reikciv to hold his hand, while they stand before the presence of the Master of Ceremony.

" . . .And do you Princess Suirtiva Reikciv, promise to act upon Odaroel Beezubul's request?

" Make that, act with excellence upon my every request. "

The Master of Ceremony was about to make the correction when Nud came stumbling into the hall, tripping over a deacon's foot he fell to the floor, yet he does not take time to argue at the deacon, but hurries to get back to his feet in order to release the door, which he does so by pressing a button in the control panel on the wall. The heavy door slams loudly; fastening to its base. The slamming of the door draws the attention of those who did not see Nud fall. Nud is too excited to worry about the big disturbance he has caused, he quickens his steps down the aisle almost to a jog and climbs the steps to the alter. The same alter on which Beezubul is trying to get married.

" I...I need to talk to you, " he said trying to catch his breath between words.

" What is wrong with you? " asked Beezubul, as he grabbed a hold of Nud's arm and pulled him over to the side. " What was the problem with the bell? "

Nud holds his right hand to his chest, as he tries to catch his breath, " We are under attack, " he whispered.

Beezubul is shocked to think they have had the nerve to try again, he knows that if they are back then they have increased their numbers as well. He cannot tell the true nature for Nud's excitement and he sees the disturbed looks on the faces of his guest.

HE WILL LIE!

" My friends! Nud tells me, that his deacon's have started their celebration for the union the princess and I will form. So he has closed the door to keep our eager friends out. Even though they send their EKTENE, I think this union is going to be hard to form if they do not control themselves. " He pauses and looks about the nave. " Let us continue. "

The guest believe Beezubul's lie. They even applaud Nud's untimely interruption for the news they think he has brought. Nud bows weakly

Beezubul spoke of blessings from the Slime Dwellers, well, they have wishes, but they are of being some place other than where they are. For where they are deacons lie dead or dying, as many more fall to join their ranks all through the fortress. Maiko's Thieves continue to slash and bash their way through.

Stroke has joined Diddily, who seems to be going even better than before for his anger has taken control of every muscle in his body. He completely ignores The Pain in his shoulder as he forces his way through.

" Stroke, we must find the others, " said Diddily.

" Do not worry, kid, they will be out as soon as we have more support from the rear. " said Maiko.

The Slime Dwellers must have been listening for there are Slime Dwellers advancing towards their front. The battle here appears to be in their favor.

" Here comes the calvary, " said Stroke.

But there were more Thieves advancing from the rear.

" Look, my brother, we have a calvary of our own, " said Maiko knowing that his men will keep them busy. " Come, this is the best time to move, " Maiko used his fist to get pass the man in front of him. Then takes lead way through the Slime Dwellers and one of the Thieves takes on his opponent to finish him off.

Stroke and Diddily follow his lead and only fight their opponents long enough for the next Thief to come and steal their life. Then they push forward.

Each man uses a different form to express himself. Maiko uses strength and savvy, then he services as many as possible with his sword. Diddily is cool, relaxed and cunning; this is all back by fast hands and a sharp blade. Stroke makes use of an art form he has studied for many years and his moves are as swift and agile as the tiger they were meant to imitate, and move for move he only seems to improve, as he makes use of his blade to enhance the combination.

Maiko grabbed a torch from its spot on the wall in the corridor. And any Slime Dwellers, who dares to venture too close, soon feels the heat, as their robes are set a blaze

Diddily finds himself forced into a corner away from the middle of the floor. Stroke sees him, but he can not help at the moment, for he has found a worthy adversary, one who seems to be better than Stroke was expecting, which also means they are getting closer to the core.

Suddenly, there is a familiar sound coming from his opponent's utility belt, a sound Stroke is happy to hear. It is the musical buzzing of a recharged laser. Stroke steals it from his belt and fires.

" Sorry, I never fight fair, " he said, then takes aim at another who dares to come too close.

Diddily did not have time to observe Stroke's actions, for he was too busy fending off the four, which had him cornered.

"DIDDILY! " Shouted Stroke.

He glanced over toward Stroke, who was pointing up towards a chandelier, for and instance he turned and shot, then pointed again at the chandelier located conveniently over Diddily's head. And Diddily understands while still fighting he watches as Stroke takes aim at the support line of the chandelier.

" Alright, kid, this shit works for Clint Eastwood and one shot is all it takes and I've got three. " Then he shoots another, who has dared to come too close." Well, I've got two. "

Two shots are fired. Diddily lounged from between them when he saw the first. And it was lucky that he did, because Stroke must have fired the second just to clear the weapon.

Maiko pulls Diddily to his feet. " Are you alright, kid? "

" Yo, dude, " said Diddily, on being lifted up by his sore arm. " I was doing fine until you helped me up. "

" Sorry, kid. "

Stroke walked over and slapped him on the same shoulder.

" Shit, man! Whose side are you guys on? "

" Are you alright? " asked Stroke.

" O yeah! I'm doing just fine, " he said rubbing his shoulder.

" You're doing great, kid. This is going to be easier than I had thought, " said Stroke.

" Yes, my brother. But we should get to the Hold to free the others. Then we must hurry to find Beezubul. "

" Beezubul? Beezubul's a pussy! I might just handle him myself, " says Diddily looking at Stroke, who says nothing. But he does give him one serious look.

" Okay, I know don't get cocky> "

" Damn straight. Well, not until we get the boys back together, " he adds with a smile.

" We need waste no more time, " insists Maiko, as he starts the run down the.

They travel back the way they fled to escape. They find Maiko's Thieves have over ran most of the fortress and they have found the treasury room of the Slime Dwellers. But the Thieves know the celebration will have to wait until the fortress is under complete siege.

Maiko rounds the corner ahead of Stroke and Diddily. Seeing three Slime Dwellers, he drops them before they even know what hit the first one. Diddily picks up his pace and runs pass Maiko, for he remembers where he is going for he too has pick been this way before. He recalls the door, which opens into the holding room, but he forgets his shoulder in his excitement and he has also misjudged the weight of the door.

"Auuugghh, shit! That muther is heavy. "

" Step aside there, young blood, " said Stroke taking hold of the door.

And Maiko is the first to enter. He runs to catch the jailer as he tried to run off to the far end of the Hold. Maiko slowed his advance and began to cross his steps as he faced the jailer with his sword pointed at him. The jailer continues to walk slowly backwards still watching Maiko's sword. Then he can retreat no longer and he is forced up against a cell.

" Okay, the party is over. How about we get down to some real work, "

Maiko's voice has caused all of the soon to be released men to feel relief. They crowd forward against the cell doors.

" I am glad to see your face, " said Cush. " It sure took you long enough to get back. "

" Dawggon'! You guys really smell bad, " said Stroke, shaking his head.

Maiko scrambles around the Hold in search of the keys, then he remembers the jailer. " Hold on, my brothers, I will have you out of there in one moment. "

" Don't worry, they aren't going anywhere. Besides, I think they like it in there," He said laughing loudly.

Blaze knows he has not noticed that Rebel is not standing amongst them.

" Stroke, !" he shouts. " There is something I need to tell you about The Rebel. "

" What can you tell me about that I don't already know? " He said.

As he caught that smell again. " Whew, boy! Man you really stink. Why don't you back on up a few feet? "

" All I want is to hear one of the Rebel's bullshit lines. Hey, Rebel! Get up here and let me see your ugly muther . . ." He fell short of what he was about to say as Cush, Sledge and Blaze cleared a path making his viewing of the Rebel's body easier.

" He's dead, " said Blaze, as he looked back at Rebel' s body.

Stroke grabs hold of the cell door and pulled his face hard against the bars. ." No, no, no, no! We came back! He can't be dead. "

Maiko returns with the jailer. " Open it! Hurry, I want them out. " He says and smacks the jailer's head. And the jailer wastes time as he nervously fumbles with the keys. He is new on the job you know.

" I told you to hurry? " said Maiko, as he punched him several times in the back of his head.

" How did he die? "Asked Stroke.

" Dead! Who is dead? " Asked Maiko, as he pulled the cell door open.

" How did he die? " Stroke asked again as he entered the cell, then he stopped at the bunk where Rebel's body lied, and he stood there looking don at his friend, no his brother laid out cold and hard in its postmortem state.

" After we were recaptured, Beezubul and Nud decided to have a little party. And beezubul told Rebel that if he defeated this big dude called Eyaf, he would allow all of us to go free. "

" Damn! The fifty-two fake out. And Rebel went for it? "

" He had no choice. They would have only killed us all, anyway. These boys are sick."

" He lost? "

" No. He won. But, he was beaten down really bad. Yet sill, he was able to reduce Eyaf to nothing but a memory. Then Beezubul told us to leave. And that's when Rebel received the wound that killed him. " Said Sledge.

" Shot in the back? "

" Yeap shot in the back."

" By who? "

" That bitch Beezubul, he shouted 'To The Pain' and Rebel fell. "

" That's not all, Stroke, " said Blaze, " Beezubul is marrying the princess at this moment. "

Stroke turns his head away from Rebel's body and walks toward the front of the cell. He sees Diddily, who cannot control his feelings, and he wept. Stroke walks over to Diddily and pulls him close.

" Be strong, little brother. "

Cush remembers what Rebel asked him to tell Stroke. He walks up behind him as he releases Diddily.

" The Rebel told me to tell you to kill Beezubul, he said to keep it in the bond. "

He knows what he meant. " Let's go, kid. "

" I 'm ready. "

" Get your sword or any sword and wet it with as many Slime Dwellers blood as you so desire. But Beezubul's blood will only wet mine; " He had started walking before he was midways through his sentence. The others hurry to strap on their weapons in order to catch up.

Blaze secures his weapons, and then he remembers the jailer and the smell he cannot forget. He searches the jailer out and finds him in a poorly lit section. The jailer knows that revenge is what Blaze has on his mind.

" Please, I beg you. Do not kill me, please, do not do it. "

Blaze has nothing to say, he draws his sword and smiles. There will be no pity for this Slime Dweller or any other.

Sledge shows the way through to the main hall. But Stroke walks as if he knows where he is going. He takes to the ramp that lead to the upper section like a man who had spent some time in New York as a kid.

The Slime Dwellers believe there is strength in numbers, which may be true. But what they witness is numbers with strength. Stroke sees the evidence as well for the Army of Thieves leaves a trail of death everywhere it travels.

" Okay, boys, we're going to kick some ass now! " said Stroke as he plunged into the mist of the battle. " WHOAH! " He shouted.

Blaze grabbed Diddily's arm. " Looks like he is really beginning to enjoy this shit. "

Diddily flinches from The Pain in his shoulder, where Blaze placed his hold much too tight. Then he looked at his sword.

" You know what the sad part is? "

" No. What is it? "

" So am I. " He said, and then he followed Stroke's lead and let out a yell for the Rebel.

Blaze is determined not to be out done by Diddily or Stroke, so he rushes in as well.

Just a few moments earlier the Army of Thieves had found them out numbered, but now they have support from their king and his new brothers. Now they are the aggressors and they force the Slime Dwellers back causing them to lose ground and men. Back they are driven, back toward the door they must enter to save the princess.

The Deacons of Slime realize that no matter how hard they fight it will be to no avail. Then suddenly, to add to their dilemma the Slime Dwellers find their avenue of retreat has been cut off by even more Thieves, as they have successfully fought their way through the fortress.

" Mercy, mercy, " begs on of the deacons dropping to his knees.

" You want mercy? " said Cush, as he grabs the deacon by the throat.

. " Alright, then tell them to drop their weapons. "

" Drop your weapons. They have won and, there will be no need to continue. "He said.

One deacon speaks out. " He does not speak for me we will fight. "

Sledge pulls his laser and shoots the one who spoke. " Okay, are there any more free agents? If so step forward. "

They drop their weapons. Cush still has the one deacon by the throat. " Very good. But you will all still die if any harm has befallen my sister. "

Maiko still thinks this man deserves no mercy, as he suddenly remembers his face. " Do not concern yourself with this one, my brother, he will probably be dead long before you see your sister. Do you remember me, Executioner? " He asks, as he pressed his sword so hard under the man's chin it draws blood.

Maiko's men rush the remaining length of the corridor.

" We can not get the door open, " shouts Ayogia.

" What? Then I suggest you try blowing it, " orders Maiko.

" Yes, Maiko, we will do as you say. "And Ayogia signals for the Thieves to send forward one of their heavier weapons and then begins what will be a drawn out battle with a well-fortified door.

Stroke awaits the opening of the door with the others, he decides to walk over to where Cush is standing, " Say, dude, why didn't you tell me that the princess was your sister? "

There comes an interruption from Ayogia before Cush can answer.

" Our weapons are exhausted. This is no good! " Said Ayogia., then expired one more shot. " Do you see this is no good, I tell you. "

" Do not try to tell me what is no good. I want you to keep blasting at that door until it is nothing more than ember! "

Cush has his chance to answer. " There was no need to tell you she was my sister. She being my sister would not have had effected the way you fought or anything else. We would still be where we are, standing here in this hall with no way to get to her, " turns to look at the door and it still stands, even though it has begun to glow red from the heat of the blasts.

Diddily has over heard what Cush has said. " That's where you are wrong, " he says, as he walks. " Hey, Stroke, why don't you get one of the prisoners to tell you another way to enter? "

" Okay, kid, But why do you think they will tell me? "

" Because you have a bullshitting way about you, ' said Blaze finding a need to intervene.

" Yes I do don't I. " said Stroke with a smile as he walked over toward Maiko, who was trying to kill a little time, and he was doing so by placing small cuts on the one he recognized as the Executioner of his little brother and all his men when he came on that first Steal.

Stroke watched, then he spoke " Having a good time?"

" O yes, I am like how you say ' Jamming'. "

" Jamming, hugh? " He said rubbing his chin. " Do you mind if I talk to this one for a moment? " asked Stroke looking the executioner in the eyes.

" Be my guess. I will just go down here and play with one of his friends. But let me know as soon as you are finished. I have nothing else to do until the door opens. " Maiko walked down the line, cutting each Slime Dweller as he walked down the length of them stacked against the wall.

Stroke smiled at the executioner.

" Turn it on, Stroke, turn it on, " said Sledge, watching him as he began.

" You know Maiko is going to kill you very slowly. You know that, right? " Stroke said, but he received no answer. " Okay, here is the deal. I promise you a quick death and you better take that because knowing him he will probably feed you to the Barunzeies or something. "

Maiko hears him from the other end of the line. " I never thought of that, but it sounds like a good idea. I will keep that in mind, " Maiko turned to see how well his men were doing with the door and accidently stabbed a deacon with his sword.

" Um, got to be more careful. " said Maiko.

Stroke laughs, and then turns attention back toward the executioner. " Listen we are running out of time, so what do you say? "

" I say ask me tomorrow. "

" Okay here it comes, the power of persuasion, " said Diddily.

" What is this power of persuasion? " asked Cush.

And just as if they were on stage singing it in three-part harmony the answer comes.

" INTIMADATION. "

Stroke lends hard on his sword as he pressed the flat thickness of it against the executioners throat. " Yo, dude, be advised, it doesn't matter to me how you wish to die. But if I don't hear something from you now, then you will die . . . NOW! "

The deacon's swallows then starts to form something in his mouth, which Stroke believes to be his first words. But the only answer he receives is a glob of spit sprayed on his face.

Stroke uses his left hand to wipe the spittle from his face, and then lowers his sword from the deacon's throat. The slime dwelling executioner brings to his lips a smile, and so does Stroke. But the executioner's smile has become askew, and he slides from his spot on the wall down to the floor. Stroke waits until the Slime Dwellers' body is free of his sword. That deacon is now dead, so Stoke steps down to the next one.

" I can't believe they teach that stuff in college, " says Blaze.

" What stuff? " asks Sledge?

" Psychology. "

" Well, I don't plan to go through the same shit, again. So, if you wish to die, just let me know. "

This deacon has a different look on his face, a look of fear. " I . . .I . . .I know how . . .Yoouuuuuu . . . caaaaaannnn . . .geeeeett . . . get . . . iiinnnnn . . . in, " said the scared stuttering deacon as water rolled down his leg.

Stroke stares at him, " Well, start talking. "

FIFTEEN

THE ELEGY

BEEZUBUL KNOWS THE FORTRESS IS under attack and he begins to feel threatened. The guests are becoming uneasy as the heat from the door becomes more intense. Nud's

Confidence lies in how long the door will sustain the blast. But he cannot afford to take any chances. He turns and speaks to the guards nearest him.

" Take point at the door, I want you to shoot any and everything that comes through that door if it opens. "

" As you command. " says sergeant. Then he motions for his guards to take up positions at the door.

And once again, the ceremony must be stopped and Beezubul must try to quiet his guest, who seem to be on the brink of panic and Nud's security measures have not made matters any better.

" Everyone should stay in their seats. The door can sustain anything they have. Do not worry; by the time they get that door open it will be too late. "

One of the guest stands. " Exactly, who are they, and why must we stay if you are having problems? "

Beezubul knows this guest well. " Kobeck, if you do not sit down and shut your mouth, then I will be forced to personally come down and tear your esophagus out with my bear hands! " said Beezubul.

The snow flurries still mixed with the frozen rain as Cush, Stroke, Blaze and Sledge stood on top of the watch tower over- looking the west side of the cathedral, which is where the deacon had lead them. The slimy walks over to the edge of the tower and looks over and points. " Here! If you drop down here to the balcony, your entrance will be easy. '

The boys walk over to peer over the side of the tower.

" Okay, lets break out the rope, " said Blaze.

Sledge dumped the rope where they all could get at it.

" Tie the lines off here. It looks sturdy enough, " instructed Cush as he rubbed on the figure carved in the stone.

Stroke prepared himself to grab the first line secured and when it was properly tied off, he took hold of the line and fastened it to the rope seat he had fashioned from what he knew.

" Stroke, what do you think you're doing? " asked Sledge.

But he did not answer.

" Know you don't think you're going in by yourself? That would be suicide. They have more firepower than you. "

He smiled, " You're right. So, why don't you give me one of those lasers you have there. '

Sledge gave him one of his laser, for he knew if he did not Stroke would just go without it. And he watched as Stroke tucked the pistol in front of his utility belt firmly.

Blaze has the other line secured, but Stroke makes the leap a lone for he has no need to wait for support.

Diddily stands beside Maiko, who has taken charge of getting the door opened for they are not sure what Nud has for them on the other side. Yet if they can force their way through the door it will better his friend's chances. Diddily is not pleased that he was left behind. " I wish they had taken me along. Shit! It doesn't look as if we will ever get this door opened. '

" Do not start, again. You know, you could not have made the drop with your shoulder the way it is. "

" Awe, my shoulder is fine. "

Maiko grabbed Diddily's shoulder. " Come on, man! What the hell did you do that for? Everyone's a comedian around here! "

" Yes, kid, your shoulder is fine. You're in great shape. " He said, then walked away from Diddily over toward the door.

Stroke rappels himself down the side of the tower to the balcony. Dangling from the line, he sees two deacons standing inside in front of the huge windows, but they have their backs turned. Stroke drops down quietly and fastens the rope. He readies the two lasers without being heard by the guards. Looking through the glass doors, he sees Beezubul at the far end of the nave, and then he finds what he was looking for and that is the rest of the guards and the release lever for the doors they had been trying to blast through.

The light of the suns barely peeks under the horizon and it is moving up slowly. He knows that it is his turn for he holds all the right cards. He steps back from the glass doors and fires two shots from each laser, which send the guards flying from the walk at the top of the stairs. He kicked the door open and continued to blast away more deacons as he came through.

Working with surprise and two lasers, he has no problem forcing the few Slime Dwellers remaining away from the door, as they run to seek cover. The deacon's blast at him from the area they have found to cover themselves. The deacons force him down along the right side of the double staircase, where he lays flat while still firing at them through the hand railing.

Blaze comes through the doors and throws Stroke another laser, and then they both lay down suppressive fire and put it down heavy on the Slime Dwellers. But soon Blaze too must seek cover and he is forced down along the same side as Stroke.

" Glad you could make it, " said Stroke.

" You didn't think I was gonna let you have all this fun by yourself, did you? "

" No I guess not. "

" I think they might have six left. "Says Stroke, and then another blast cuts through the air just over their heads.

" Ah you can make that seven, but that guy's a bad shot. Lets just hope that none of the guest are armed. Damn!"

" What's wrong? "

" Man we could sure use some pyro, " he said , just before the deacons sent another series of shots .

" Where is Cush? "

Blaze turns to see Cush dropping onto the outer balcony, " He's out beating off, as usual. "

" I'm going to need support from both of you, while I run an open the door. Otherwise, we'll be pinned up here."

" No way, Stroke, I am going, " insisted Cush.

" What there is no time to argue. "?

" You are right. We do not have time to discuss this. Here, Blaze you better takes my spare weapon. "

" What about you? "

Cush held up another weapon.

Beezubul held the princess close, not for affection, but protection. " Do not allow them to come any further. Keep them back! "

The Slime Dwellers begin to blast constantly at the balcony and their shots begins to tear away chucks of the stone railing the boys are using for cover.

But they remain where they are as they wait for the number of possible shots to decrease and when it does, Cush is going to take a chance at running the ten or so meters in order to reach the lever that will open the huge secured door.

" What's your count, Blaze,? " asked Stroke

" Ah, I'd say about twenty – four. "

" Sounds good, I counted twenty – three. "

" Okay, Cush, are you ready? "Asked Blaze.

" Let's move, dude, " he answered.

" Just as soon as Stroke and I start firing at them, I want you to jump up and haul arss for the lever!"

" Haul arss/ Yes, haul arss. I understand. "

" Alright, Cush, get here where I am, " said Stroke shifting from the stairs as he made sure to keep his head down. " It should be easier to start the run from here," stroke crawled up to the balcony and laid down next to Blaze.

Blaze looked over at Stroke, " You ready? " asked Blaze.

" Yeap, I'm ready. "

" Okay then, we stand up and start firing on three. "

" Copy three. "Said Stroke

" Copy three. " said Cush.

" One . . Two . . THREE!"

Blaze and Stroke were on their feet and they have a better angle, which they take full advantage of as they blast away at the deacons.

The Slime Dwellers have their hands filled trying to return shots at them. And Cush has started his run to release the lever.

" GET THAT ONE HE IS TRYING FOR THE DOOR! " Shouts Beezubul.

Nud turns and fires a shot which takes Cush off his feet, stopping him just short of the door.

" YES, NUD, GOOD SHOT! " says Beezubul. with a smile.

Nud turns toward Beezubul and bows. He thinks he has stopped Cush the same way he stopped The Rebel.

Stroke redirects his shots toward Nud. " That mutherfucker got Cush, "

But just like The Rebel, Cush has the will to survive, so he collects himself and manages enough strength to roll the last few feet to the lever.

Blaze sees him. " Keep shooting, Stroke. Cush is trying to make it. Thhaaattt's ssss right, . . . Thhhaaatt'sss right."

With Blaze and Stroke still laying down suppressive fire, Cush pulls himself up the wall, and then falls against the release lever for the huge secured door.

" NNOOOOOO, " Shouts Nud blasting at Cush while running toward the door.

Blaze sees Nud and he sends several shots his way as he still runs towards the door. The door begins to open.

" THE DOOR IS OPENING! FIRE AT THE DOOR! " He orders.

Maiko has lined the Slime Dwellers in front of the door. And Nud and his deacons end up shooting their own brothers as they expire their weapons. As the Thieves enter strong and hard. They are way too much for what Nud and Beezubul has left, and they know they cannot stop this crew, but surrender is not an option.

" DROP YOUR WEAPONS OR DIE! " Shouts Maiko.

" THEN WE WILL DIE, MAIKO, " Insisted Nud. " BUT IT WILL NOT BE AT YOUR HANDS, THIEF! " Nud begins to move slowly toward him, and his deacons follow their lord, even though there can be no survival against so many.

Stroke and Blaze walk down the stairs to join the others, Blaze stops to help Cush to his feet.

At the alter stands Beezubul, who has not released his hold on the princess.

" STOP YOU FOOLS!" He shouted, using his power to freeze them all.

And I do mean all: All The Thieves, All The Deacons, All The guest and everyone else within a hundred meters of him.

" NOW YOU SHALL WITNESS THE DEATH OF THE PRINCESS. IF I CANNOT HAVE HER, THEN NO ONE WILL. "

" Damn, that bastard! " said Blaze, still trying to move.

The ring Stroke was given begins to glow with a very strange light, and he realizes that he is not effected by Beezubul's spell like everyone else . He says nothing as he walks pass the Thieves, who stand frozen in a ready fighting position.

" Stroke, why have you not been effected? " calls Maiko. " STROKE!"

Stroke remained silent, because he did not have an answer. But he continued to walk down the length of the aisles toward the alter.

Beezubul watched as Stroke neared closer." YOU THERE! HOW DO YOU RESIST MY POWER? " Asked Beezubul, who suddenly feels he needs more support so he draws his laser.

" STOP! DID YOU HEAR ME I SAID, STOP! STOP OR I WILL KILL HER."

Stroke does not stop, he continues. " DO NOT WORRY, PRINCESS, HE KNOWS MY TRUTH IS SRONGER THAN HIS. HE DOES NOT HAVE THE BALLS TO HARM YOU. THIS IS ALL JUST A FRONT, FOR HE KNOWS THAT YOU ARE THE ONLY THING KEEPING HIS WORTHLESS FORM ALIVE. "

" TO THE PAIN, YOU FOOL. " Shouts Beezubul as he watched Stroke, who was still walking slowly towards them." I KNOW I HAVE NOTHING TO GAIN OR LOSE BUT TIME. "

Stroke listens, but the words fall short of the fear they were intended to cause. And Stroke had already picked the spot where he wants to shoot Beezubul, and it is the arm he is holding the laser, which is resting against the temple of the princess.

" BEEZUBUL, YOU ARE A VERY AMUSING MUTHERFUCKER.
"

Then with a quick twist of his wrist, Stroke takes that shot and it is a clean and perfect shot. " BUT I AM NOT LAUGHING. "

Beezubul was slightly burnt by the shot, but it was enough to break his grip on the princess and has also broke the spell he had on the others.

The princess is free, and she runs to the aid of her brother.

Beezubul snares angrily at Stroke, " HOW DARE YOU?"

" HOW DARE YOU? STEAL THE PRINCESS FROM HER HOME.

THEN HAVE US DRAGGED FROM OUR HOME. AND HOW DARE YOU KILL MY BEST FRIEND. " Stroke stands with his laser still pointed at Beezubul. " BUT YOU KNOW WHAT; YOU CAN NOW START TO REGRET ALL THAT YOU HAVE DONE. BECAUSE I AM GETTING READY TO GIVE THE REBEL A FAREWELL SHOW. "

" DO WHAT YOU THINK YOU MUST DO. BUT I HAVE NO REGRETS. "

Beezubul adjusted his posture, thinking he was about to be shot.

" NO WAY, HOMEY, YOU'RE NOT GOING OUT LIKE THAT. YOU SEE, I DIDN'T BRING MY SKINS TO BEAT FOR HIM. SO I GUESS YOUR ASS WILL JUST HAVE TO DO. NOW DRAW YOUR BLADE !"

And the battle resumes as, Maiko signals for his men to move on the Slime Dwellers. Blaze looked toward Maiko, then he looked at Nud.

" HEY, NUD, MY FRIEND MAIKO HAS SOMETHING FOR YOU, " He said pointing behind Nud, who turned about to have a serious right jab smashed in his face.

Nud finds that he is no match for Maiko, who is now using the moves he has seen done Stroke, as well as, the tricks used by Diddily. Nud is forced into submission and he drops to his knees. And starts to beg for his life.

" YOU HAVE WON, MAIKO. PLEASE, NO MORE, I BEG YOU, NO MORE. GO HOME AND TAKE ALL MY TREASURE WITH YOU, BUT PLEASE SPARE MY WORTHLESS LIFE. "

Maiko is sicken by the thought of Nud trying to bargain for his life. " YOUR TREASURE? WHAT DO YOU MEAN YOUR TREASURE? I DO NOT KNOW WHERE YOU HEARD THAT, BUT YOU HAVE OBVIOUSLY BEEN LISTENING TO THE WRONG CONVERSATIONS. " Maiko moved closer to where Nud Knelt.

" AND AS YOU ONCE SAID TO ME, ' I THINK YOU WILL HEAR LESS WITH ONE EAR. "

Nud knew what was about to happen and his fear caused him to flinch, and he moved his head just as Maiko started the swing of his blade. Maiko is disappointed, for instead of an ear, Nud lost the left side of his head.

" Fool! You made me miss, " Maiko starts to laugh. " I always knew Nud had a small brain and look; there is the proof on the floor. "

It has been written and it has been said, now let it be written again. Beezubul must die and Stroke must be the slayer.

Beezubul stands with his sword in hand, ready to begin. Stroke is ready as well and he begins to see mental pictures of The Rebel's face. This was his brother from another mother. He knows he must win, for too much depends on his victory.

Now all those who were before preoccupied with some other task are now giving their undivided attention to Stroke and Beezubul, as they carefully look one another over.

Beezubul is no fool. He realizes that no matter what the outcome of this final battle shall be, he knows that he will die. But if he has a chance to kill once more, well he has one thing he likes to say. " TO THE PAIN! " He says leering at Stroke.

" TO YOUR PAIN! AND TO MY GAIN. "

" WHAT IS YOUR NAME? "

Stroke smiles and decides to go to another level of the game, as he slowly circles about him while dragging his blade on the floor. And Beezubul must pivot in order to keep his eye on him.

Stroke adjusted his eye patch, " I am many things to many people. I am what makes it hard for you to sleep at night. I am your darkest fear. I am what your mother should have warned you about. For I, my friend, am death. "

" Well, death, I think you better reassemble your thoughts, for I am death to you. And I do not think that what you bring will be strong enough. "

Stroke' s arrogance forces him into the first surge of their battle. He swings his sword furiously, causing Beezubul to retreat in order to better his footing.

" Is that strong enough for you?" asked Stroke.

Beezubul takes one more step backwards as Stroke ceases his attack. He lifted his sword, and then brought it down over and over again, in order to prove that he is just as strong as Stroke. And he will now have his turn at being the aggressor, moving on Stroke quickly, he slashes at his leather jacket, while forcing him back to regain some of the ground he lost. He attempts another overhead blow.

But Stroke zagged left, when Beezubul thought he was going zig right, causing Beezubul to miss his target. Stroke used his mouth to make a sound like a hi – hat frizzle, as he used his right leg to land a perfect inside roundhouse.

The force of the kick sent Beezubul spinning across the platform. Stroke smiles knowing his kick has taken a big bite out of him. And he goes at him hard, but Beezubul is still able to resist his attack, even though Stroke has began to alternate his swings; Parry left, parry right, then thrust and thrust again. Every deathblow Stroke attempted he found that Beezubul had a counter of equal force.

Their violent movements in battle has forced them off the alter platform. Yet they continue to battle through the crowd, which had gathered closer to get the ringside effect.

Beezubul is once again in control; he forces Stroke back down the length of the aisle. Their swords cross and remain temporarily locked together. Beezubul grabs Stroke's arm and sneers in his face, and Stroke sneers back.

Then, Beezubul sees the reason for Stroke's ability to resist his power.

" WHERE DID YOU GET THAT RING?"

" I GOT IT FROM A FRIEND, WHO WISHES YOU DEAD."

" YOU ARE AS STRONG AS THE OTHER FOOL, BUT I WILL KILL YOU SOON AND I WILL HAVE MY RING BACK, TOO. "

" WHEW BOY, WHAT'S UP WITH YOUR BREATH? SMELLS LIKE YOU BEEN EATTING A SHIT SANDWICH. YOU SHOULD DO SOMETHING ABOUT THAT BREATH. "

Beezubul drives Stroke back by giving him a hard right fore arm to the mouth, then he opens up with a series of swings which drives Stroke back even further.

Stroke is not able to see the object lying on the floor behind him. His peripheral vision is limited due to the patch over his left eye.

" STROKE, WATCH OUT BEHIND YOU! " Warns Diddily.

Only the warning comes too late and Stroke trips over Nud's empty shell and splashes in a pool of blood, letting his sword fly half way across the hall.

Diddily aims his pistol; he is ready to stop Beezubul where he stands looking down at Stroke.

" NOW YOU WILL DIE, MY FRIEND, " said Beezubul with his sword held high above his head.

" No, now you will die, snake face, "said Diddily

Maiko knocks his pistol up as he pulled the trigger. " You nor I must interfere in this. It is a personal matter. "

Beezubul looked back down toward Stroke after the shot flew over his head and he could see Stroke was still a bit shaken from the blow he received when his head hit the floor.

Stroke tries to focus his eyes on Beezubul's face, but he could only see the position of his sword. Stroke rolled over weakly, and then managed to time a left back kick with the landing of the sword, as it struck down hard on the floor after missing its target.

The back kick arrived on Beezubul's lips good and solid, sending him into a row of benches. His sword flies through the air, until it is lodged in the back of one of the benches.

The momentum from the back brought Stroke to his feet. He tried to shake some of the cobwebs from his head, as he removed the torn leather jacket.

Beezubul was trying to steady himself by resting his weight on a bench; he's only a few feet from Stroke, whom had already started to regain his composure.

Stroke shook it off and started up behind Beezubul. And on reaching him, he snatched him about, and then delivered a quick combination of punches, while he used his mouth to imitate the sound of a drum roll.

Stroke lifted Beezubul's head and smiled at him, then he threw a right upper cut, that damn near tore his head off, and he sounded off like a heavy crash cymbal as he did. The punch sent Beezubul from his feet and Stroke watched as he crawled toward the platform.

Stroke cracked his neck and followed.

Beezubul could feel him as he approached; he stood as he fought off the effects of the blows for he had a few tricks of his own. Beezubul began to spin as Stroke neared him, he stumbles into a few of the spectators, as he removed his cape and threw it over Stroke's head. Then Beezubul takes advantage of Stroke's blindness and he punches him over and over again. Before he snatched the cape from his head so he could better place his blows.

Beezubul had beaten Stroke down to the floor, but he used his fist in a double clutch to finish him off.

" I WANT MY RING BACK, NOW! " Then he makes an attempt to remove the ring, " FECES! IT WILL NOT COME OFF! "

Beezubul sees his sword stuck in the back of the bench. He was tired and weak as he staggered toward the bench where the sword rested.

Stroke's will to survive prevails, forcing him up on both knees. But for now he can only watch as Beezubul stopped to clear his moth of some blood, and he watched as Beezubul spat the blood on the floor.

Beezubul felt something in his mouth, and he used his tongue, then reached in side his mouth to remove the loose tooth. He looks at it, and then flings it across the hall in aggravation. Beezubul reaches his sword and takes hold of the hilt, and begins a feeble attempt of retrieving it.

Stroke is still trying to stand and he use the corner of a bench to try and pull himself up.

Beezubul finds the sword is wedged much more securely than he thought. And as he struggles to remove it, Stroke succeeds in his quest to stand, but he begins to cough violently.

Beezubul turns to see Stroke is tying to make his way forward, as he fights against the strong cough that rattles his whole body. Beezubul knows now that he should have killed him and then removed the ring. He begins to struggle even harder to remove his sword, he places his left foot on the bench and uses both hands to try and wiggle it loose. The wood starts to give; he is closer to freeing the blade.

The sword is free, and Beezubul turns with the hilt clenched firmly in his right hand. Stroke is closer than he had thought and he grabs a hold of Beezubul's arm stopping the blade in full force. And while still holding his arm Stroke used his right leg to kick him three times; Once in the ribs and then twice in the head. Then Stroke bent Beezubul's wrist until it snapped and the blade fell free.

Stroke displayed a spinning side – kick, sending Beezubul face down on the steps of the alter. Then Stroke moved upon him with a chop to the back of his head. " GET UP YOU FILTY BASTARD! "

Then another blow, this time in the small of his back. Beezubul gasped in pain.

" YEAH YOU LIKE THAT? HUNH . . .WHAT WAS THAT YOU SAID?

' TO THE PAIN '. WELL HOW YOU LIKE THAT? " Said Stroke as he stood over Beezubul. Stroke reached down and pulled Beezubul's left arm, and dragged it up under his chin, then he locked on a death hold.

" YOU PUT ME AND MY FRIENDS IN YOUR HOLD! WELL, HOW DO YOU LIKE THIS ONE? TO THE PAIN, MUTHERFUCKER, TO THE PAIN!"

Beezubul does not have the strength to break free of the hold. As Stroke cranked down even tighter.

" I AM GONNA BREAK YOUR FREAKIN' NECK, SON! "

Beezubul struggles at Stroke's grip with his free hand, he can feel the life being choked out of him, and he knows this will not get him loose.

Beezubul reached under his stomach and starts to work one of his belts loose.

Stroke applied more pressure. " AUUUUUGGGGHHHHH! SSSSSHHHHHIITTTT! " He yelled in pain.

" TO THE PAAAIIINNNN! " Yelled Beezubul still beneath Stroke.

Beezubul had stabbed Stroke in the leg with a small very sharp knife, which was concealed as one of his many belt buckles.

The knife was small but very effective, and it was more than enough to get Stroke to release his hold.

He released Beezubul as he limped hurriedly up onto the platform of the alter. And as the pain rushed to his brain, Stroke realized that he had been toying with a killer, and he should have finished Beezubul a long time ago. But those were only secondary thoughts, and he had put himself where he was now. And now all he knew was the pain as his nerves sped the message to his brain.

Beezubul was coughing and gagging as he rolled to his back.

The suns are being set free and the horizon begins to glow from the ferrous light. But no one here took note of that as they watched the two chiefs battle, with no mercy.

Stroke tried to place his weight on his uninjured left leg, as he pressed his back against the wall. He saw a laser on the floor, and it was the same laser he had shot from beezubul's hand earlier. He held his right hand just above the knife, and then he reached over with his left hand and placed it on the small dagger. The blood follows the knife out, flowing freely from the gapping wound.

Beezubul staggered down the aisle back toward his blade. Stroke removed his belts to get rid of some of the weight, then he tore his black tank top tee shirt and bit down hard on his lower lip, while he applied the shirt as a turn- a- kit over the wound to help slow the bleeding. He held his head back and closed his eyes and tried to ignore the pain.

Beezubul lifts his sword, then turns back to face Stroke with the blade of his sword gleaming in the light of the morning suns.

Stroke looks down at the laser lying on the platform, he slides against the wall moving closer to the pistol, and he moves as slow as the suns light creeping across the for of the nave as it shines through the broken windows making a very moody light. Stroke forces himself away from the wall to test the stability of his right leg. And he finds that it will not be able to hold his weight. So he tries to limp toward the laser, which is less than three meters away.

Beezubul does not move slowly, he quickly leaps up the stairs of the platform as Stroke tries to cover the last few feet with short hops. Beezubul stops Stroke's advancements by kicking him in the wounded leg. Stroke spins then drops to his knees.

Stroke takes hold of the gold cross around his neck with his right hand.

Beezubul looks at the back of Stroke's head, and then grabs a hold of Stroke's hair and with one quick swing he removes the braid, with the razor sharp edge of his blade.

Beezubul smiles at the hair in his hand, and then throws it a few feet in front of Stroke.

" LOOK WHAT YOU HAVE LOST! "

Stroke looks briefly, thinking Beezubul will deliver the final blow at any second. But what he receives is a kick to the back of his head.

" I SAID LOOK AT WHAT YOU HAVE LOST, BEFORE YOU LOSE MORE! "

Stroke stretched his body across the floor, as he attempted to reach the laser with his right hand. He could not reach it.

Beezubul smiled down at Stroke.

" PLEASE, GOD, JUST A LITTLE MORE, " he prayed, as he strained to reach the laser.

Beezubul had had enough of the games; he looked down at Stroke with a savage vengeance. " TURN NOW AND TELL ME YOUR REAL NAME! YOU SAY DEATH AND I AM LAUGHING AT YOU. " He held his sword high above his head. " I SAID TURN AND TELL ME YOUR NAME. " And this time he grind his boot into the injured thigh.

" AAAHHHH! GOD, HELP ME! "

" WHOM ARE YOU TALKING TO? " asked Beezubul, as he watched ready to commit the his final act. " TELL ME YOUR REAL NAME! I SAID TELL ME! "

Stroke turned over to look up at Beezubul, who was standing directly over him and the light drifted up across his stomach, as he relinquished his hold on the cross.

The light continued to move further, where it struck the cross lying on Stroke's chest. The cross-reflected the light in its' shape. And that reflected beam hit Beezubul's face with great intensity burning at his eyes.

Stroke cannot believe what is happening as his left hand feels the laser.

" TO THE PAIN! " Shouts Stroke. And along with the stream of light from Stroke's cross there is another, caused by the laser in Stroke's hand.

The blast from the laser throws Beezubul off the platform, as it burns a hole through his head.

Beezubul's body lands hard against a row of benches, with the thudding sound of dead weight with a splashing sound, as his life's fluid pours from his shell.

Stroke laid back and closed his eyes, " My name is Stroke. "

SIXTEEN

INCARNATION

THE BEGINNING OF A NEW day. The darkness, which covered the land, is gone.

Sledge, Diddily and Blaze rush to help Stroke to his feet. Then they all stand holding each other, for the are glad it is finally over.

The princess helps her brother over to where the rest of the boys now stand. Stroke sees her coming and he carefully pushes his friends aside; while standing with the support of a sword. He is now face to face with Reikciv and they stare into one another eyes.

Stroke begins to realize that among all the reasons he has fought for, the chance to see her face he has fought for the hardest. And he has won that right. But that right comes also in a wrong for he has lost his friend, his brother.

He takes the ring from his finger and places it on the left ring finger of the princess. Then with his left hand he pulls the scarf from her face and lets it fall to the floor.

" Happy birthday, princess. "

The princess is even more beautiful than he had imagined. He places his left hand on her wrist and pulls her close, until he was able to wrap his arm around her waist. He holds her tightly against his body and watched as a tear rolled down her cheek. She lifted her head up and kissed him.

Balaam enters with king Revilo and Queen Sesma.

" STOP THAT THIS INSTANCE. " Shouts Balaam causing them to break the kiss. Balaam moves his right hand slightly across his face and freezes all the members of Quest.

" My daughter, " called King Revilo. " My son. "

Reikciv ran to her father, the king and said, " my dear sweet loving father. "

" My darling, darling baby, it is going to be all right now. '

" Father, what is happening? " she asked with tears in the well of her eyes.

" Balaam knows what he is doing. These men are not from Zandoria. There was some strong magic out into effect in order to bring them here. They must return to their world. "

They stop to watch Balaam, as he did what he did best. Only this time his slight movements made the boys of Quest fade away, and they will rematerialize aboard the ship Deliverance. The blanket covering The Rebel's body falls flat on the surface of the bunk on which he laid, for he too will return home.

" I must go now. It is time to return them all home. They are needed here no longer . . . I shall return. " With a farewell salute to the King, he slowly fades away.

" Father, do not let him do it. Do not let Balaam take him away from me." She cries and her Father feels the magic. Her father the King.

Deliverance is hurled through space traveling pass stars and making them look like streaks. Soon it begins to slow as it approaches the very outer regions of Pluto and the speed is even less as it enters the earth's atmosphere, then even slower as they approach a small section of the planet known as Slovannah, Georgia.

Deliverance lands on the same spot the controller had placed it before. The doors open and Balaam walks out. " Come with me, " he orders, leading the boys out of the ship.

They follow him off the ship and into the arena, where their real bodies has been all the time. Balaam had cast a very complicated spell, one part stopped time, while the other part drew from them their WILL TO SURVIVE.

Balaam reunites their WILLS with their real bodies, and then walks back out to Deliverance. " Farewell, my friends, until we must meet again, " He snapped his fingers as the door slid shut.

The spell has been broken. Quest runs through the back stage crowd toward the stage. Still hidden from their fans by the darkness. The crowd begins to chant.

" WE WANT QUEST! WE WANT QUEST! . . ."

The letters are lit and the word QUEST shines in large yellow neon. The next sound comes from a yellow Washburn guitar and the spot light shines down on THE REBEL.

The Rebel is pulling hard on those strings, while Stroke recites the opening line from the theme song for Quest. And as the beat changes the crowd begins to feel the groove.

Quest performs all of the favorites with the high energy, which only comes from being on stage. They thoroughly enjoy giving a good performance on the stage, which they designed. For the guitarist there are ramps that stretch out from twenty fee high stacked amps and speakers on both side of the stage and the walks extend out high over the crowd at a distance of about thirty feet. Then there is also another special effect added when Stroke's acoustic set of skins rotates away from him and a Simmons SDS8 kit replaces it. The Slanted ramps on either side of the drum platform allow for even more fun for the boys to play on. And for the final song Stroke does his big drum solo without visible skins. Stroke had got with a couple of Engineers and the measured he reach of both his acoustic and his electric set of skins and with his jacket on he could play either kit without sitting behind them. NICE ENOUGH FOR YA?

Balaam made sure to clear their memories of what had happed, well all except The Rebel, whom he allowed to remember because of what had happened to him. So as he made the audience scream at the boss sounds coming from his fingers on the strings, He was experiencing brief mental flashes of the things he had missed on Zandoria. He tries desperately to ignore the images, but they continued to the end of the show.

The concert is over. Quest has given a awesome, breathtaking show. The boys rush from the stage with the crowd still wanting more.

" Man, listen to that crowd, " grins Diddily with much excitement, " Can we do one more? "

" No way, Kid! We've got a long night ahead of us, " explained Blaze.

The Band goes into the green room and the house lights come on, and their fans

Know they have seen all for tonight. The crowd slowly begins to depart.

Back in the green room. " Okay, guys lets get out of this sissy stuff and into some street clothes, " said rebel as he throws his shirt onto the dresser counter. " Tonight will be like no other night you have known before. "

Even with all the chaos of everyone trying to get dressed at the same time, they manage to change in less than ten minutes.

There comes a knock at the door. " Alright, dude, the big car rides are waiting to take you to ADVENTURE'S INN, " Said Bobby with his head sticking through the slightly opened door.

" Slow your roll homey, we're almost done. "

Bobby closed the door and walked away shaking his head. " I work for a bunch of nuts. "

The were about ready to boogie when Sledge looked at Stroke.

" Hey, dude! You don't look too happy for someone who has just given

One of the hottest drum solos I have ever heard and in his hometown, even. Come on gemme some. " Said Sledge and waited fort so dappage.

" Yeah, that shit was pretty hot, " said Stroke as he gave him that dappage.

" But check this, guys, I don't think I'm gonna be able to make it to the party tonight. I've got a painful feelin' inside me. Feels like I'm coming down off a very bad trip. I feel cold and empty. It and it hurts all over, it's like I have suffered a great lost . . . Ah, F it! " Stroke rubbed the cross around his neck.

" Yeah, I got a funky feelin' in me, too" said Sledge.

Everyone else suddenly made themselves busy with other tasks.

" Anyway, you dudes don't need to hang out too late either. We've got a early call for the trip to Jay ville. "

" Okay, mom, see you in the morning. " said Diddily.

" What's the matter dude you don't like to hang out with the white boys anymore? "Asked Rebel.

" Don't try to hit me with that shit. " Stroke caught himself. He lifted his backpack and pulled it over his left shoulder. He decided to leave before he really got pissed.

" Wow! Something must really be bothering him; he usually falls for that black white shit. " Said Sledge.

Stroke saw Bobby as he exited the green room and he decided to give him a few last minute instructions. " Hey, Bobby, that was a great set. Real smooth like. "

" Thanks, cuzo, I know if I want to keep my job, it's gonna have to stay that way. Cash is thicker than water. Peace. "

Stroke laughed. " Don't worry, it's not that thick. Hey now! Walk with me . . . I want all the gear on the rode to jay Ville to night. "

" Cuzo, you alright? Did you forget that we set up the leapfrog crew last month? The Jayville show is already set. This gear goes to San Antonio, Texas. "

" Yeah! Yeah! Yeah! I knew that. . . . Anyway the boys and I will arrive in the chopper by twelve at the latest."

" Yeah the boys told me about your new toy. It must be nice. Well, anyway I had bought you something, too, but I had left. So I'll have it for you in Jayville. Cool? "

" Cool. "

" STROKE! STROKE RENEGADE! OVER HERE, OVER HERE.
"

Stroke turns feeling that he knows the voice and he breaks off the conversation with Bobby. " Hey, cuzo, how's bout doing me a favor and take this over to Evette," He asked Bobby passing him his bag, as he pulled on his jacket. Then he walked toward the direction from which the voice came. And there she stood, being held back by two

Oversized security guards.

" Dawggon'! How many times have I told you guys, that ruffling up the females is bad for your health? "

" May I talk with you please? "

He smiled as he heard the voice again coming from behind the wall of muscle.

" Come on, Fellas, let the lady pass, " he said, reaching between them to pull her through.

The guards stepped aside to allow her through. She walks out into the light. Stroke is impressed by the way she is dressed, but even more by the way her eyes seem to catch every light in the room. He finds her beauty exceptional.

" Hey there, pretty lady, Now what can this country boy do for ya? "

She stared into his eyes and said. " Hello, Stroke. " She paused and smiled and it was like enchantment. " I am a reporter for the Eastern Star..
"

" Damn, I should have known, " he said and started to turn. " I don't do interviews. Didn't anyone tell you that. You are gonna have to talk to my publicist. "

She grabbed his arm. " Stroke, please don't walk away. "

He turned to see if this reporter had really grabbed a hold of his jacket. But as he looked in her face, he saw something in her eyes he could understand; it was a look of real pain. But still he wanted to leave her standing there, if it was an interview she wanted she could catch one of the boys when they come out.

" This is all about you. I was hoping to do an exclusive on you, " she said as if she had read his mind.

He was looking in those eyes again. " You know what? "

" What? "

" You have a freaky glow in your eyes. Its almost like I know you . . . Boy that's kinda creepy, too. It's almost like your eyes are smiling at me."

She smiled for him

" And your real smile is just awesome. " he said showing all twenty eight's. " Okay, I'll give you that exclusive. But under two conditions. "

" What are those conditions? " She asked – not that it mattered. The answer would still be 'yes'. She stepped a little closer.

" First of all, I want you to tell me your name and second, I need a date for late supper tonight. "

" My name? Yeah it's ah . . . " she paused, " Vicki . . . Vicki Ravitrius. Where are we going for the late supper? "

" Ah I know this nice place on Hilton Head Island."

Stroke walked her on arm over toward his car. Evette's engine sounded, then her horn was blown for the guards could clear the dock doorway.

Outside the rain had stopped but wetness still remained and the night lights

Were glowing on the black top streets. Stroke drove Evette out of the arena and made his way out into the main traffic with a little help from grounds security.

Back inside the arena, The Rebel was busy packing up his favorite guitar, yeah that yellow Washburn. And as he pulled on hi jacket he felt something in one of the pockets. It was the envelope ha had been given earlier; He looks at the envelope, which had been addressed to Quest. He opens it as he sits down. He read what had been written:

Quest,

Rebel, Sledge, Diddily, Blaze and Stroke T. Renegade. You must help us. The planet of Zandoria has been placed in danger by Nud the Lord of Slime and Beezubul.

If you do not help, they will be able to hold the Princess Reikciv until Beezubul can receive the power and that power will be matched by none.

PLEASE HELP,
BALAAM, SORCERER

Rebel runs out of the green room, " Hey, Bobby, where is Stroke?"

" He just left here with this fine little honey. Hell her name should have been honey. She was that damn fine. "

" What did she look like? "

" Dessert. "

" Dessert? Really what did she look like? "

" What? She looked like a freakin' princess."

Rebel ran toward the dock door and saw Stroke's car at the signal light. The light turned green before Rebel could make the run across the lot. But he did manage to get a close enough look at who was in the car with Stroke.

Rebel stood there and thought back on all that had happened on Zandoria.

" Damn! And Balaam didn't even say thanks. "

Blaze walked up behind Rebel with a pair of shoes in his hand, he hands Rebel his shoes. " I knew he was lying . Just running all that game on the boys 'bout feeling incomplete. Bullmutherfuckin shit! I'd say, mate, once a hawk always a hawk."

" Don't worry, I've got a feeling that we will be seeing him again tonight. Hey you gotta light? "

Blaze passed him his lighter, then looked up to see what the dude standing next to him was pointing at.

" Well, I be dawggon' "

" What is it? " asked Rebel looking up. Then he smiled as he saw the words, 'THANK YOU QUEST', were spelled across the night sky.

" Well, he said thanks after all, " then he touched the flame of the lighter to the note. And stuck the lighter in his pocket.

" What did you do that for? "

" Do what? " asked Rebel slipping into his shoes.

" Never mind. Ah, can I have my lighter back? "

Stroke sits in his car smiling, then he looks again at his lovely passenger as the motor hummed gently and the lights shined on the street, he reached over and turned on the radio.

" . . . Even more oldies on The Que, " said the disc jockey. Then a song started, and it was one he had no problem recognizing from the first note, it was ' Just The Two of Us ' Bill Withers and Grover Washington,jr.

" May I ask my first question now? "

" Sure, ask away. "

Okay, what was the reason for changing you name? And why did you choose Stroke?"

He smiled; this is the one question he cannot answer right now because it would not be smooth at this moment. But if she is lucky or maybe it will be his luck. Anyway, that answers . . .

" Too early for that one. So I'm gonna pass on it 'til later. Cool?"

" Yeah, Cool."

As Stroke let his mind traverse over the possibility, he realized that he no longer felt THE PAIN

THE END